AMMON'S HORN

or

THE MYSTERY OF THE BRAIN

ALSO BY PIERRE MAGISTRETTI

Glial Man: A Revolution in Neuroscience (coauthored with Yves Agid)

Biology of Freedom: Neural Plasticity, Experience, and the Unconscious (coauthored with Francois Ansermet)

AMMON'S HORN

or

THE MYSTERY OF THE BRAIN

Pierre Magistretti

AND

Christine Magistretti

OTHER PRESS
NEW YORK

Poetry excerpt on page 131 from "Romance Somnámbulo" by Federico
García Lorca, translated from the Spanish by William Bryant Logan in *The
Selected Poems of Federico García Lorca*, New Directions, 1955.

Hippocampus image on page 370 provided by Professor Corrado Càlì.

Production editor: Yvonne E. Cárdenas
Text designer: Jennifer Daddio / Bookmark Design & Media Inc.
This book was set in Baskerville and Helvetica Neue
by Alpha Design & Composition of Pittsfield, NH

1 3 5 7 9 10 8 6 4 2

Library of Congress Cataloging-in-Publication Data
Names: Magistretti, Pierre, 1952- author. | Magistretti, Christine, author.
Title: Ammon's horn, or, The mystery of the brain : a novel /
Pierre Magistretti and Christine Magistretti.
Other titles: Ammon's horn
Description: New York : Other Press, [2023]
Identifiers: LCCN 2023006269 (print) | LCCN 2023006270 (ebook) |
ISBN 9781635423600 (paperback) | ISBN 9781635423617 (ebook)
Subjects: LCGFT: Thrillers (Fiction) | Novels.
Classification: LCC PR9160.9.M34 A83 2023 (print) |
LCC PR9160.9.M34 (ebook) | DDC 823/.92—dc23/eng/20230524
LC record available at https://lccn.loc.gov/2023006269
LC ebook record available at https://lccn.loc.gov/2023006270

TO AMBROISE, BÉRÉNICE, AND HENRI,

OUR THREE WONDERFUL CHILDREN

"Ammon's Horn," is the name that ancient anatomists gave to the hippocampus, one of the brain areas involved in memory, and where the initial pathology of Alzheimer's disease occurs.

OPERNHAUS, ZURICH, SWITZERLAND

DECEMBER 14, 2017

Fred Lindenmayer was about to conclude the meeting of the Opernhaus board when he felt his phone vibrating inside his jacket. He looked at the caller ID, excused himself, and left the room. It was Heidi, his personal assistant. She knew he was in a meeting and would never call if not for a very good reason.

"Fred, I'm so sorry to disturb your meeting, but this is an emergency."

Fred immediately thought about his wife. "Has something happened to Meg?"

"Yes, Fred, I'm afraid so."

His heart skipped a beat. "What happened? Where is she?"

"She is at Sprüngli's, in the manager's office. They couldn't find your cell number, but they had the office number and—"

"What the hell is going on?" Fred was getting impatient, and Heidi knew better than to drag out her explanations.

"Apparently one of the saleswomen at the chocolate shop recognized her and called the manager. Meg has been wandering through the shop and the tearoom in a state of agitation asking everyone when the chocolate Easter eggs would be available. She is now having some tea and has calmed down, but she doesn't remember her name and doesn't seem to know where she is." Heidi could not hear anything on the other end. "Fred, are you there?"

"Yes, yes, Heidi, I'm listening," he replied. He felt cold fear closing in on his heart as he paced up and down the corridor outside the meeting room while nervously rattling the keys in his jacket pocket. "Please tell them that I'll be there in about twenty minutes, I'm leaving the meeting now."

Fred rushed back into the meeting room, whispered an excuse into the board secretary's ear, grabbed his computer bag, and left without another look at the people around the table, who had stopped talking. He ran down the imposing staircase of the Opernhaus, holding on to the handrail as he felt his legs going wobbly. Upon reaching the ground floor, he bolted to the right, heading toward the side door. His driver was waiting and within seconds they were on their way.

This was the moment he had been dreading ever since Meg had been diagnosed with Alzheimer's two years ago. From this point, nothing could stop the decline of her condition. He felt helpless and angry at the same time.

When the car pulled up at Sprüngli's on Paradeplatz fifteen minutes later, Fred felt like they had been driving for hours. The manager's assistant was waiting for him at the door and took him up to the office without a word. When she opened the door, Fred saw Meg sitting there with a cup of tea she was cradling with both hands. She raised her head toward him with an empty look in her eyes.

Fred nodded to Mrs. Niggli, the manager, and went to kneel by Meg's side. He gently took her hand. "Hello, my darling, how are you?"

Meg looked at him and dropped the cup on the floor. The crash made her startle and she stood up.

"Would you like to go home, sweetheart?" he asked.

Fred took hold of her arm, but she withdrew it violently and stepped back, almost falling over the chair she had been sitting in.

"Who are you?" she replied. "I don't know you. I want to stay here and have another cake while waiting for my Easter eggs."

Meg was shouting, raising her arm and threatening to hit him. Large halos of sweat showed on her silk blouse. As Fred took hold of her arm to stop her, he noticed the smeared makeup on her face and her untidy hairdo. What had become of his impeccable-looking wife?

Noticing Fred's dismay, Mrs. Niggli stepped in and gently taking Meg's elbow guided her toward the door. "Why don't you and I go choose another cake, Mrs. Lindenmayer," she said softly, "and then I will take you to your car."

Meg looked at her, delighted. "Yes, thank you, my dear, and let's not forget the chocolate eggs."

Fred followed them to the elevator, and once out of the door, Meg seemed to recognize José, the driver, who was holding the backseat door open for them.

"Hello, José, what a great time I had here. Let's do it again soon." She shook Mrs. Niggli's hand and lowered herself into the car.

Fred got in on the other side and asked José to drive them home.

In the car, Meg fell into a deep slumber and Fred called her neurologist. Though Professor Trümper was about the leave the hospital, he assured Fred that he could meet them at their home within half an hour.

———

Meg woke just as the car was pulling up at their front door. She looked at Fred and seemed to be surprised. She smiled at him. "Hello, darling, why are you in the car with me? We did a great job finishing the Christmas shopping, didn't we?" She did not move to get out of the car.

Fred stretched both his hands toward her to signal he was helping her out of the car.

"Hello, my Meggy," said Fred helping her out of the car. "Why don't we go in and have a drink?"

"That would be lovely, but I first need to look at my shopping bags."

Fred felt tears welling up in his eyes as he was talking to her, "José will bring your bags inside once he has parked the car, don't worry."

Meg followed him in, and Fred handed their coats to Ida, the housekeeper.

When he turned to talk to Meg, he saw that she stood very still, as if rooted to the floor of the hallway.

"I don't know this place, why don't we go home," said Meg in a shaky voice, "and I'm not sure I want to stay here. But I'm really thirsty. May I please have some tea?"

"Of course, my Meggy." Fred guided her to the library and asked Ida to bring some tea and cakes. Once settled in her favorite armchair by the fireplace, Meg went back to sleep.

LINDENMAYER RESIDENCE, KÜSNACHT, SWITZERLAND

APRIL 28, 2018

Standing at a window framed by a heavy brocade curtain, Jonathan Boswell waited for the next contestant to arrive. When his boss, Mr. Lindenmayer, had first told him about the award, he had been moderately enthusiastic. At this stage of his life, he was never more than moderately enthusiastic about anything. However, he had not anticipated the effect of seeing the young contestants.

The first contestant, Sarah Majewski, had arrived early for her appointment that morning. She had run up the steps then slowly ambled back down. With big, dreamy eyes, she stared at the stone house. She was a tall, slender woman. When Boswell opened the door, she greeted him with a strong American accent. He had adopted his most avuncular tone and had led her up the stairs to the drawing room, seating her in a comfortable armchair to wait for Mr. Lindenmayer. He wasn't worried about her. He felt sure she was a contestant that he would be able to manipulate.

Next had been Philip Caldwell-Tyson. The strong jaw and stocky build did not fool Boswell for a minute. He could not have said precisely what had given Philip away. He certainly didn't reveal his sexual orientation in his gestures or even in his manner of walking or in his British accent, but it was quite clear to Boswell that the man was gay.

The third contestant, Jean-Pierre Abdoulayé, might be less easy to manipulate. He had arrived at eleven o'clock on the dot. A short, wiry man with dark skin and a French accent, he had run up the steps and pressed the gold button twice, and then, when Boswell tarried, a third time. Despite his annoyance, Boswell trusted that he had adopted a relaxed demeanor that in no way revealed his displeasure. "I'm sorry to keep you waiting," he said, in a breezy manner. "Mr. Lindenmayer is in the drawing room." He pointed him to the stairs, but did not bother to accompany him all the way. It was too bad for him if he got lost.

After Lindenmayer's lunch break, Boswell led the fourth contestant, Yucun Fang, into the cloakroom, where he reviewed her appearance. "Very nice," he said, admiring the shiny black hair that gleamed beneath the light. He almost whispered "my accomplice" but decided not to, fearing it might make her uncomfortable. He approved of her outfit. In the navy blue skirt and white shirt, she almost looked like a schoolgirl. The pumps accentuated the shape of her legs. He led her all the way to Mr. Lindenmayer, right up to his chair. Bowing, he introduced her before tiptoeing out of the room.

Now Boswell was most eager to meet Edoardo Gardelli, the fifth and final contestant, who should have arrived ten minutes ago.

CITY CENTER, ZURICH, SWITZERLAND

APRIL 28, 2018

The afternoon traffic was at its worst at four o'clock, as Edoardo Gardelli tried to navigate his way through Zurich from the airport. Although concerned about arriving late for the meeting with the wealthy Swiss businessman, Edoardo still felt upbeat. His plane from Milan had landed on time. He had been confident that he would arrive at Fred Lindenmayer's house in Küsnacht, a nearby suburb, at five. But now he was stuck on Limmatquai—a street in Old Town that runs parallel to the Limmat River.

Edoardo was looking forward to meeting with the creator of the Lindenmayer Award, as he had put much hope in being chosen as a candidate for it. His knowledge of the man he was about to meet was limited to the scant biographical notes included in the ad when the competition was announced in scientific journals. After discovering the ad in *Science*, he googled Fred Lindenmayer. But apart from a few business articles about the Lindenmayer financial consortium, there was surprisingly little information about him. What Edoardo did learn was that although Lindenmayer could have run with the international jet set, he didn't. He even managed to avoid publicity in the financial press despite being known as the scion of one of Switzerland's wealthiest families. An architect and owner of a ski resort in the United States, Lindenmayer had moved back to Switzerland to take over the family business when his older brother had passed away in 2015.

He wondered if Lindenmayer would be shy and withdrawn or arrogant and distant like many moguls of finance could be. Even more mysterious was the man's motivation for creating the award. Why was this prominent businessman interested in brain research and how much did he actually know about the field into which he would be pouring so much of his fortune?

Edoardo didn't notice the traffic light turning green. Immediately cars started honking behind him. When he took off abruptly, the tires squealed.

Reaching Bellevue Platz at the end of Limmatquai, he saw blue blinking lights: On the scene of an accident were an ambulance and two police cars. What a mess. He cut the engine; there was no way he'd be moving for a while.

He took a moment to check his reflection in the mirror to ensure that he looked presentable after his flight. Not bad, he thought, seeing his Mediterranean features reflected in the rearview mirror: black hair, hazel eyes, tanned skin. He wore his wavy hair brushed back with a touch of gel, hoping the length compensated for his receding hairline. He was dressed simply but elegantly in khaki trousers, a striped white-and-blue button-down oxford shirt, and a navy blue Armani blazer.

It struck him how happy he was, even now, trapped in traffic with the clock ticking on an appointment that could change his life. He'd been blessed with a happy disposition and the good luck of having been raised by a loving family. Up to now, there was no denying that he had been very fortunate. He was also completely committed to his work. After many years of conducting research on the brain, he was still fascinated by what Woody Allen defines as his "second favorite organ." Ever since high school, when he'd dissected a cow's brain in biology class and learned how much there still was to discover about its functions, Edoardo had been hooked.

He loved the idea of knowing what his brain was doing at that moment as it reacted to the flashing lights, the cars honking, and the exhaust fumes from running engines. He imagined his nerve cells firing as each sensory impression aroused one of the systems that allowed him to connect with the external world; the neurological mechanism was exquisitely precise. He thought of the neurons in his retina being activated by the light and sending signals at a speed of approximately two hundred miles per hour to specialized centers in his brain that processed visual information and alerted him to what he was viewing. At that very minute, the information from the streets of Zurich was being integrated and stored in a distributed memory system, not just one single area of his brain concerned with memory but many different ones.

Awe-inspiring!

"*Vorwärts, vorwärts,*" the firm voice of a policeman exclaimed. *Move ahead.*

As the cars in front of Edoardo finally moved, he reached for the ignition key. He crossed Bellevue Platz at a slow pace. Soon he was accelerating on Seestrasse along the water. He couldn't wait to reach Küsnacht. He remembered once before visiting this rich neighborhood of Zurich's Goldküste, a playground for millionaires who purchased estates created by star architects. He had been eight years old and came with his parents and two sisters to visit his godmother. Seeing the road sign indicating the entrance to the village, he sighed with relief.

Fred Lindenmayer's secretary had given him very precise directions—how could it be otherwise for a Swiss—and within three minutes he was ringing the doorbell of Seestrasse 33. Unfortunately, this meant he was ten minutes late.

A distinguished but rather uptight gentleman in his late forties greeted him at the door. He was dressed in a black tight-fitting suit. "I'm Jonathan Boswell, Fred Lindenmayer's personal assistant. I hope you had a safe trip, Dr. Gardelli."

"Yes, thanks, Mr. Boswell. It was fine except for the traffic jam."

"Dr. Boswell," the man corrected, his smile disappearing. "Please follow me into the drawing room." He turned, leading Edoardo through the large round entrance hall and up a marble stairway.

The change in the assistant's tone of voice surprised Edoardo. He must have missed Boswell's title in the letter that accompanied the application papers he had received from him.

The assistant opened the door to a small drawing room and asked Edoardo if he cared for a drink. While Boswell poured him a glass of water, Edoardo observed him. Of medium build, Boswell had a long face, narrow nose, and steely gray eyes behind small metal-rimmed round glasses. His hair was reddish-blond and cut very short. Edoardo wondered what kind of doctorate he held, maybe in finance or economics, given who his employer was.

Boswell handed Edoardo the glass and informed him that Mr. Lindenmayer would join him shortly, before politely excusing himself. Edoardo looked around the room: The Chippendale furniture was exquisite and the peach-and-cream-colored walls were the perfect backdrop for the half-dozen paintings. Most of the paintings looked as if they could be authentic masterpieces, but one in particular caught his attention. He walked across the room to check the signature on the lower right corner: Henri Matisse. "Oh my God," he exclaimed in surprise. It could have been one of the great works he had viewed in a Matisse exhibit in Madrid a few months earlier.

"You must be wondering if it is an original," a deep voice said.

Startled, Edoardo turned around to face a tall, broad-shouldered man who extended his hand.

"Hello, Edoardo, I'm Fred. It's a pleasure to meet you."

"Likewise, Mr. Lindenmayer."

Fred Lindenmayer was casually dressed in corduroy pants, a button-down shirt, and a navy V-neck cashmere sweater. As they shook hands, Edoardo noted the intense expression on his host's face; he had deep blue eyes, a generous mustache, and a full head of silvery hair. Between the firmness of his grip and the steadiness of his gaze, he radiated authority.

"Come on, *mein junger Freund*, sit down and let me satisfy your curiosity about the Lindenmayer Award."

Lindenmayer had introduced himself in English, but used this amiable expression in his native German. Edoardo knew the American version was "my young friend" and appreciated that Lindenmayer had used it to put him at ease.

"And, yes, it is a Matisse."

"I recently visited an exhibit at the Thyssen-Bornemisza Museum while I was in Madrid for a meeting on Alzheimer's," Edoardo said as he took the seat Lindenmayer offered. "It looks very similar to one that was there."

"Actually this is the same one. It just came back a couple of weeks ago." Fred's smile broadened, reminding Edoardo of a proud father. "But let's get serious. What about some California wine? I know from your application letter that you appreciate fine wines."

Beside the decanter, Fred picked up a bottle from the delicately carved wooden basket that allowed several bottles to be stacked in individual compartments. He handed it to Edoardo: a 1985 Stag's Leap Cabernet Sauvignon Cask 23.

"This is almost impossible to find these days. It is one of my favorites," Edoardo said with enthusiastic surprise. He returned it to Fred with a grin.

"I thought so, which is why I chose it." Fred poured the beautifully smooth dark red wine from the decanter.

Edoardo wondered why this wealthy Swiss businessman would want to give an endowment of a hundred million US dollars to establish an institute for Alzheimer's disease research.

Fred sipped from his wineglass. "I'm sure you would like to know what this is all about, Edoardo, so let me tell you my motivation for this competition."

Nodding, Edoardo followed his host's example, enjoying the taste of the rich, fruity Cabernet.

"You see my wife, Meg, who has been my right hand, my business partner, my confidante, and, most of all, the love of my life, was diagnosed with Alzheimer's disease in 2015. At first, I refused to accept what her neurologist told me, that there is no cure. I contacted the best-known neurological institutes around the world and I even hired a medical student to research the literature of the disease. But I soon found out that not only is there no cure but not much can be done to slow down its progression. In the last twenty years, we have learned nothing new."

"I'm so sorry to hear about your wife, sir," Edoardo said with genuine sadness.

Fred paused and waved his hand to offer more wine. "I'm sorry about getting a bit personal. But I want my candidates to understand what motivated me to set up the competition."

"I understand," Edoardo said.

Fred looked up at a painting of a lovely young woman with emerald green eyes that hung over the fireplace and Edoardo wondered if it was a portrait of his wife as a young woman.

"Ultimately," Fred continued, "I owed it to her to fight with her, for her. My thoughts went to all the families coping with Alzheimer's patients. I concluded that I was very lucky to be healthy and affluent and that I had to do something to help all these other people who might not have the energy or the means to assist their loved ones."

Fred took a sip of his wine and looked at Edoardo with his steady gaze. "That's why I decided to make the best of our terrible fate, Meg's and mine." He leaned forward. "I want to fight with Meg against this illness and the best way, as I see it, is to contribute as much as I can toward igniting research on Alzheimer's." He leaned back in his chair. "But I'm talking too much, I'm sure you must have questions for me."

Edoardo found himself grappling with what to say. "Hmm, yes, of course. I guess, I'm wondering about the practicalities of the competition? How is it going to work? What do we need to do?"

Fred lifted one hand. "You hit on exactly the right questions: Dr. Boswell will brief all of the contestants about the technicalities of the competition tonight at the dinner you will have with him"

Through the open door, Boswell had followed all of Fred's discussion with Edoardo. He was sitting at his desk in a small adjoining room, which had become his office, and he wondered why he had told Edoardo to call him doctor instead of mister. What upset Boswell was his own lack of control and what the slip had revealed to him about his own feelings. Until now his performance had been flawless. He was certain that not one of the competitors had guessed his less than charitable feelings toward them. It was not the strain of maintaining the performance. It was not because Edoardo was the most charismatic of the contestants. It wasn't even because Edoardo was one of those people you could tell had never really suffered, a man blessed from the start with wealth and intelligence and a loving family. Unlike other competitors, Edoardo didn't really need to win the award. It would just be another feather in his cap. It was because he saw himself in Edoardo. That was what he could not forgive. Boswell had also once had all the opportunities this young man had. "I might even have dressed the same way, only I would have worn a tie," he thought, getting up from his chair and staring out the window at the courtyard where Edoardo's rental car was parked.

The courtyard reminded him of a similar one at Mara's house in Johannesburg. And he thought back to his first meeting with Henry McCall, the president of McCall Diamonds and, more important, the father of the woman he would always love more than any other. McCall had welcomed him graciously enough into his home. At that point, of course, Boswell was only Mara's boyfriend and did not present any real threat. McCall had been only too happy to show him around the opulent house with innumerable servants and an immense garden with a pool. Looking back, Boswell thought that there was only one moment that foreshadowed McCall's future behavior. Why? Boswell wasn't sure, but he still remembered Mara coming down the marble staircase. He had never seen anyone more ravishing. She wore a light green moiré dress with a string of pearls that glowed against her neck. Upon reaching them, her father said, before Boswell could speak, "You look lovely, my dear. It will not be easy to find a husband who matches your glamour." She did not say anything but took a seat beside Boswell and listened to her father grill him about his scientific achievements.

Now, hearing his boss's melodious voice explaining the reason for the competition, he wished that he could trade places with Edoardo. But that was not possible. He had closed that door a long time ago. What upset him most was the realization that he had not overcome his feelings of envy and regret. Far from it. They had simply been suppressed. And in the wake of these feelings, Boswell's need for a certain white substance had also reemerged as if the two were connected. He reached across his desk, crushing a delicate piece of paper between his fingers. Then, realizing that he had damaged the origami that Yucun had given him, he tried to undo the damage, but it was beyond repair so he threw it into the wastebasket. He must act and not just take what he was being dealt. First, he would put in a call to Cuno Milic, to get some cocaine. Next, he would call Yucun. He needed to make sure he could gain her complete devotion. She did not yet know what he had in mind for her. It still irritated him that Fred had refused to give "his dear Jonathan" the solution to all of the riddles of the competition. Fred had insisted on a complicated system involving a Webmaster, which required the hiring of the annoying Bobby, who was already getting in Boswell's way, and a notary. It was all completely unnecessary as far as Boswell was concerned.

After accompanying Edoardo to his rental car, Fred turned to look up at the house. He thought he saw someone move back from the window, but it was probably his imagination. He had enjoyed talking with each of the contestants. Their enthusiasm was contagious. He must find Meg to tell her all about them. Although he knew that she didn't always follow everything he shared with her, he couldn't bear to change the way he communicated with her. He talked and talked to fill the silence. He could almost always find her sitting in her favorite armchair by the window in her boudoir, a room she had never used before her illness, laughing at the very notion of a boudoir, but now increasingly she spent more and more time in its sanctuary.

As he approached her boudoir, he heard voices and immediately recognized Boswell's. Such a good man, he thought, always so solicitous of Meg. He had come to depend on him more and more. It was hard to believe that he had hesitated hiring him. Boswell's manners were stiff, but once one got used to it, one appreciated his thoughtfulness. He always seemed able to antici-pate Fred's or Meg's needs. Fred stood in the doorway watching Boswell help tuck a mauve mohair blanket around Meg's legs. She seemed to feel the cold more, whether because of Alzheimer's or because she simply did not move around as much, Fred did not know.

"Thank you, Jonathan," he said. "So very kind of you. Please feel free to leave. It was quite a long day."

"Yes, sir, I just have a few things to attend to."

"What did you think of our contestants? I feel very fortunate. Each one is such a talented scientist and they come from such diverse backgrounds."

"I must say I was particularly impressed with the Chinese candidate...hmm...Yucun?" said Boswell.

"Quite remarkable, particularly given the obstacles she must have had to face. I'm looking forward to telling Meg all about them." He pulled up another armchair, identical to the one Meg was sitting in, so that they could sit close to each other. Then he leaned forward and took her hands in his. "Sarah was the first candidate. Something about her reminded me of you when we first met."

Meg smiled mischievously at him. "Is she good at tying ski bindings?"

Fred laughed, remembering that the first time he met Meg, when he had come around a curve too fast and plowed right into a fir tree. After brushing off the snow, he had noticed a dazzling young woman looking at him, smiling, and handing him the ski that had come off.

"That was a very lucky fall," he said.

SAVOY CLUB,
ZURICH, SWITZERLAND

APRIL 29, 2018

Hans, the maître d' at the Savoy Club, was looking at the four gentlemen sitting in the smoking lounge. They seemed to know one another very well, as there was an ease in their conversation and a lot of laughing. Hans of course knew Mr. Lindenmayer because he visited the club quite often for business lunches. But who could the other three gentlemen be, Hans wondered. He had never seen them at the club. And Hans would know—he had an extremely good memory for faces and had developed quite an acute sense of observation during the many decades he had been working here. As the discussion grew even more animated, Hans decided that it would not be a good moment to ask if they wanted any refills for their drinks. Mr. Lindenmayer would call him if he was needed, and so Hans stepped back into the room behind the bar.

Discretion is indeed what this exclusive gentlemen's club is all about. Founded in 1891 as an overseas club by Swiss gentlemen who had been expats, the club has its seat at the Savoy Hotel on Paradeplatz, across the street for the famous Sprüngli chocolate shop.

Fred was laughing and puffing on a Cuban cigar as he turned toward the group of his closest friends, with whom he had brainstormed over the last few months about the award.

Gunnar said, "I would like to know why you have chosen the mysterious and very charming Sarah as one of the competitors."

"You old playboy, you haven't changed a bit since we were trying to seduce French girls on our trip to Chambord so many decades ago. And I'm sure Jacques and Piergiulio also remember that you always tried to be the first to speak when we met up with girls at the locals' bar in Amboise."

"You were a sly fox with your Swedish charm," added Jacques, with a twinkle in his eyes. "You'd have thought that between a great-looking Italian," he said raising his glass of Islay malt to Piergiulio, "a well-groomed Swiss guy," he nodded to Fred, "and a very humorous Belgian," pointing a finger at himself, "the girls would not be completely taken by you my friend."

"But so it was, gentlemen, what can I say." Gunnar was quite content with himself. "And believe me, my great charm is still working today!" His friends booed him.

"Enough ego trip, my dear Gunnar, let me get back to answering Piergiulio's question about the final choice of contestants," Fred said. "I must admit it was quite difficult to choose in the end. And to come back to Sarah, my heart went all wobbly when I saw her coming through my office door for the interview." He paused for a while before continuing with a dreamy look in his eyes. "Sarah is the spitting image of Natacha, my first real love, whom I met at university."

"I certainly remember her," Jacques interjected, "all Fred did during his second year in architecture in Zurich was to woo the beautiful Natacha, writing poetry for her, taking her on romantic outings, and talking only about how you missed her when she was not with you. How could I forget her? I hardly saw you during that year!"

"And I have the feeling you still resent her because of that," Fred replied, "but anyway, this beautiful love story ended when Natacha decided to leave Zurich for an exchange year in the States. So of course Sarah, being also of Russian heritage, and most of all a brilliant scientist, was an obvious choice for me."

"Fine, we can understand that, but then what about Yucun, who is the opposite of Sarah?" asked Piergiulio. "You tell us she is very shy and seems to be completely ill at ease when you talk to her."

"Well, that is exactly what intrigued me," admitted Fred. "Her uneasiness and shyness was exactly what got me interested in her. After talking to her, I was also feeling very compassionate about the way life had treated her and her family. With a mentally disabled sister and parents who had lived through the horrors of the Cultural Revolution, life in China must have been very hard during her young years. I hope the award, and of course the chance to win it, will sort of compensate for all the years of deprivation she has suffered. I am also told that her research project is at the cutting edge."

"I understand, your old Saint Bernard feelings coming up again," Piergiulio added to try and lighten the atmosphere. "We know what a generous man you are, my dear Fred."

Fred raised a hand to call Hans. "I do think we need a refill before moving on," he suggested, and his friends all nodded in approval.

"Now let me tell you about the three other contestants," Fred offered, "before we get too drunk. I will start with a bit of an ego trip, as Edoardo reminds me so much of myself. Not only were we both born with a silver spoon in our mouths but he loves good wine and is an excellent golfer."

His friends burst out laughing. "Good for him," said Jacques, "but with regards to you, we have always wondered what came first for you: your wife and children or golf and wine."

The others howled with delight as they felt quite tipsy now, being on their third whiskey.

"Seriously, are you still interested in my choice of the other contestants or shall we go through for dinner?" Fred asked, seeing that they would all be quite drunk if they didn't have some food sooner rather than later.

"Okay, okay," Gunnar said, "tell us quickly about the Brit and the Frog."

"Fine, let's start with the poor Frenchman you call a frog," Fred went on. "When I started talking with Jean-Pierre, his heavy French accent reminded me of a fellow ski instructor when I was working in Aspen with whom I had a lot of fun and who became a close friend. But of course that is not all. Jean-Pierre has the same positive attitude I have toward life in general, and I'm much impressed with the originality of his research on glial cells, which make up half of the brain. Indeed, my dears, I've learned that neurons only make up about half of the brain. Glial cells are the future in neuroscience."

"Hooray for glial cells then," cheered Piergiulio. "I'm starving, but let's just have a few words about the Brit, please Fred."

"Fine, fine, I can see you bunch of drunkards do not really care." Fred was really enjoying himself. "But here is to Philip. You may remember that before I took over the family business from my brother a few years ago, I took a crash course in corporate management at the Oxford Centre for Management Studies, where I met Winston, a wonderful Brit called Winnie by his friends. He had, like Philip, the most incredible aristocratic British accent I have ever heard. But on a more serious note, I must say that Philip impressed me considerably with his sharp intelligence and attention to detail when talking about science."

At this Fred got up and declared: "It's time to move to the dining room, gentlemen, for some serious wine after these few drops of malt!" And he was cheered extensively.

LINDENMAYER CORPORATE HEADQUARTERS, ZURICH, SWITZERLAND

APRIL 30, 2018

A very auspicious beginning, Boswell thought, as he observed numerous journalists entering the large conference room. "We need more chairs," he instructed a young intern. "The press conference is about to begin," he announced. There was no doubt that the Lindenmayer Award was generating a great deal of interest. Thanks to yours truly, he thought. He had suggested to Fred that they specify on the invitation the amount—a hundred million US dollars—for the award without giving any further details. "Bound to titillate," he'd said to Fred. He remembered using that word: titillate.

They couldn't have chosen a better setting. No one could fail to be impressed by the top floor of the Rotes

Schloss on General Guisan Quai, a huge castle-like red-brick building designed in the 1890s. The room offered a wonderful view of the Arboretum and Lake Zurich. Paintings by Segantini, Anker, and Hodler, along with two sculptures by Giacometti, were a testimony to the deep-rooted Swiss tradition and wealth of the Lindenmayer family, who had been pioneers of the industrial revolution in Zurich at the end of the nineteenth century.

Even from the back of the room, Boswell could see that Fred was impressed by the turnout. He kept glancing around at the sea of journalists. Almost all of the major Swiss newspapers and many international publications had sent correspondents. There was a nice mix of science and business journalists. They didn't often cross paths. But it was a fairly rare event, Boswell thought: a wealthy businessman donating a significant portion of his personal fortune to set up a private research institute. He had also urged Fred to include, on the invitation, the purpose of the proposed institute: research into a cure for Alzheimer's. Another brilliant suggestion of his that would no doubt lead dear Fred to suppose that Boswell's every move was dedicated to the success of the award when nothing could be further from the truth.

As Fred took the stage for his introductory remarks, Boswell did not feel obliged to listen to the prepared statement given by Fred. After all he had already read it. In fact, he had suggested a few alterations.

As Boswell was looking around the suddenly quiet room, he noticed that annoying Bobby waving at him. Perhaps he could pretend he didn't see him. No, the man was now creating quite the stir. He would have to pay attention and, no doubt, Bobby was getting agitated over absolutely nothing. It really was quite frustrating that Fred had felt the necessity to hire him. "I know you would like to do everything," Fred had said, "but we must hire a Webmaster."

"Whatever for? I'm quite capable of overseeing everything. I'm up-to-date on the latest technology."

"Yes, yes, my dear Jonathan, I'm sure you are. But, if nothing else, it's better for cybersecurity reasons."

"Are you anticipating some trouble?" Boswell had been unable to restrain himself.

"I can see that I've worried you," Fred said, patting his arm. "But really, trust me, it's all for the best."

"Yes?" Boswell said now, turning to Bobby who had come up to where he was sitting. "What is it you need? What is so urgent?"

"Someone has hacked into my e-mail account," Bobby said, his voice quivering.

"I'm sorry, but really, there's no need for alarm. It happens all the time." Boswell waved at him as a sign that he wanted to be left alone. "Besides, what could you have in your e-mails that's so important?"

"It's the timing." Bobby was wringing his hands.

"I think that you are reading far too much into it. Now, if you told me that all the contestants' e-mail accounts had been hacked into, I might be more alarmed."

"Do you think I should let Mr. Lindenmayer know?"

"Of course, not. Why worry the poor man? Let him enjoy this moment. He's been looking forward it."

Boswell pointed to Fred, and Bobby finally turned around and left the room, looking resigned. Boswell felt quite frustrated by this exchange with Bobby, as it reminded him there had been absolutely nothing of consequence in Bobby's e-mails. All the man seemed to be interested in was organizing dart competitions with friends in some pub.

There was suddenly a brief silence followed by loud clapping. Fred must have concluded his remarks. When Boswell moved closer to the podium, he saw quite a few people with tears in their eyes. He wished he could still feel that kind of emotion, but the truth was that nothing—except for onions—could bring tears to his eyes these days. Now Fred was taking questions.

Fred pointed to the affiliate of the *Neue Zürcher Zeitung*. "Yes, Rosemarie."

"Fred, the press kit says that you had more than two hundred applications. How many did you expect? And how many did you submit to the selection committee?"

Fred smiled. "I didn't know what to expect. I guessed that the amount of funding involved would be a strong attraction. I presented thirty-five candidates to the committee, out of which five were selected over Skype for an interview with me. We had anticipated choosing only three contestants, but in view of the scientific excellence and the outstanding personalities of the five scientists I interviewed, I recommended to the committee that we keep all five as contestants."

"What were the selection criteria?" asked Dietmar Wegener, from the *Frankfurter Allgemeine Zeitung.*

"The committee members insisted on having a group of contestants representative of diverse gender, geographical and cultural backgrounds, scientific training, as well as personalities and life skills. Personally, I was eager to select adventurous individuals who could think outside the box, who could show that they were driven by a genuine desire to cure diseases rather than being obsessed with the conventional indicators of scientific success, such as impact factors of journals and all that nonsense." Fred made this last statement with a touch of impatience in his voice.

Tony Hunt, a spry young journalist from *Nature,* waved his hand. "I'm sorry, Mr. Lindenmayer," he said when Fred signaled for him to speak. "This sounds ambitious, but if I may, also very idealistic, even a bit naïve. With such atypical selection criteria, didn't you worry that only mavericks would apply, or even out-casts, rather than serious scientists?"

"Sometimes the best minds are considered outcasts because they don't follow the conventional paths. In addition, the notion of an outcast is relative. I think I have a pretty good eye to spot individuals with the 'right stuff' for the job, even in this particular context," Fred assured him.

"Mr. Lindenmayer," Carmen Sandoval from *El País* broke into the discussion, "how is the competition going to run, practically?"

Fred stroked his mustache with two fingers. "Let me give you a brief overview on the rules and procedures of the competition. It will last a maximum of thirty days, starting today. After this press conference, the award team will meet with the contestants for a briefing. Each of them will receive an iPhone and iPad and a bank account with twenty thousand euros for their expenses. The award team consists of Dr. Jonathan Boswell, my personal assistant, who will act as chief executive; Mr. Bobby Cochran, our Webmaster, who will serve as liaison between the team and the candidates; and, of course, myself."

"Could you give us some clues about the riddles that were mentioned in the press kit?" asked Ghislaine De Rochefort, the science correspondent from *Le Monde*.

"I can't tell you much at this point, as you can imagine. But I can explain how the contestants are going to deal with them." Fred outlined the concept of the five riddles and how each riddle was comprised of two components: a historical part and a scientific part. "To begin with, the contestants have to figure out the historical location and actually travel there. On site, they'll search for the clue that will give them the solution to the neuroscience component of the riddle."

"It's difficult to imagine these riddles. Can you give us an example?" Ghislaine persisted.

Fred seemed to hesitate, then he shrugged and continued, "Why not? We discarded several riddles that were proposed by the selection committee. Here's one: 'In the waters at the feet of the Virgin; lost in her dreams, she was wandering unconscious.' We rejected this one for being unbalanced. The second part is too easy: Who wanders unconscious while sleeping, as hinted by 'lost in her dreams'?"

"Someone who suffers from somnambulism," offered the red-haired Cecilia Rossetti from *La Stampa*. "That would reflect the part having to do with the brain."

"Yes, easy indeed." Fred nodded. "And also limited to a rather particular aspect of neuroscience, a sleep disorder. But who has a clue for the historic and geographical reference in the first part of the riddle?"

"Fatima," João Nunez de Carvalho, the Portuguese-born correspondent from *Le Temps*, said triumphantly. "The Fatima sanctuary dedicated to the Virgin Mary is located only a few miles from the ocean."

"We are not talking about that Virgin," Fred said.

A long silence ensued during which Boswell noticed that many in the audience were smiling, having understood the challenge awaiting the contestants.

"If such a distinguished group as the one present in this room cannot find clues to the first part of the riddle, it means that we have set the difficulty at the right level," Fred said. "The Virgin we are talking about is the Jungfrau, the imposing mountain near Lake Thun in central Switzerland. Its name means 'virgin' in German. The link between the first and second part of the riddle is *La Sonnambula*, the famous opera by Bellini in which a romance between Amina, who suffers from somnambulism, and Elvino, a local farmer, unfolds in a village on the foothills of the Jungfrau."

Cecilia Rossetti's arm went up. "When will the contestants receive the riddles?"

"Tonight at midnight they will receive the five riddles via e-mail. They can then choose which riddle they want to solve first. As soon as the contestant thinks she or he has solved a riddle, they send an e-mail to our Webmaster, with the answer and a picture of herself or himself at the historical location with our on-site representative. At each location, we have contacted a staff person and informed them about the competition. This contact person will be able to tell the contestant if the solution is correct. If it is, the contestant can move on to the next riddle. The first contestant who has solved all five correctly, within the next thirty days, will be the winner."

A hand was raised and Fred called on Franz Marmier, head of the business and economics desk at the *Tages-Anzeiger*. "Mr. Lindenmayer, I was wondering if you could tell us more about the benefits the winner of the award will enjoy. And also, may we put some questions to the contestants directly?"

"Absolutely," Fred replied smilingly, "it may be interesting for you to get to know them on a more personal level than what you can gather from their résumés in the press kit. I'll just give you a short insight into the position the winner will hold at the Lindenmayer Institute for Alzheimer's Research. This scientist will first participate in the design and construction of the new institute. She or he will be responsible for hiring the necessary staff and outlining a strategic plan for the first five years. And, of course, the winner will become its first director."

A Canadian journalist from the *Toronto Star* raised her hand. "Yes, Dominique."

"Fred, can you tell us why you think that your institute will perform better and do more insightful research on Alzheimer's?"

"That's a most challenging question, and I'm going to give you a simple answer. As you know, we Swiss usually think we're the best, so I simply acknowledged that fact and went ahead with my idea!" The reporters broke out in laughter, prompting Fred to add, "For those of you who aren't Swiss, you can at least observe that we also have a good sense of humor."

He continued, "On a more serious note, the five scientists we've selected are among the best in their age group—early thirties. They bear the 'special' qualities, like being able to think outside the box. In my view, all the elements for success are there. It appears that this is a good moment to introduce our young scientists so that you can ask all the questions you didn't dare put to me."

Boswell joined Fred on the stage, followed by the five contestants. "Ladies and gentlemen," Boswell said in his deep voice, which commanded attention, "please keep in mind that our contestants still have a long day ahead of them with briefings, a dinner reception, and the exciting moment when they'll receive the riddles at midnight. Be so kind as to keep your questions brief."

As the three men and two women took their seats behind a table facing the journalists, an elderly gentleman in the front row called out, "I'm Christopher Lawson from *The New York Times International Edition*. If I may make a suggestion to my honored colleagues," he craned his neck, "why don't we agree on two questions that we put to all five candidates? As I seem to be the veteran among you, I'll claim the privilege of age. Here is what I'd like to know."

Directing his attention to the contestants, Lawson asked, "First, what was your motivation to apply for the award, and, second, why do you think you were chosen?"

"The French have a reputation of having a big mouth and an even bigger ego," Jean-Pierre declared, as he sprang up from his seat, percolating with energy, and reached to click on the microphone standing on the table. He was short and wiry with a sly smile. "I'm Jean-Pierre Abdoulayé and my motivation was simple: after all, you have to do something in between the meals," he said in his heavy French accent.

"It's definitely not the answer we would have expected," Lawson fired back with a robust laugh. "Why do you think Mr. Lindenmayer chose you as a contestant?"

"Now on a more serious note," Jean-Pierre continued, "what I'm really interested in is to make the importance of glial cells relevant in studying neurodegenerative diseases like Alzheimer's. And as to your question about choosing me as a contestant, I would say probably for my charm and good looks," the French-man stated, titling his head like a dog waiting to be petted.

"We are obviously not going to get any serious answer out of you," another journalist said.

Boswell had to repress a snort of contempt. He had tried to chat with the man himself. Beneath the Frenchman's charm was a steely determination to succeed. Jean- Pierre was not about to divulge anything he didn't have to.

Call him a snob, but Jean-Pierre's origins were rather unimpressive. His father was a butcher and his mother a clerk. No doubt Jean-Pierre didn't have any family background that would help him in his career, and this award could be his unique chance at scientific success.

Suddenly Boswell's attention turned back to the contestants, as it was now Yucun's turn to speak.

"Do you think, Dr. Fang, that you could give us some more detailed information on your participation in this competition?" a correspondent from the *China Daily* asked.

"With pleasure," said Yucun, her cheeks rosy from the excitement of speaking with the media. "My motivation is to honor my parents, who have not had the opportunities that are offered to us today. They were victims of the Cultural Revolution." A silence followed this statement. Good girl, Boswell thought; always effective to trot out the story of a victim who has made good. Yucun continued in a measured voice: "As for the reason for choosing me for the competition, I imagine it's due to my research in the field of Alzheimer's and my scientific accomplishments."

Coming after the levity of the French candidate, these declarations changed the mood in the conference room, reminding people of the seriousness of the endeavor. There was an awkward pause as the reporters looked down and scribbled in their notebooks.

Boswell got up and tried to launch the discussion again by addressing Sarah Majewski, whom he had found warm and easy to talk with. "Dr. Majewski, maybe you could give us some input from a different angle," he suggested, extending his hand toward the attractive, young scientist.

She hesitated, obviously not quite sure how to reply. Boswell surmised that she had probably never attended a press conference.

"I was just thinking that I wasn't prepared for these kinds of questions. I could tell you anything about my research, but why I was chosen?" She stalled, as if she were afraid to say the truth. "Probably my scientific ambitions and my track record in publications showing that I'm capable of thinking outside the box, just as Mr.

Lindenmayer mentioned in his opening remarks," she added, leaning forward to look at Fred who was sitting at the end of the table.

She continued by explaining candidly that the award also presented a unique opportunity for her to change the course of her career in a significant way at this stage in her life.

Boswell then turned toward Edoardo Gardelli and Philip Caldwell-Tyson. "Well, gentlemen, it is your turn. Who will go next?"

The scientists looked at each other, each gesturing for the other to speak. Finally, Edoardo spoke up. "I believe Mr. Lindenmayer chose Philip and me because he is a Baptist and I'm a Taoist. But that's another story and I'd be happy to explain this inside joke to you after the press conference. On a more serious note, I think that my work on the role of the tau protein as a culprit in neuronal death has made a mark in the field of Alzheimer's research. That must be what the Selection Committee found would be a good contribution. As to my motivation to apply for the award, I would say that I see it as a real intellectual challenge and I love it! And now last but not least." He turned toward Philip.

Philip cleared his throat. "This is a difficult exercise for a Brit who definitely doesn't like to talk about himself," he started, a slight twitching of his lips betraying that he was not finding it difficult at all. "I applied to the competition as a challenge to myself. There is a tradition in my family never to take the easy road. So we keep looking for unusual challenges that will allow us to do better than our parents or siblings. Maybe this is also why Mr. Lindenmayer chose me, because to the Continentals, such British weirdness is quite attractive. And last but not least, as Dr. Gardelli mentioned, I'm a Baptist and he is a Taoist, so the committee probably figured we would be complementary."

The journalists seemed to appreciate the light-hearted tone the candidates had adopted and several were signaling to ask new questions. But Boswell had an appointment he had no intention of missing. He moved to bring the press conference to an end.

"Thanks for coming, everybody," he said, ignoring raised hands. "We'll keep you updated on our contestants' progress by e-mail during the coming weeks."

LINDENMAYER RESIDENCE, KÜSNACHT, SWITZERLAND

APRIL 30, 2018

All contestants had been invited for dinner to Fred and Meg's beautifully situated house on Lake Zurich in Küsnacht. Fred had planned for this evening to be special, particularly for Meg, who had expressed the wish to meet the contestants.

It had been quite an emotional moment when Meg had joined them for predinner drinks in the drawing room. She was almost her usual self, warm and welcoming, but she moved very slowly from one person to the next to shake their hands. After they had all taken a seat on the off-white couches facing a beautiful old fireplace in a semicircle, she told Yucun, Jean-Pierre, Sarah, Philip, and Edoardo how much she admired

Fred's dedication to push for a radical change in Alzheimer's research. She also emphasized how much she wanted them to hear about her struggles with the disease. She knew Fred was always very discreet about her condition, but for her it was important that these young scientists, who would probably dedicate most of their life to Alzheimer's research, heard her side of the story.

"You know," she explained, "this award is the best medication Fred came up with, as it gives hope to all of us who have been diagnosed with Alzheimer's."

She looked at Fred and took his hand, her eyes expressing all the love she had for him, but also the great distress she was in, not knowing for how long she'd be able to share her feelings with him.

"You are all wonderfully dedicated scientists but I realize how difficult it is to understand this illness. I'm talking to you now, but only a few months ago, I got lost in town, not remembering my name or what I was doing in the shop where Fred came to pick me up." There she paused as if she was trying to emphasize what she was saying, but she seemed to have a hard time going on and remembering what she was about to say.

"Sweetheart," Fred moved closer to her on the couch, "maybe you would like to retire, it has been a long day." He felt that dinner with all of them would be too much for her, and he was getting up to help her out of the room. But Meg sat up straight on the couch and raised her hand to indicate that she was fine and wanted to continue to speak. Fred noticed that her eyes started to wander off, looking at the people around her with a blank expression.

"Meg, darling, maybe I could take over and explain what you were going to say? You may have exhausted yourself a bit while talking." Meg looked at him with tenderness, and nodded her head in approval.

Fred continued, "What Meg means is that how you see her tonight may be very different from how she will be tomorrow. Tonight she is here with us, but in a few hours or days, her mind can suddenly switch off, particularly when she is in unfamiliar surroundings, and it will be like she is in another world, not recognizing the people around her."

"Thank you, my love." Meg squeezed Fred's hand. She was looking at the five young people sitting across from her and she smiled. "And also I want them to know about the award, and"—she was searching for the word—"the research, but I can't remember what I wanted to say."

Fred put an arm around her shoulders and drew her closer to him.

"For both Meg and myself, it is important that everybody understands what hope this new institute is giving Alzheimer's patients. As Meg sees it, the institute is an innovative opportunity for you, promising scientists, to change the course of research in this field, and for patients like her, she describes it as a rainbow of hope."

At this, the scientists' faces, which had shown concern and sadness while listening to the Lindenmayers, lightened up and the discussion switched to the award. They told Meg and Fred how excited they were to start the competition the next day. They would receive the riddles at midnight, and they seemed like a group of children about to go on a treasure hunt.

The contestants were intrigued to hear from Fred how this idea of an award came about. He told them about the brainstorming weekend he had organized at Swiss Creek with a number of trusted old friends. He told them about his past life in Aspen, at Swiss Creek. How he had met Meg, their first date, their wedding, when their children were born, and all the wonderful family trips they had taken to Europe to introduce their children, Barbara and Steven, to their European roots.

It was this reminiscing that gave him the idea to embed the contest in a European setting, giving the contestants an opportunity to learn more about Europe and its traditions.

"Yes," Meg interjected, "our honeymoon to Venice and Vienna was indeed so beautiful, and also the trip we took when Steven was born to..." And Meg looked at Fred with questioning eyes. "Where was it again? Paris? No, no it must have been Madrid, but..." And she hesitated again.

"Don't worry, my darling, our honeymoon in the south of Spain was indeed a remarkable experience, and so were the many trips we took with the children to Europe."

An animated discussion followed and the contestants all wanted to ask more questions about how Fred came up with the idea of designing a competition with riddles.

As the next question from Jean-Pierre was about to fuse, there was a knock at the door and Ida announced that dinner was served.

Ida immediately noticed that Meg was exhausted, and she came straight over to her. Fred's arm was still around her and she was leaning her head on his shoulder. Her eyes were closed. Fred and Ida helped her get up and all the scientists stood to say goodbye. Meg hugged each of the young people close, saying what wonderful children they were and that she and Fred would take them on a trip to Venice or Vienna. As Ida led Meg out of the room, a heavy silence fell on the party.

"Okay everyone," Fred announced, trying to keep the sadness out of his voice, "let's move to the dining room."

As Fred and the contestants sat down at the beautifully laid dinner table, Ida brought Meg to the library where she had left a dinner tray. The housekeeper helped her settle into her favorite armchair by the fireplace. Meg was looking around as if to figure out where she was. As her eyes moved to the picture frames on the fireplace mantel, Ida noticed a spark coming back into Meg's eyes. Ida started describing the pictures for her: Fred and her in Aspen just a few weeks after they met fifty years ago; their wedding in a flowery meadow above the resort; pictures of Barbara and Steven as babies, toddlers, and then college graduates. Meg saw her whole life sitting there in picture frames, and a few tears started rolling down her cheeks. Ida saw the tears and tried to console Meg by enticing her to eat her dinner. Ida rolled the tray table in front of Meg's armchair. She was hoping that Meg would enjoy her favorite meal: veal and mushrooms in a cream sauce, one of the highlights of Zurich gastronomy. Meg looked at her plate but did not make any move indicating she would start eating.

Ida discreetly put the fork and knife into Meg's hands and told her that she had prepared her favorite meal in honor of the contestants. Meg's eyes seemed to light up and she started eating slowly, still looking at the family pictures in silence.

PHILIP'S APARTMENT, LONDON, ENGLAND

MAY 1, 2018

As Philip waited in the small apartment he kept in his parents' town house in South Kensington, he could not sit still. He kept jumping up from the leather couch to walk over to the window of the living room that looked onto a communal garden. He had checked on the roast several times. The smell wafted into the living room and should have contributed to a cozy atmosphere, but instead it made him almost ill. He was filled with anxiety at the thought of Julian's disappointment when he would tell him that he had not been able to tell his parents the truth about his sexual preference.

There was no denying it. He was at a low point. He seemed unable to come up with an answer for the first riddle he had chosen to solve. He kept going over and over it. *Federico García Lorca chanted the waters, where the houses of cross and crescent blended, surrounded by the scent of orange blossoms, in a symbol of regenerating life.* The waning light that the floor-length windows cast across the polished wood floor seemed unspeakably sad.

Philip retrieved his iPad from the glass-top coffee table. He scanned for the hundredth time various biographical websites about the writer: "One of the greatest Spanish poets and playwrights of the twentieth century. He was born in 1898 in Fuente Vaqueros, a small town in southern Spain. Moved to Madrid in 1919 to study at the university. Befriended Salvador Dalí, Luis Buñuel, and other Spanish intellectuals of the time."

He skimmed through the next section before reading it again. "The first account of his homosexuality dates from his time in Madrid. It's believed that Lorca fell in love with Dalí, who did not return his sentiment. He also had a passionate love affair with the sculptor Emilio Aladrén Perojo, which ended when Emilio married a wealthy Englishwoman. Lorca suffered from a major emotional breakdown after his separation from Emilio; he moved to New York City to study English at Columbia University."

The information was very interesting but didn't seem to shed light on the riddle. Perhaps he should take a look at some of Lorca's poetry. The first poem he pulled up was called "Song of the Horseman." On one side of the page was the Spanish and on the other the English. The Spanish sounded so much more compelling, he thought. It was impossible to translate poetry satisfactorily. "Córdoba," he read. "Distant and alone." The words seemed to describe his feelings, but Lorca was describing a black nag. There might be something to Córdoba, he thought. "The houses of cross and crescent" might refer to Christianity and Islam. The history of Córdoba was paved with encounters between the two religions. If this was the case, then the "chanted waters" must refer to the Great River or Guadalquivir, the second-longest river in Spain. He may finally have discovered a clue to the riddle. He couldn't believe it. He would have to travel to Spain.

This discovery was encouraging, but he wanted to finish reading about Lorca's life. "After a short stay in Cuba, Lorca returned to Spain in the early 1930s and began writing more openly homosexual works, such as 'Ode to Walt Whitman,' and a drama, *The Public*. These works were published in limited copies; their homosexual content certainly had something to do with the restricted distribution. After the beginning of the Spanish Civil War in July 1936, he moved from Madrid to his hometown of Granada to be on safer grounds. However, on August 16, he was arrested and three days later savagely murdered by Nacionales insurgents."

A figure stood inside the doorway. For a moment, Philip imagined that it was Lorca himself who had entered, but it was Julian.

"You should be more careful," Julian said. "You left the door open."

"Did you know that Lorca was murdered?"

"Yes," Julian said. "Executed by a firing squad."

"Why?"

Julian shrugged. "The exact reason is a mystery. What does it say?"

Philip read, "It's clear that, in addition to his liberal views and sympathy for leftist ideas, García Lorca's homosexuality was intolerable for the conservative movement led by Francisco Franco, who would succeed in overthrowing the Spanish government three years later. Even after the fall of Franco's regime in 1975, major efforts were made by Lorca scholars and by his family to conceal the poet's homosexuality."

This last paragraph seemed directed at him: He felt like a coward. He turned off the iPad and placed it carefully on the coffee table. He stared at Julian. "I'm sorry," he said. "I just couldn't tell them."

"That's too bad because I can't take it anymore. I can't be with you until you can be completely open." Julian shrugged and then walked out of the apartment.

As Philip listened to the door slam shut, he tried to remember why he had such a hard time acknowledging his homosexuality to others. He could have done his coming out while studying at Oxford, but his only form of "rebellion" had consisted in switching from history, a family tradition, to science. This switch had created enough of an uproar and confusion in his family. His parents could not understand his interest in science, even though he had tried to explain his thrill upon attending a class on experimental biology where he had discovered an interest in research and decided to pursue his new passion by getting a PhD in zoology. He enrolled in a graduate program at the University of Cambridge, where he had joined the lab of a professor who was working on the mechanisms underlying the development of the nervous system. When he first met Julian, while attending a summer course at Cold Spring Harbor Laboratory on Long Island, they were both dating women. Philip immediately felt attracted to Julian's easy elegance and graceful stride. Julian was not only a chemist by profession but an enthusiast of poetry, an unusual combination, which Philip appreciated. It was only a year later, when they ran into each other again at the annual meeting of the American Society for Biochemistry and Molecular Biology in Atlanta, that they'd acknowledged the sexual attraction between them. Now they lived together in Pasadena, where Julian was working on his PhD in chemistry at Caltech and Philip was working as a postdoc on the molecular mechanisms of neuronal death, a topic that eventually drew him into Alzheimer's disease research.

Philip sighed and went to get his phone in the kitchen to book a flight to Córdoba. But the iPhone was not on the kitchen table where he was sure he'd left it. He spent the next half hour looking for it, trying to call it from Skype so that he could hear it ring, but to no avail. Then he remembered Julian had told him that he had left the entrance door open. Could it be that someone had entered his apartment while he was working on the riddle? He returned to the kitchen where he had also left his wallet and it was still there on the table, but it had been emptied of the £500 he just taken from a cash machine that morning.

"Not my lucky day." Philip felt quite disheartened. "First the row with Julian and now my iPhone and money stolen, what a gloomy day indeed."

CÓRDOBA, SPAIN,

SPRING 1973

After their alpine-themed wedding in Aspen, Fred had wanted to take Meg on a surprise honeymoon through Europe. After landing in Madrid they rented a car and decided to drive south in search of some warmth and sunshine. Meg had always wanted to visit Spain's southern cities—Córdoba, Granada, Seville. In college she had chosen Spanish as a minor and was enthralled by a course on Spanish history in the Middle Ages and the Renaissance. Fred could quiz her on almost any subject related to those periods, and he felt she would certainly be very keen to visit all these places she had studied inside out.

The two days in Córdoba would stay with them as a very special memory, as it was there that Meg suspected she might be pregnant. In fact, Steven was almost named Christoforo in memory of Columbus, the Italian explorer who had spent several years at the Royal Spanish court in Córdoba. Luckily for Steven, they had changed their minds by the time they returned to Swiss Creek and figured out that an Anglo-Saxon name would be more appropriate when living in the United States.

ZURICHHORN PARK, ZURICH, SWITZERLAND

MAY 1, 2018

As Yucun walked along a lovely tree-shaded path in Zurichhorn Park, with its breathtaking view of the Alps, she wondered how her meeting with Jonathan would go. Since her arrival in Switzerland, they had met only in the presence of other people, with the exception of two minutes in private before he had led her up the stairs to meet Mr. Lindenmayer.

She remembered their first encounter at the library of the UCLA Medical Center. At the time, she had been a postdoctoral fellow in the group of Barry Fishman, a prominent neuroscientist. Jonathan had been working as a librarian. She was searching for a book published in the early 1980s on vasoactive intestinal peptide (VIP), a neurohormone originally discovered in the gut but later identified also to reside in the brain. In a recent article, she had found a reference to this book, which described how VIP could boost the energy metabolism of cells. She was impatient to get hold of the text as she had the intuition that, by increasing the delivery of energy to neurons, they could be prevented from dying. The idea could have significant implications for Alzheimer's, she had thought, with excitement. As it turned out, from that day on, her work in Fishman's lab focused on energy metabolism in neurodegenerative diseases—with very promising results. She suspected that her research carried considerable weight in her being selected for the award competition by the committee, which acknowledged the originality of her approach.

The library had been nearly empty the day they met as a result of a game between the Oakland Raiders and the Green Bay Packers; but, like Jonathan, Yucun couldn't have cared less about football. She asked for his assistance and they struck up a conversation. She was much intrigued by this librarian who could discuss VIP like a true scientist. But when she asked him about his previous job, his answer was vague. Although she often shied away when meeting new people, the exchange with him had been so interesting and unusual that she looked forward to her next library visit.

But she didn't have to wait to see him in the library. A week later, Yucun ran into Jonathan in one of the sandwich bars on campus, and they had lunch together. One day, after many shared lunches, he invited her to his apartment to watch a movie and they ended up spending the night together. Their affair blossomed after that; but it wasn't a love story. All along she felt that he was holding something back. At first, she imagined that he was seeing other women while he was dating her. When she found out that wasn't the case, she concluded that someone from his past must have hurt him. He refused to talk about past lovers. In fact, he did not like to talk about the past at all. Perhaps, she imagined, he'd had to look after a sickly parent or sibling and this had prevented him from achieving his full potential. Or perhaps he had sacrificed his career for a woman and followed her all the way from South Africa to America. It's true that he didn't really strike Yucun as the self-sacrificing sort. In fact, he was quite impatient with illness. She recalled that the one time she had been ill, he had made up various excuses not to be at her bedside.

A few months after their affair began, Jonathan was offered a job in Switzerland and he soon left for Europe. At UCLA, their relationship had little to do with love, a word that had never even been spoken between them. But when he moved to Switzerland, Yucun was taken aback by her reaction to her loss. Jonathan left a bigger void in her life than she had anticipated; she missed him terribly. The two had kept in touch via e-mail, and when the call for candidates for the Lindenmayer Award had been launched, Jonathan encouraged her to apply.

She had been close to finishing a rather successful postdoctoral period and was looking for a position as an assistant professor in the States. Her work on boosting the energy metabolism of neurons as a neuroprotective strategy had attracted attention, but to her surprise and mortification, when she looked for a job, she had not been offered one despite coming very close several times. When Jonathan told her about the competition, she was excited. This might be the answer to her difficulties in finding a job. Indeed, if she did win, she would get the kind of job she was dreaming of. And it would also allow her to move closer to Jonathan, as the Lindenmayer Institute would be built in Switzerland.

Secretly, she had been overjoyed by Jonathan's faith in her abilities—and his apparent wish to have her live nearby. She was even more thrilled when, a few months later, she received news that she had been selected as a contestant and was to fly to Zurich for a meeting with Fred Lindenmayer.

The last time she had been alone with Jonathan was the evening of his move to Zurich. Yucun had accompanied him to the airport and their parting at LAX had been unexpectedly emotional. Not certain if she would ever see him again, Yucun's eyes had filled with tears when Jonathan leaned over to say goodbye at the departure gate. He, however, had remained quite composed and dry-eyed.

When she reached the inlet where she had agreed to meet Jonathan, Yucun lay down on the pebbled beach. She closed her eyes and enjoyed the weak spring sun. There was something different about Jonathan, she thought, but she could not put her finger on what it was: a suppressed excitement. Perhaps she was imagining it.

Feeling a hand on her shoulder, she opened her eyes. "Hi," he said, lying down beside her.

Suddenly, he drew her closer, into a passionate embrace. She almost pulled back. He laughed, feeling her movement of surprise.

"I've missed you," he said and then he whispered, "my little accomplice." An odd choice of words, she thought, but before she could respond, he suggested that they go to his place. His enthusiasm for her was so obvious that it was hard to resist.

"Oh yes, please," she said.

She took his hand and they started walking toward the parking lot where he had left his car.

LICEO PARINI, MILAN, ITALY

MAY 1, 2018

As Edoardo approached the table and lectern, from which he was to lecture the students of his former biology teacher, Giovanna Bianchi, he tried to shake off his misgivings. He had hoped to arrive early so that he could speak with Giovanna and suggest having lunch with her. Instead, he'd had to dodge a man with the kind of face you imagine in nightmares. The man had a square jaw and a scar across one cheek. Edoardo had the feeling he had seen him the day before in Zurich as he left the press conference. He had mentioned him to Bobby, though he felt slightly ridiculous at the time. But now he was certain the man was following him. Edoardo'd had to run the last few blocks. He almost regretted deciding to come to Milan today, right after the start of the contest. But he had promised Giovanna so many times to come and talk to her students, this was a perfect opportunity before setting off to wherever the first riddle would take him. And he was also eager to see his parents again.

After setting up his computer for the PowerPoint presentation, Edoardo removed the lectern and sat directly on the table. Out of the corner of his eye, he saw Giovanna raise one eyebrow. She shook a finger at him, as if he were still her student.

Remembering his mind-set and priorities at the age of these students, who were in their high-school years, he had decided to start with some provocative statements about men and women.

"The human brain weighs about 1.5 kilograms, for men, and about ten percent less for women," he stated. When the female students reacted with noisy protests, Edoardo smiled and explained that, even though the female human brain weighed a little less, it had more gray matter, basically meaning more neurons.

"I suppose you're interested in knowing what neurons are?" Edoardo asked the group who had caused the interruption.

"Not only that," a good-looking blond girl with a tight ponytail said, "we'd like to know which one of us is the more intelligent sex: males or females."

"This is of course a classic, but not particularly relevant, question. I don't mean that offensively," he added when the questioner frowned at his statement. "For some tasks, there may be a slight gender difference. For example, women seem to be more apt at verbal fluency. As far as spatial orientation is concerned, the two genders appear to use different strategies. But—and this is the important thing to remember—the main point is that there are more differences between individuals within the same gender than between the two genders as groups. We're above all unique individuals with our own abilities and weaknesses, independent of our sex."

Edoardo's last remark generated murmurs among the students.

"Let me give you some basic information on the structure and function of the brain and then maybe we can discuss how the human brain is unique. The brain is made of billions of cells, which are the elementary units that allow the processing of information. These cells are divided into two great categories, the neurons and a less well-studied cell type, the glial cells. Neurons are specialized cells, which consist of three main parts. At one end are many branches called dendrites—you may think of the branches of an oak tree—that receive signals from other neurons. These signals are then integrated in the cell body," Edoardo said, pointing at the next PowerPoint slide.

In keeping with the analogy of the oak tree, Edoardo instructed the students to look at the cell body as the part of the neuron where all the branches converge. Finally, he told them that neurons emit signals from a single extension called the axon. From the axon's end, the neurons send messages to other neurons through a specialized structure called the synapse.

In an enthusiastic voice he said, "The human brain contains about one hundred billion neurons, and each is in contact with about ten thousand others through their synapses. This means that there are about one thousand trillion synapses in the human brain, an absolutely astounding number!"

Here he paused to smile directly at the students. One girl in the first row was staring at him with unabashed admiration. A few others were nodding or scribbling in their notebooks. "Do you follow me so far or do you have any questions?"

Edoardo's eyes met Giovanna's. He still found her attractive even though she must be in her late forties. Of course nothing had ever happened between them.

"Moving on," he said, pleased, and switched to the next slide. "The efficiency of the information transfer at synapses is not constant, as it may change over time. This 'plasticity' of synapses, as neuroscientists call the process, is the basis of memory. I realize that the issue of memory is a pressing one for you these days. How many of you will take the baccalaureate exams this year?"

About two-thirds of the students raised their hands.

"Excellent," he exclaimed. "What that means is that your memory will be put to work quite intensively over the next few months. Let me tell you what we know so far about the mechanisms of memory."

Edoardo turned toward the screen. "We still don't know all the details, but what is clear is that the neuronal circuits that store memories do so by modifying the efficiency in the transfer of information between neurons at the level of the synapses. So let's say that certain circuits have been involved in processing a given bit of visual information. The synapses in that circuit will become more efficient, or what neuroscientists call 'facilitated.' When we remember something, these facilitated synapses are reactivated simultaneously. This mechanism is thought to provide the neuronal basis of memory."

The next picture on the screen showed the skyline of New York at night. "Take a simple image as an example. Imagine a skyscraper at night with thousands of windows that light up one by one. You can generate a pattern of illuminated windows that represent a given picture—for example, a Christmas tree. In the brain, these illuminated windows would correspond to the facilitated synapses. With Alzheimer's disease, it's as if several of the windows are not lit. If a certain number of these windows are not lit, then the patterns of the remaining illuminated windows will not be sufficient to generate a picture, meaning a memory."

Edoardo paused to allow the seriousness of his last statement to sink in and noted the hush in the room.

"The key to understanding how the process of memory works so efficiently is embedded in the notion of 'neuronal plasticity,'" he continued. "The secret of memory lies in the fact that brain circuits are continuously being rewired, providing the brain with the unique capacity to integrate new information in the context of existing information. Our brain is highly dynamic, the structures of synapses change with experience. The efficiency of synapses is modified not only in the sense of facilitation but also, in some cases, in that they become less efficient. This is probably the mechanism through which we forget events."

Following the lecture, a small reception was held in the teacher's lounge. Mozzarella, prosciutto, salami, and crackers were served, along with cans of soda and bottles of water. As Giovanna approached him, Edoardo was surprised by the powerful sexual urge he felt for her. It didn't make any sense; he was happily in love with Benedetta. But the memories of his adolescent sexual fantasies—Giovanna undressing slowly for him; images of her naked breasts and small waist—were flashing in his mind. As she drew near, her perfume, with its hints of vanilla and jasmine, caused his heart to speed up. She smiled at him with her full lips, her bluish-green eyes sparkling. He needed to say something clever to lessen the tension building inside of him.

"Did I tell you about the riddles I have to solve while traveling to various European countries?" he asked.

"What are you talking about? The Lindenmayer Award?" she replied, putting her arm around Edoardo's shoulders. He felt himself becoming aroused—which was utterly embarrassing and making it nearly impossible for him to focus. He pulled away from her and grabbed a glass of water.

"I am so proud of you. I wish I could take some time off and travel across Europe with you," she said. This was too much for Edoardo. He felt an urge to kiss her. As their lips came closer, Giovanna said, "Yes, I'd love to be close to you."

But Edoardo hadn't even heard her. As he was leaning toward her, he noticed the man with the scar, looking through the open window a few feet from them. Before Edoardo could step back from Giovanna, there was a flash as the man took a photograph of them. Edoardo looked for the door that would lead him out of the room—and fast. He was determined to catch the man.

He squeezed her arm. "I'm so sorry. I won't be able to have lunch with you. An emergency. I'll call you."

He hurried out. The street was deserted, except for an old man playing the accordion. As Edoardo drew nearer to him, intent on asking him whether he had seen the man with the scar, he realized that the accordionist was blind. He wandered down one street then another but there was no sign of him.

ON THE TRAIN TO PARIS, FRANCE

MAY 1, 2018

On the TGV from Zurich to Paris, Jean-Pierre folded *Le Monde*, which he had been reading for the last hour, and looked up. His eyes fell on a seedy-looking character sitting two rows down from him on the other side of the aisle. He had the feeling he had seen him before. The man was wearing dark glasses and a baseball cap, so Jean-Pierre couldn't really make out his face. But his long greasy hair sticking out from under the cap, the big gold chain with a medallion hanging from his neck, and his open shirt definitely gave Jean-Pierre a sense of déjà vu. Now the man got up and walked down the aisle; as he passed by Jean-Pierre he gave him a big shove on the shoulder and then leaned down toward him as if to apologize. But he murmured, almost into Jean-Pierre's ear: "You stop award or you'll be in danger." Then he walked down the aisle in big strides as the train was entering Basel station.

By the time Jean-Pierre understood what had just happened and regained his composure more or less, he wanted to follow the guy, but at that moment new passengers were boarding the train and he couldn't get past them.

"Well," Jean-Pierre thought, "I really would have liked to punch him, too, and ask him what this was all about." He decided to let Bobby know once he reached Paris. Now it was time to look at his first riddle. He had chosen this one as it had something to do with France and one of its most famous kings, François I. This meant he could stay in France in these first few days of the competition.

He took out his iPad to read the riddle again: *The jewel of François I, King of France, harbors the secret of life recognized by a noble Francis four centuries later.*

"A king of France, that should be easy for me," he thought. But he had no clue what the reference to the jewel meant. "Wait a minute," he thought and chuckled. "If they're talking about the family jewels, in the French sense, they harbor the secret of life. After all, that's one of the testicle's main functions."

At this point, he was murmuring and smiling to himself. *"Mon vieux*, old chap, let's be serious. In Madame Martin's history class we learned all the names of French kings by heart." But he couldn't remember much else about these monarchs' lives and achievements. "Maybe that part was taught in later years when all I thought about was playing football so I could become a star of the French football league."

He leaned back smiling, feeling nostalgic. He suddenly noticed that the elderly gentleman sitting opposite him was also smiling.

"Oh, dear, you must think I'm very strange. But let me assure you, I'm completely normal. I was just reminiscing," he said.

"Don't worry. I was actually thinking how wonderful it is to have a smiling travel companion," the gentlemen said in a friendly voice. "There are too many grumpy people on the train who have something to complain about: delays in the schedules, the food, the noise, you name it."

Jean-Pierre agreed with the older man's observations and they continued their conversation about travel. Jean-Pierre explained that he had never really traveled much before but that the Lindenmayer competition had provided him with the opportunity.

His travel companion's eyes widened with interest

and Jean-Pierre quickly told him about the award and how it involved solving riddles.

"What a fascinating story! Tell me more about the riddles."

"This is the one I am trying to solve." Jean-Pierre handed him his iPad.

The older man read it quickly. "Quite intriguing. Do you have any clue how to solve it?"

"I'm not sure. I was trying to recollect my history lessons, but I can't seem to remember much about François I, certainly nothing about any kind of special jewel. I thought of '*Le collier de la reine*' (the queen's necklace) in Alexandre Dumas's *The Three Musketeers*. But the musketeers were King Louis XIII's personal guard, and that was two centuries later. I don't remember any other jewel story."

The gentleman handed him the book he was reading. "I may have an idea, actually."

Jean-Pierre looked at the title of the book: *Histoire de l'Architecture Française: de la Renaissance à la Révolution*, by Jean-Marie Pérouse de Montclos.

"You're probably wondering what architecture has to do with jewelry. Some of our architectural masterpieces may be called jewels, especially if we have a castle in mind."

"I must confess, I never thought of that," Jean-Pierre said.

At this stage the gentleman burst out laughing. "Let me explain. But first, let me introduce myself: I'm Aristide Bruneau. As we are travel companions, with a common intellectual endeavor, I feel we should know each other's names."

Jean-Pierre reached for Aristide's outstretched hand and shook it warmly, excusing himself for not having introduced himself first. After all, his parents had taught him that you always introduced yourself first when meeting an elder.

"Well, Jean-Pierre, let me tell you my theory. I used to be a high-school history teacher and I was always particularly interested in the Renaissance. When I re-tired a few years ago, one of my former students asked me to help her with the research for a doctoral thesis in which she analyzed the development of Renaissance architecture by comparing castles in France and Italy. One of the castles in our country is considered to be a jewel of Renaissance architecture." Aristide paused and looked directly at Jean-Pierre. "It's the castle of Chambord in the Loire Valley."

Jean-Pierre was stunned into silence by this stranger's knowledge and cleverness.

"Yes," Aristide said, "the jewel in the riddle could well be that castle."

BLOIS, FRANCE

1967

Madame Lachaux, the owner of the café in the Hôtel le Médicis, called her daughter Elise out of the kitchen, while the four young men settled down under the big plane tree in the courtyard. With a wink, she told Elise to take their orders, as they would much prefer to see a beautiful young girl than an old matron like herself.

Elise approached the table and saw that the four young men were actually quite attractive, and she was eager to find out what they were doing here and where they came from.

Fred was the first to notice her approaching. "Okay, guys, now here is a good-looking girl, but I saw her first, so you let me do the talking!"

"Hello, I'm Elise," she addressed them in English, as she had heard Fred's last sentence about him doing the talking. "What can I bring you?"

"Actually, we would like to take you and your friends out for dinner tonight," Fred said very self-consciously, but still blushed a little when Elise lifted her eyebrows and asked if there was nothing she could bring them to drink now.

"But why not for dinner later," she added with a chuckle. "Let me see if some of my friends are free and interested in meeting you." She turned around and headed back to the kitchen to prepare two cafés au lait and two diabolo menthe, a sparkling lemonade with mint syrup.

"You are so bold, man." Jacques van Engelhorn nudged Fred with his elbow. "I have never seen you so direct with a girl before."

"Well," Fred replied quite proud of himself, "Swiss girls are not that easy to approach, as you well know. You've been in Zurich six months and what is your track record? Only one girl you were able to lure into your bed!" The two other young men burst out laughing.

"Well," Gunnar Johansson said to Fred, "let's see if the fair Elise accepts your invitation and can convince her friends to go out with a bunch of foreigners."

Fred contemplated his cousin from Sweden and was about to assure him of their success, when Piergiulio

Mazzoleni di Cordaro, his childhood friend, cut in and reminded them how they had all been able to convince their respective parents that this was to be a cultural trip to the Loire Châteaux, when all the four of them wanted was to meet French girls.

SWISS CREEK RESORT, COLORADO

MARCH 2017

Fifty years later, Fred looked at the men seated around the scarred pine table. They had just sat down for drinks and were talking animatedly. His cousin Gunnar was reminiscing about the famous trip to the Loire Valley when he, Jacques, Piergiulio, and Fred were students, and the others roared with laughter. Fred smiled, thinking how funny destiny sometimes was. Indeed, Jacques fell madly in love with Catherine, one of the girls they met on that trip. They ended up marrying and were still living happily ever after. Fred decided to interrupt their lively discussion because they needed to get down to business.

He lifted his glass addressing them: "Dear friends, let me welcome you officially to this brainstorming weekend. As you know, this is where Meg and I met and got married more than forty years ago. It's also here where we started working together in the development of the Swiss Creek ski resort. As many of you remember, we decided to settle here against my father's wish for me to return to Switzerland to work with him in the family business. It turned out to be the right decision, since through the venture we made with a Japanese real estate consortium, we managed to make the resort a resounding success. I see this as a good omen for the new project I want to launch today with your help. I'm not going to repeat the objectives of this brainstorming as I had the opportunity to discuss them with you individually on the phone. But now that you've met, I'll tell you all about each other."

Fred turned to the elegant, sharp-featured man on his right who sported a perfectly knotted bow tie under his V-neck sweater. "Max Fernshaw is chair of the Department of Neurology at UCLA. I've known Max since he was a medical student more than thirty years ago. His parents were among the first people to buy a chalet here in Swiss Creek. You may recall that two years ago we returned to live in Switzerland, so I could take over the family business after the sudden death of my brother, Hans-Peter. Shortly after being back in Zurich, Meg started showing signs of confusion and forgetfulness. I wasn't worried at first; I thought she was just adjusting to a new environment. But after a few months my children urged me to have her examined by a neurologist. Of course I called Max." His voice thickened with emotion. "He came to see us in Zurich and diagnosed Meg with probable Alzheimer's disease. His help and support have been invaluable to Meg and me since then."

Fred was glad when he was interrupted by a knock on the door, as he was getting a bit emotional. "Yes, come in! Hello, Daisy," he waved his housekeeper into the room.

"Dinner is ready, sir."

"Thanks. Gentlemen, shall we move to the next room for dinner? I'm sure Daisy has outdone herself tonight in your honor." As everyone rose, chatting, he thought how lucky he was to have this group of accomplished, amiable men as friends.

Once they were comfortably settled in the dining room, Fred finished the round of introductions and suggested it was time to reveal, in detail, the purpose behind the meeting. "The bottom line is that I want to do everything I can to cure Meg. Obviously this sounds like a rather naïve wish and, most probably, it is. I'm realistic. However, I want you to help me find an innovative and, most of all, efficient way to support research on Alzheimer's disease. First I'd thought of making a major endowment to one or several existing laboratories at the forefront of this type of research. Max was very helpful in my inquiry into the best research groups. But, after careful consideration, I've decided that such a conventional way of supporting science was not for me. As much as it may surprise you, I ended up being deeply disenchanted and skeptical about the way bio-medical research is conducted these days. You might think: 'Who is Fred, a businessman, to judge how science is carried out?'

"And you may be correct," he continued. "But there are two things I've learned over all these years in business: first, how to solve problems; and second, how to select the right people to do it. Quite pretentious, I know," he added with a grin. "But what's struck me is the fact that most scientists appear to be more concerned with research that will 'sell well' to funding agencies, or which holds the potential to make the editors of high-profile scientific journals salivate, than to be committed to solving a problem. Scientific research has become like everything else in our society: It follows fashions and trends and has to be flashy. Image is everything."

He paused to catch his breath. "Sorry, my friends, I get carried away when I talk about this. I'm angry that so many brilliant brains are sacrificed on the altar of scientific fads." He turned to his guests with an inquisitive look. "Max, you have opened my mind on this issue, so I hope you won't contradict me on this."

"Quite the contrary," Max snapped, as if he couldn't wait to unleash one of his favorite tirades. He had piercing gray eyes, which he widened now in response to Fred's comment. "The end result of this regrettable situation is that most research is conservative: There is no risk-taking when designing new projects. Scientists are expected to describe, in their grant proposals, experiments that they will be performing two years later. How can this approach result in discoveries, if projects are so predictable?"

Max's jaw was set in contempt. "From the scientific-journals end, the situation is just as bad in terms of not encouraging creativity and originality of research. All the editors are preoccupied with is the 'impact factor' of their journal—which is a measure of the frequency with which articles published in a journal have been cited over a given period. One of the pernicious effects of this 'quantification' of quality is that it puts pressure to publish articles likely to be highly cited because the subject is fashionable. If your journal has an impact factor of more than ten, or even better, twenty, you're in business; under five, its viability is in question."

Max nodded at Fred, who ran his hand through his silvery hair before saying, "I understand that this kind of frenzy influences the choice of journals in which young scientists want to publish and, therefore, the kind of projects they want to be involved in. Yes, it's a vicious cycle since one of the measures that search committees use to appoint scientists to their first faculty position is the impact factor of the journals where they have published their work."

Fred continued in a determined voice, "I want to break this vicious cycle, at least as far as research on Alzheimer's disease is concerned." He sighed deeply. "My dear friends, we need to invent a mechanism that will favor the emergence of a new breed of young scientists, driven by risk and curiosity, rather than being constrained by unimaginative granting procedures and conventional publishing fashions."

"Certainly a great idea," Jacques piped in.

Jacques was a large, ruddy man with cropped grayish-blond hair. A professor of international law at the Université catholique de Louvain in Belgium, he'd been Fred's legal adviser ever since the two men met in Zurich while Jacques was in law school and Fred was studying architecture at the Swiss Federal Institute of Technology. "But, it will take several years to implement. What kind of mechanism do you have in mind?"

"I am—we all are, in fact—no longer in our prime. We can't wait for a new generation to emerge. Somehow, we need to identify this new breed of scientist."

"I have an idea," Brian Malcolm-Jones, a professor of medieval history at Cambridge University, said. "I've always been a keen admirer of individuals who can combine excellence in science with a genuine sensitivity for other fields, like history or art."

Fred had met Brian a few years earlier on a cruise to Antarctica. One evening, after their wives had retired to bed, they'd discussed the problems of aging over beers. In an ironic twist of fate, it turned out that both their wives had since been diagnosed with Alzheimer's disease.

"I suggest the following procedure," Brian said. "We publish a call for applicants in the best scientific journals. The age limit should be thirty-five. With Max's help, Fred puts together a panel of senior scientists who will select the best candidates, chosen on the basis of their achievements. I take care of the rest with some friends from Cambridge." He smiled and his face brightened even as the skin around his eyes and mouth crinkled. "Maybe even some from Oxford—after all, there are a few reasonably good scholars in that university too."

"What do you mean you'll take care of the rest?" Gunnar asked gruffly. The tall, muscular CEO of Johansson Industries in Sweden didn't look very happy.

With a barely perceptible twist of his lips, Brian said, "We'll ask the finalists to write an essay, say, on their favorite piece of art. It could be a painting, a sculpture, a poem—"

"Please let's be serious," Gunnar interrupted. "We're not talking about the selection of the best altar boy in the parish. We want to identify the most qualified scientist to help find a cure for Alzheimer's. Don't you agree, Fred?"

"There is something to what Brian is saying, I think," Fred said diplomatically. "The idea of a selection process by a committee is a good idea. But we know that this won't be enough. We want people who have the ability to think outside the usual scope of their work. They should be gifted with intense and sensitive minds. I don't know exactly how to include Brian's ideas, but they are definitely worth considering."

As Gunnar rolled his eyes, Piergiulio, a senior partner at a prominent private bank in Milan, cleared his throat. Piergiulio and Fred had known each other since they were children; their parents used to spend summer vacations together. In his early seventies and still wiry with a thicket of dark hair, Piergiulio now acted as Fred's financial adviser.

"Because of my line of business I usually focus on money. I'm assuming that the selected candidate will receive some kind of monetary prize. But how can this make a difference in the fight against Alzheimer's disease? We need to give him or her the tools to develop daring, original research projects, unconstrained by administrative and financial limitations, at least up to a reasonable point."

Tapping his foot, Gunnar said, "Let's be practical. The best tool for a scientist is a laboratory. We should therefore build a research institute for the selected candidate. It's as simple as that."

"Wow," Piergiulio exclaimed. "We're talking big money here."

"Yes." Fred nodded. "And we should be. This cause is a worthwhile enterprise. I don't mind putting a good chunk of my capital into it."

The discussion digressed to the topic of architecture: Who should design the institute, where it should be built, and how large it should be. Soon, however, Jacques brought this spirited conversation to a halt. "Gentlemen, all this is entertaining, but let's get back to business. We still haven't decided how we'll select the candidates."

Fred stood up and paced in front of his friends, looking from one to the next. "I have an idea—it might be a bit crazy or naïve. But I have a good feeling about it. What about an international contest that would challenge a group of scientists in accomplishing tasks that would require the skills we discussed: entrepreneurial skills, an innovative and creative mind for problem-solving, scientific achievements, and...artistic sensitivity? We could call it, very modestly, the Lindenmayer Award."

The silence that followed was impressive after the noisy chitchat that had filled the room just moments before.

Piergiulio raised his glass. "A toast to our dear Fred, may he be as productive and creative for many more years to come! But now," he winked at Fred, "let me ask you this: Could you elucidate your idea more clearly for us because I haven't the faintest clue what you are talking about, nor does anybody else if I read them correctly."

"Indeed so," Brian said. "Before we can start planning, we need to figure out what kind of challenges we want our scientists to face."

Max jumped in with the suggestion that the five scientists be awarded a grant for a pilot project, which would test a completely original hypothesis about the cause of Alzheimer's disease. "They could test this hypothesis in the laboratory of their choice; after eighteen months, a meeting would be organized, with the best Alzheimer's specialists attending, in which the candidates would present their data. The hope would be that from the initial results obtained by the young scientists some novel lead for therapy would emerge."

"Hmm, not bad. I like the idea of sponsoring innovative pilot projects," Gunnar conceded. "However, we run the risk that the more senior scientists attending the meeting will steal the best ideas and implement them in their own laboratories."

"That's very likely to happen," Max admitted. "Still, Fred wants to move this field of research ahead quickly. This approach may well achieve that goal."

"Yes, but this would be unfair to the candidates," Fred said.

"How about bringing together the five scientists in a single place, for example a laboratory that we would lease for a limited period of time, say two years? Have them work in some kind of Manhattan Project for Alzheimer's disease, putting their competences and ideas together," Max proposed.

"You're far too idealistic," Gunnar said, sharply, again. "Science is a rat race nowadays. No one, particularly at an early stage of his or her career, would agree to share the best ideas with four other colleagues. And what about intellectual property if a major discovery resulting in a new drug emerged from this joint project? Forget it." He dismissed the idea with a wave of his hand. "We'd need to mobilize Jacques's legal skills for the next ten years."

"All these ideas are still much too conventional. I want something that hasn't been done before," Fred said, disappointed.

Piergiulio, who had been quiet for a while, raised his index finger as if bidding at an auction. "What I'm about to say will sound a bit crazy. But here it is: What about a kind of treasure hunt? Do you remember, Fred, the incredibly exciting treasure hunts my mother used to organize for us during the summer vacation when we were children? We had to use all the skills you described as necessary for your group of scientists. The riddles were really challenging for kids of our age, even demanding courage at times."

Max clapped Piergiulio on the shoulder. "Excellent! Given the nature of the subject for which we want to select the winner, we should give the competitors a number of scientific riddles to solve within a given time. The riddles should, of course, make reference to issues in the field of neuroscience."

"I'm in favor of that idea too," Brian said. "But may I suggest that we add some historic component to the riddles? This will really show us if the competitors have the capacity to think and reason outside their field of work."

Delighted, Fred said warmly, "My dear friends, we have made considerable progress." He glanced at his watch. "But it's one o'clock in the morning and we all need to get some sleep. Why don't we postpone the discussion about the riddles until morning?"

The atmosphere was cheerful as everyone wished each other good night. Left alone, Fred sat in his favorite wing chair in front of the fireplace and made notes in preparation for the next meeting. Across the top of the first page of his tablet, he wrote in bold letters, "Advertising the Contest and Selection of Candidates."

The award competition will be advertised in ten of the major scientific and medical journals, and the members of the selection committee will also inform their networks about it. The potential candidates will be asked to send a motivational letter with their résumé, as well as two letters of recommendation. The candidates must have published at least four original articles in the field of Alzheimer's research in leading scientific journals. The age limit would be set at thirty-five.

The applications should be addressed to Fred directly, who would make a first selection with the help of his assistant, Jonathan Boswell, and the selection committee, which was to be composed of his group of friends plus two to three leading scientists in the field of Alzheimer's research. The committee would select a number of potential candidates who would be interviewed, and the finalists would be notified by the end of 2017 that they were chosen to participate in the contest.

As he started on the "Rules and Procedures" section he realized that this was the complicated part. He scribbled down all the questions that he could imagine. By the time he put his pen down, the fire had gone out and it had become quite chilly in the room.

Fred shivered and looked to his left, out of the floor-length windows framed in polished wood. The moon was shining on the snow-covered mountain peaks. He sighed, contentedly. It would be easy to fall asleep here in his comfortable chair. But he hoisted himself up to join Meg in the bedroom.

The next day was devoted to refining the major details for the competition. Fred's friends agreed to serve on the selection committee and Max offered to identify three additional experts in the field of Alzheimer's. The historic component of the riddles would bring the candidates to five different European cities where they would have to uncover the clues for the scientific section. Each committee member agreed to submit additional proposals for the riddles.

MOSCOW, RUSSIA

MAY 2, 2018

As the plane landed at Domodedovo International Airport in Moscow, Sarah wondered if her grandmother, her beloved Douschka, as she called her, would still be alive.

The day before Sarah had received a phone call from her mother in Minneapolis, telling her that her grandmother had had a stroke and was in critical condition. Doctors had indicated that there was little chance that she would survive. "Oh my God, no, not Douschka, she seemed to be in such good health," said Sarah, asking for more details. Her mother explained what she had been told by the hospital. She knew that Sarah would not hesitate for a second to drop everything and fly to

Moscow. "Are you sure? You are at the beginning of the contest. Darling, it is so important for your future."

"How could you even think that I would hesitate," said Sarah in an angry voice. "I am taking the first flight to Moscow out of Zurich, and I will meet you there."

"Passport, please."

Lost in thought, Sarah hadn't realized she was next in line at passport control. "Thank you, miss, and have a nice stay in Moscow," the customs officer said to her in English, handing her US passport back to her.

Outside the airport, Sarah was lucky to find a cab right away. The driver spoke English and was eager to practice the language with her, but Sarah was so preoccupied that she answered his questions with a yes or a no. She was imagining her grandmother in the intensive care unit at the hospital. Was she conscious, was she suffering? she wondered. After a long silence Sarah explained to the cabdriver what had brought her to Moscow.

He nodded solemnly then raised his hand to touch the cross that hung from his rearview mirror. "I wish you the best," he said, in strongly accented English. "I pray for you."

CÓRDOBA, SPAIN

MAY 2, 2018

As the plane landed in Málaga, Spain, Edoardo was jolted awake and looked around bewildered. He was obviously on a plane and hearing the flight attendant's announcements in Spanish, he remembered that he was on his way to Córdoba.

The evening before in Milan he'd had dinner at his parents' house with his godmother, Tina. He had enjoyed every moment of their time together, as he hadn't seen her for two years. Each time they met, he feared that it would be the last. Tina had by now reached the honorable age of ninety-four, and even though she still had her legendary sharp wit and quick mind, her body was rapidly failing her, as she had told Edoardo when they last talked on the phone. Edoardo had suggested cooking dinner for her, as she loved his pasta carbonara. The last time they had dinner together was in Zurich at Tina's favorite restaurant.

Indeed, on every important event in his life, Tina had taken him to the Kronenhalle. The first time was when he was about to start school at the age of six. On that visit, she had told him about the art that hung on the restaurant's walls.

"Look at the paintings," she said. "They are by Giacometti, Picasso, Matisse, Miró, and Chagall, among others."

The Kronenhalle was a mythical place, much more than just a restaurant. For decades, it had been a very popular and famous meeting place for artists. The Swiss writer Gottfried Keller, the painter Arnold Böcklin, the writer James Joyce had been regular guests.

Tina was a formidable lady. Of Jewish origins, she was the only daughter of a strong-willed mother and grew up surrounded by three older brothers who were overly protective of her. She seemed destined to marry into another Jewish family and become a mother of many children, like her mother before her and her grandmother before that. Instead, she decided to become a lawyer and help the less fortunate in their legal battles. Not only did she become the first woman lawyer to plead in the Supreme Court in Switzerland; she also became the first woman to plead in a military court.

Despite her charm, vitality, and intelligence, it seemed as if she would miss out on the one experience in life that nothing could replace. She was unable to conceive. Instead of resigning herself to a life without children, she had looked after the children of other women, especially Jewish women's children who had fled Germany during World War II. Some of these children lived with her for a time, while others spent their vacations with her. She paid for the education of many of them.

Edoardo was her youngest godchild, a godchild in the religious sense, as she had assisted his baptism in a Catholic church. In those days, it was quite unusual for a Christian child to have a Jewish godmother, but Tina had been a very close friend of Edoardo's grandmother, who had died when Edoardo's father was only ten years old. For a long time, Edoardo's grandfather had been devastated by his wife's death and Tina had opened her house to her friend's children who visited often. When Edoardo was born, his father had asked Tina to be his son's godmother. They came even more frequently to her house in Zurich after their father remarried a woman who didn't care for his children. To Edoardo's father and his siblings, Tina had become like a second mother.

Tina was one of the people who'd had an enormous influence on Edoardo's life. She had made him aware of the responsibility each one of us has to be a good human being, and she had stressed the importance of humanistic and ethical values. She had taught him everything he knew about music and art. Tina had come frequently to Milan, and during these visits she had taken him to places that were special to her. It was just the two of them. In his younger years, it had been an outing to a public park or a lake. When he got older, as an adolescent, she had taken him to concerts or the opera, and as a young adult they had visited art museums and galleries. Every outing had included a lesson in geography, science, or art, and Tina and Edoardo loved to discuss what they had seen and what they had learned.

From an early age, Edoardo had loved his godmother, but as he grew older he realized that her qualities were extraordinary. With her, he could discuss any topic, whether it was fights with his sisters or friends, worries about school, difficulties with his girlfriends, or even his sex life. Nothing was taboo.

"Tell me, Edoardo, how are you fairing with the competition?" she had asked him, almost immediately upon her arrival at his parents' home. "My youngest godson may well become a celebrity. I'm so proud of you, but you seem preoccupied." Her eyes twinkled with excitement.

"Right on target, as usual, my dear Tina." He suddenly realized that he could challenge her with the one of the riddles he had tried to solve on the train to Milan. "I'm actually counting on your vast knowledge of the world to give me a hint for the riddle I'm working on now. If we figure it out together, I promise to take you on a romantic escapade to whichever place the riddle suggests."

His godmother chuckled. "Romantic, at my age? You must be joking. But tell me about this riddle of yours."

He explained the riddle then asked, "Do you have any idea which river García Lorca chanted the waters of?"

"It's the Guadalquivir and it flows through Córdoba," she fired off without hesitation.

"I'll be damned. Your mind is so fast even at—" He stopped in mid-sentence, afraid of being rude by bringing up her age.

"At my advanced age," she said, completing his sentence for him, with a tender smile.

"And Córdoba? How did you think of that city?"

"Well, my dear boy, I spent a few eventful, dangerous, but highly romantic months as an exchange student in Spain in my early twenties."

"You never told me about that," Edoardo said, wanting to know more.

"I often wonder how my life would have unfolded if I had stayed with Carlos. He was so handsome and brilliant, but he was married and decided to return to his wife and children," she explained with a sadness in her voice he had never heard before.

"Did you ever see him again?" Edoardo asked.

"Yes, once. Our paths crossed in New York, on Fifth Avenue. We ran into each by chance. Nothing had changed and we spent a passionate two days together. After that, we never spoke again, and I suppose he must have died because he was much older than me."

The flight attendant announced that passengers could now use their electronic devices. Groggy from his daydreaming, he checked his iPhone. He hoped to see a message from Benedetta, but instead he found a text that read: *If you do not quit the Lindenmayer Award competition immediately, we will be obliged to send this photograph to Benedetta.* He peered at the photograph, which was blurry. It was of Giovanna and him. They appeared to be about to kiss, lips inches apart. How could he explain it to Benedetta? If he told her that he had been tempted but, in the end, had remained true to her, would she believe him? Should he quit the competition? On the other hand, he hated the thought of being bullied into giving up. But did he want to run the risk of losing Benedetta?

"*Basta*, enough," he mumbled to himself. "I'll get a good night's sleep and then I'll call Fred in the morning and tell him exactly what has happened."

Satisfied with his decision, he found the driver of the limousine he had booked in the arrival hall, and in a flash they were out of the airport. In Spanish, Edoardo told the driver the address of the sixteenth-century palace in the old city of Córdoba, which had been converted into a boutique hotel. After checking in, he went to the bar and ordered a Laphroaig, his favorite single-malt whiskey. But he couldn't really enjoy it, as his thoughts kept wandering back to the text message and photograph. He was very tempted to call Benedetta and tell her everything, but he was afraid that she wouldn't believe him. He would prefer to tell her in person. Soon he returned to his room, threw himself on the bed—without taking off his clothes—and immediately fell asleep on top of the covers.

The next morning, he woke up in his elegantly furnished room that faced a courtyard; a citrus smell from the orange trees wafted through his open window. He felt energized, with renewed optimism. "It's ridiculous to let myself be swayed by stupid threats," he thought. "How can I, Edoardo Gardelli, an accomplished scientist, let myself fall into hysterics just because of some threat?"

He called Fred and explained his predicament. "It's very embarrassing," he said, "but the photograph makes it look as if I'm embracing Giovanna."

Fred reassured him and told him that he was thinking of hiring a detective to look into these latest threats. "Please forward the text with the photograph," Fred asked. He sounded so dispirited that Edoardo felt obliged to reassure him.

"It's okay, Fred, I'm sure it will all be resolved in time. I'm very eager to get to work on the Guadalquivir riddle."

"Thanks," Fred said. "But do keep me posted if anything else happens."

"I promise," Edoardo said, hanging up.

Looking at his breakfast tray, which had just been brought up, he grabbed a cup and poured coffee out of the thermos flask. On the desk, beside the tray, he noticed a brochure on the sightseeing highlights in Córdoba.

"Let's see where I should start today." He read introductory remarks in the brochure:

Córdoba was the center of a sophisticated and rich Hispano-Islamic civilization along with Byzantium and Baghdad. In the tenth century, at the peak of its development, Córdoba was renowned for its

*intellectually advanced culture and its libraries, far
outstripping the still-undeveloped Christian north.
In the late eleventh century, Córdoba became part of
the Kingdom of Seville and continued to thrive as an
intellectual center until the Christians reconquered it
in 1236.*

He continued reading through the brochure until a
name caught his attention: Cristóbal Colón.

Delighted, he exclaimed, "My hero when I was in
primary school!"

He recalled how his grandfather had given him a
book for his tenth birthday about the great explorers.
His favorite one had been Christopher Columbus; he
wondered now what the famous explorer's connec-
tions with Córdoba had been. It stated in the brochure that Cristóbal Colón (as Columbus was called
in Spain) was granted an interview in Córdoba with
King Ferdinand II of Aragon and Queen Isabella of
Castile who, by their marriage, had reunited the two
largest southern kingdoms. They had recently con-
quered Granada, the last Muslim stronghold on the
Iberian Peninsula. The interview took place in 1492
in the Alcázar de los Reyes Cristianos, where a sculpture commemorating that moment could now be seen.
It was during that interview that Colón negotiated his

journey. He settled in Córdoba while preparing to sail and had a son, Fernando, with the beautiful Beatriz Enríquez de Arana.

Continuing to leaf through the brochure, Edoardo stopped at the page describing the Saint Cathedral of Córdoba, the Mezquita, the Catholic cathedral, which was built inside the mosque in the twelfth century. He thought, "How typically Catholic to build churches everywhere, even in the middle of a Muslim place of worship."

The most striking feature of the Mezquita is that, in-congruously, the "mosque" contains a Christian church (Córdoba's cathedral). What one sees from outside is confusing: a huge, flat-roofed, low-lying square building with a gigantic baroque church jutting up in the middle. In the year 786, Abd-el-Rahman I started building a mosque on the site of a Christian basilica.

When the Christians reconquered Córdoba in 1236, instead of bothering to build a new church, they simply "converted" the building to Christianity and set up an altar in the middle—a pattern they repeated in all the Andalucian cities. In the sixteenth century, this modest Gothic insert was enlarged and given its current baroque style, resulting in the strange hybrid which we see today, with its ornately carved altar and pews.

Edoardo reflected: "This Muslim-Christian back and forth seems like a promising place to start." He decided to visit the mosque as soon as he finished breakfast. He poured himself a last cup of coffee. If only he could stop visualizing the photograph of him and Giovanna.

LINDENMAYER CORPORATE HEADQUARTERS, ZURICH, SWITZERLAND

MAY 2, 2018

Bobby had just turned on his Mac and was looking at a white beach with palm trees on his screen saver. "Isla Saona is where I'd like to be now," he thought, recalling the camping trip he had taken years ago with a local friend to this island at the tip of Dominican Republic. But instead, he had to deal with the problems relating to the competition. He wondered if he should tell Boswell about the latest issue with the iPhones. Philip and Jean-Pierre had called him to tell him that their iPhones were not working anymore. He immediately called the Swiss phone company, which handled all the contracts for the Lindenmayer Corporation. The company explained that they had received an e-mail from each of the candidates concerned, asking them to temporarily disconnect their number. Having received copies of the two messages, he could see that both Philip and Jean-Pierre had apparently sent them. But this was impossible. Someone was playing a joke on them. Remembering Boswell's response to his hacked e-mail account, Bobby decided that he would not tell him.

He threw a dart at the board on the wall of his office. Oban, his brown-and-white Scottish terrier immediately rushed to get it.

"Shoot," Bobby said to Oban. "I forgot that Boswell's still here."

Boswell had made very clear his dislike of Bobby's favorite pastime. He had actually made a point of entering Bobby's office and telling him that the sound the darts hitting the board was distracting. He could not tolerate it. Bobby would have to play while Boswell was not in the office.

"Of course, of course," Bobby said, in a very conciliatory manner, but he was thinking, "What a jerk. Everything I do annoys him." Boswell disliked Oban as well, and the feeling was mutual. Whenever Boswell appeared, Oban would start growling.

Oban had released the dart at Bobby's feet and was now sitting, looking up at him expectantly.

"Sorry, Oban, not right now. But we'll have our fun in a little bit." They would go to the Bonnie Prince, a

Scottish pub on Zähringerstrasse near the train station where he could play darts. Bobby and his dog were the pub's mascots. They were celebrities in the dart clubs and pubs worldwide. Bobby knew that whenever a game of darts was played, whether in a Scottish pub in Sydney, Tokyo, or New York, someone would always bring up his name and his famous dog, Oban. Bobby was five years old when his father had first taken him to the local pub in the village of Gullane in Scotland. That day he had discovered his passion for the game of darts.

"What do you suppose Boswell's doing in there?" he asked Oban.

He could hear Boswell pacing in his office. Bobby pictured him walking up and down, with his hands behind his back. Boswell was the only fly in the ointment, to use a cliché. Otherwise, Bobby's job was perfect. It was clear to him that Boswell resented Bobby having the job of Webmaster. What he found puzzling was the fact that Boswell was so overqualified for his job. He had a PhD after all.

"I would give a lot to know what happened," Bobby said to Oban, reflexively throwing another dart at the board. Catching a glimpse of himself in a mirror that hung from one wall, he thought he should probably cut out chocolate. He was a big man, so he could carry his weight, but lately, the stress had made him crave sweets even more. Perhaps he should have a low-calorie chocolate mousse instead.

"We all have our weaknesses," he said to Oban, then pulled out a treat from the drawer of his desk and threw it up in the air. Oban did a pirouette and caught the biscuit.

UNIVERSITY HOSPITAL, ZURICH, SWITZERLAND

MAY 2, 2018

Fred had agreed to give this speech last year when he had no idea that this would also be the first week of the award competition. But he had promised his friend Ueli Trümper, the chair of the Department of Neurology, that he would be there and he was actually looking forward to this midday event, which had been Ueli's idea for the General Assembly of the Association of Families of Alzheimer's Patients. When they had first discussed it, Fred had been reluctant to accept the invitation; he was uncomfortable talking about Meg's illness, which he knew he couldn't avoid doing in this forum. Ueli had insisted that it would be educational for the audience to hear the testimony of someone who was a public figure, one of Switzerland's leading industrialists, but who also experienced the grief of dealing with this disease. Fred finally agreed to participate since he strongly believed in the work of the association; he recognized how much it did to support families in their daily plight. The organizers had asked him to speak about his personal experience, but also about the award and how it could potentially help the families.

Fred had expected a large turnout, but there were even more people than he had imagined. The audience in the hospital's lecture hall was a mixed group. A few doctors and nurses in white coats sat in the front rows. The rest of the hall included elderly people, unusually quiet and accompanied by middle-aged men and women, most likely family members. Fred immediately recognized in some of these older people what he'd seen when Meg showed the first signs of Alzheimer's: glazed eyes indicating confusion and disorientation. There also appeared to be many students. As soon as he and Ueli stepped onto the stage people stopped talking.

Trümper was a lanky man with a swift, purposeful gait; he had a friendly smile and kind eyes. He fiddled with the edges of his wire-rimmed glasses as he spoke. "Ladies and gentlemen, dear colleagues and friends, in a few minutes it will be my great pleasure and honor to welcome Mr. Fred Lindenmayer, who has agreed to speak to us tonight about Alzheimer's disease and the creation of the Lindenmayer Award."

The only sounds from the audience came from an older man who coughed discreetly and the rustling of a young woman riffling through her notebook.

Trümper continued, "Fred's contribution to the field of Alzheimer's research will take the form of a new institute, which will be chaired by the winner of the award competition. But before ceding the stage to Fred, I feel that in order for you to appreciate the importance of his contribution, you need to be armed with some scientific knowledge of the subject."

As the lights dimmed, Fred took a seat at a small table to the side of the stage. Trümper took his place at the lectern; next to it a computer rested. When the first slide—a richly colored image of the brain shown from the side—appeared on the screen behind him, he began to lecture in a confident, clear voice.

"As most of you probably already know, what is uniquely devastating about this illness is the loss of what makes the patient a unique individual: memory, language, and the ability to think abstractly, as well as to utilize overall reasoning capabilities. The first symptoms of Alzheimer's disease are usually connected with subtle decreases in short-term memory, often related to a sense of place. People may be slightly disoriented in a familiar environment. The disease progresses slowly with losses in most spheres of cognitive abilities. In the late stages of the disease, simple tasks like feeding oneself and getting dressed without help become impossible. The patients often die of secondary respiratory complications such as aspiration and pneumonia. The average survival time between diagnosis and death is about ten years, but some patients live up to twenty years after the initial diagnosis. Today, the disease affects more than thirty million individuals worldwide. It's predicted that unless new therapies are found, one in forty-five people could suffer from it by the middle of the twenty-first century. But what exactly do we know about the causes of Alzheimer's disease? Unfortunately, not very much."

Trümper touched the computer keyboard and a series of images appeared in slow succession. "What we do know is that millions of neurons—the cells that process information in the brain—die at an abnormal rate, therefore removing elements from the chain of neurons in the very complex network of which the nervous system is composed. Thus the points of contact between neurons, called synapses, are disrupted in several places, making the brain much less efficient in processing and retrieving information. The end result is one of the main symptoms of Alzheimer's disease: the loss of memory."

He was illustrating his words with beautiful slides showing the shape of neurons and their synapses; he paused and looked out at the audience. "Please don't hesitate to interrupt me if you have any questions. Fred and I wish to have a dialogue rather than just give our presentations."

An older woman, with thinning white hair that revealed her pink scalp, timidly raised her hand. "I'm sorry," she said apologetically when Trümper encouraged her to speak up, "but I don't know what neurons are."

"No need to apologize. It's my mistake," he replied with a smile. He clicked back through the pages of his PowerPoint presentation and found the appropriate slide to illustrate his point. "Let me try to simplify this information for everyone: Neurons are cells that form the basic building blocks of the nervous system. Experts estimate that there are approximately a hundred billion neurons in the human brain. They differ from other cells in that they're specialized to transmit information throughout the body. Here's the drawing of a neuron, which shows how they communicate with each other. While very rudimentary, I hope this brief explanation makes sense." He directed the last comment to the woman kindly.

She nodded and thanked him.

Trümper carried on more quickly, knowing his audience would have limited patience with brain basics. "It's now clear that normal aging doesn't necessarily involve a significant loss of neurons. However, large numbers of them die in neurodegenerative diseases, of which Alzheimer's is one."

He readjusted his glasses. "But as I stated before, a normal aging process doesn't involve a significant loss of neurons, and the good news doesn't stop there. Until recently one of the dogmas of neuroscience was that we're born with a given 'capital' of neurons and that we regularly lose them as we age, possibly at a quicker pace later in life. But, in fact, we've discovered that the adult brain has the ability to constantly produce new neurons through a process called 'neurogenesis.' And that's why there's a great interest in the potential of therapeutic applications of neurogenesis. If scientists were to find a way to promote this process, one could envisage strategies to compensate the loss of neurons that happens in someone with Alzheimer's disease."

Trümper let the screen go back to the original handsome slide of the brain and said, "So those are the basics; but before I finish, let me give you a little history of the disease and a brief update of the scientific research in the field. In 1906, Alois Alzheimer described the case of a middle-aged woman, Auguste, who presented symptoms, which we would today relate to probable Alzheimer's disease. Upon Auguste's death, Alzheimer analyzed her brain. What he found was a much-altered organ that had lost possibly up to twenty percent of its mass."

The slide showing the shrunken brain of a patient who had died of the disease brought a gasp from the audience. Indeed, where they'd just seen the familiar plump folds and curves of a healthy brain, they now saw what looked like a shrunken walnut. "When he took tissue samples from the brain and stained them with compounds that made details of the tissue visible under his microscope, he found two unique features, which are still used today to provide the definitive diagnosis of the disease." Trümper moved to the next slide, which displayed an Alzheimer's brain section under the microscope.

"Alois Alzheimer discovered deposits between neurons: Some material accumulated where it shouldn't have been. He called these 'plaques.' He also found that dead neurons contained what appeared like bits of thread, which were entangled within the dead neuronal cell body. He called them 'neurofibrillary tangles.' This is the picture after death. The question still remains of how neurons die and what the relationship is between these strange deposits, the plaques and tangles, and the dementia that characterizes the disease.

"Over the years, lively debates about whether either one of these deposits causes the disease have animated neuroscientific circles—so much so that each side of the main debate came to be known by memorable nicknames. On one side were scientists who suggested that the plaques, made of a particular protein called beta-amyloid, were the culprits. Abnormal accumulation of this protein around neurons would somehow suffocate them and lead to their death. The proponents of this beta-amyloid protein theory, or BAP, are called the 'Baptists.' To date, we've found that several of the genetically abnormal proteins in familial Alzheimer's disease—which account for less than three percent of the cases—are related to the beta-amyloid protein."

He cleared his throat. "The disputing school of thought provided evidence that some abnormal state of the protein of which the neurofibrillary tangles were made—the tau protein—was the cause of the disease. The proponents of this theory are known as the 'Tao-ists.' Thus for years we have witnessed an almost religious debate between the Baptists and the Taoists," he said, spiritedly.

"What's most frustrating, however, is that despite what we have learned, current treatments work only on lessening the symptoms. Indeed, they have a moderate effect, decreasing the rate at which memory function is impaired without tackling the causes of the disease or permanently halting its progression."

At that point, the screen went dark, the lights came up and Trümper closed the computer. He walked quickly to the center of the stage. "And that, ladies and gentlemen, in a nutshell, is why the search for a cure needs people like the man I'm about to introduce: Fred Lindenmayer, a man whose inspiration we hope can finally move the research forward."

As Fred made his way toward the podium, a wave of nervousness washed over him. While he was used to addressing large audiences, this would be only his second public speech about the award. And unlike the journalists, many of these people had a great personal or professional stake in discovering a cure to Alzheimer's. He took a deep breath. Preparing his remarks, he'd wrestled with the question of how to begin. But he'd soon realized that there was only one way: with his personal experience.

As soon as he started to speak, his nervousness evaporated. He identified in the faces of many of the audience members the same feelings of helplessness and fear with which he struggled.

"When the doctor told me about my wife's diagnosis, I was stunned, unable to process the news. My head was a jumble of questions and I couldn't even formulate the first one. The doctor carefully explained to me the different possible phases of the illness and it suddenly hit me that Meg, my beloved wife of more than forty years, would never be the same. At this point, I temporarily lost all hope. Meg would slowly retreat into a world of her own, and everything we had shared and loved together would be gone for her. At some point, my wife would no longer even recognize our children or me. As for me, slowly and painfully, I'd lose the woman I love."

Overcome with sorrow, Fred paused and reached for the glass of water on the podium. There was no sound in the audience. But when Ueli rushed to his side and asked him if he was unable to proceed, Fred reassured him that he would finish his remarks.

"That's why I have decided to launch the Lindenmayer Award. It's time for the scientific community to make a significant breakthrough in research so that a treatment can be found. I'll only briefly outline how the award will work and leave details for the discussion. What I hope will matter most to you is the strategy behind this project, which is to identify the boldest, most confident, and most intellectually dynamic scientists committed to Alzheimer's research and to harness their talent to lead the search for new treatments and ultimately a cure."

MOSCOW, RUSSIA

MAY 2, 2018

Back at her hotel, Sarah threw herself onto her bed and broke down in tears.

Douschka had passed away a few hours before she arrived.

A knock at the door made Sarah startle. Who could it be? She was so tired and sad, she just wanted to go to sleep. She went to the door. Standing outside was a young woman in a white-and-black maid's uniform with a tray in her hand. Sarah was about to say that there was a mistake, she had not ordered anything, when the woman said, "Complimentary drinks," in Russian. The woman stepped into the room with the tray and placed it on the coffee table by the little pink sofa. Before Sarah had time to ask who had sent the complimentary drinks, the woman walked out of the room. Sarah noticed the stockings the woman wore, an ugly yellow that didn't seem in keeping with her uniform.

Wondering what kind of drink she was being offered, Sarah went over to the tray and lifted the glass and sniffed it. Vodka. How strange, she thought. She was about to take a sip when she noticed a note on the tray.

Reading it, her heart skipped a beat: "*if you do no give up award and go back hom, we can no garante your safe here in moscow, axident can happen.*"

Even though her legs were rubbery from fatigue and fear, she rushed to the door to catch the hotel worker, but of course the corridor was empty. She grabbed the phone to call reception, but then replaced the receiver and sank into the armchair next to the desk. "Don't panic," she said aloud. Lindenmayer had told her that in case of an emergency or serious trouble she was supposed to call Bobby. She looked up his emergency number on her iPhone, and then remembered that she just had to punch the 1 key, which automatically dialed his number.

After two rings, he picked up. "Sarah, is that you?" he asked. "What's going on? I hope you arrived in Moscow safely."

She was so relieved to hear his warm voice that tears rimmed her eyes. "I'm so glad I reached you! I just received a message threatening me with an accident if I don't give up the competition immediately."

"Listen, Sarah, I'm going to put Fred on the line too," Bobby said, his voice now agitated. "Just hold on for a minute."

"Of course."

Within a few seconds, Bobby connected Fred to her.

"Hi, Sarah. Fred here. Sorry to hear about the message you received. Please tell us what happened and, if you don't mind, we're going to record our conversation."

"No, I don't mind." She then recounted how she'd found the message on the tray that had been delivered to her room. After reading it aloud to Lindenmayer and Bobby, she said, "It looks like it was written on an old typewriter, not a computer. It's on a plain sheet of grayish paper with some grease stains on it. There are also a lot of spelling mistakes and no capital letters."

"Sarah, listen to me carefully," Lindenmayer said calmly but forcefully. "We're facing a serious situation here and I don't want you to be in any danger. Several of your fellow contestants have also run into difficulties. Edoardo received a threatening message, Philip's iPhone was stolen, and it seems that Jean-Pierre is being shadowed by a seedy-looking character. Now you have received this note. I will consult with a friend who is a private investigator, and in the meantime you should definitely leave Moscow as soon as possible. Why don't you come back to Zurich and continue from here. I will keep all contestants posted about any further development."

Sarah was stricken with sadness at the thought of leaving the city without being able to attend her grandmother's funeral.

"Sarah, are you there?" Fred asked.

"Yes, I was trying to figure out what to do. My grandmother just passed away."

"Oh, I am so sorry to hear that, my heartfelt condolences. It is really up to you to decide what to do next. But so you know I have already contacted the Swiss embassies in the countries where the contestants are traveling to ask them for help in getting you all back quickly. Sarah, hold on for a second, Bobby is talking to our embassy in Moscow. Stay on the line."

"Of course," she said, wiping the tears with her free hand.

"Okay. Bobby was able to talk to a diplomat at the embassy. He's on his way to pick you up if you decide to leave. His name is Michael Eschler and he'll slide his ID under your door when he knocks. Until then, don't answer the phone or open the door. You'll stay at the ambassador's residence tonight and he'll brief you about your trip back to Switzerland. We'll book you on a flight to Zurich as soon as you have made your decision."

"What do I tell the hotel?" She tried to keep her trembling voice in check.

"Tell them you're going to stay with friends for the night and that you have to go back home tomorrow because of a family emergency. That way, whoever put the message on your tray will know you're leaving the country. Good luck, Sarah, and see you soon."

"Thanks for your help, Fred. Good night."

While waiting for the diplomat to arrive, Sarah called her mother, who was staying with friends in Moscow to attend the funeral. "I'm so sorry, Mum," she said. "But there has been an unexpected turn of events in the contest and I think that I really have to return to Switzerland. I won't be able to go to the funeral."

There was a silence on the line.

"I know you must be disappointed, but the truth is that some of the contestants have received threats and I was advised to leave Moscow as soon as possible."

"I understand, darling, take good care of yourself and keep me posted," her mother replied.

Sarah could not help weeping out of sadness and exhaustion. She lay on her bed without getting under the covers. She was too shaken to fall asleep. Nevertheless, she must have dozed off because she awakened to a knock at the door. Sarah picked up the ID slid under it, as instructed. It showed Michael Eschler's name and picture. Upon opening the door, she faced three men. She hesitated, but then one of them stretched out his hand.

"Miss Majewski, I'm Michael Eschler. It's a pleasure to meet you. Are you ready to go?"

She took his hand and looked up at his broad smile. He was a tall man of medium build with round, brown eyes and dark hair that curled at this neck. Eschler kept her hand in his a moment longer than was necessary.

One of the other two men coughed discreetly and said, "Mr. Eschler, it's best if we leave now." Sarah pulled her hand away.

"You're right, Ruedi," Michael said. "Please take Miss Majewski's luggage."

While the other man checked the corridor—Secret Service, she was wondering—Ruedi took her bag and they led her toward the elevator. She could not believe that she missed seeing her grandmother and that she wouldn't even be there for her funeral. The tears came to her eyes again and she had to blink them back when she got into the elevator. Michael Eschler reached into his pocket and pulled out a handkerchief. "Please," he said.

"Oh no, I couldn't! How old-fashioned," she couldn't help exclaiming.

"I take that as a compliment," he said, smiling again.

She looked down at her shoes. There was no denying that Michael was handsome, but he smiled too often. Flirtation was the last thing on her mind. They reached the lobby, and she approached the reception desk to check out.

Five minutes later they were in the car, driving to the ambassador's residence, and Michael turned toward her. "Ambassador Greuter and his wife are attending two functions tonight and aren't at the residence. The ambassador asked me to keep you company for some drinks and dinner. I'll also be staying at the residence overnight."

"That's very kind," Sarah said. "But I'm really not hungry."

"At least have a drink," he suggested.

"All right," she said, not wanting to be rude.

The car stopped in front of the residence—a light green building with a Swiss flag hanging from a center window—and someone opened the car door for her. Michael showed her inside, where Jelena, the housekeeper, greeted them.

"I'll show you to your room," he said, gesturing to the stairs. "When you're ready, join me in the kitchen, which is down the hall. Jelena has fixed us something to eat."

They had just sat down in the kitchen when the ambassador poked his head through the kitchen door. "Hello! I'm just popping in for a minute. My wife forgot something. She's always forgetting something." He stretched out his hand to Sarah. "I also wanted to say hello and wish you a good night." He was a dignified-looking man with cropped gray hair, wearing a well-cut suit and silk tie. "I'm Peter Greuter, by the way."

"Very nice to meet you, Mr. Ambassador. Thanks so much for putting me up for the night."

"Our pleasure," Greuter replied, turning to Michael. "By the way, I've decided to send you to Switzerland with Miss Majewski to replace me at the conference on the Central Asian Republics at the ministry."

"Well, that's excellent news," Michael said, unabashedly. "Did something happen to make you change your mind about going to Switzerland?"

"Yes," the ambassador said. "A situation came up and I can't leave the country right now. I'll give you the details in the morning. How about breakfast in my study at eight?"

"Perfect, sir. Have a good night."

"Thanks, you too. Miss Majewski, I hope all your problems will be solved quickly. Catherine, my wife, will see you in the morning. Good night."

After the ambassador left, Michael gazed at Sarah. "You have the most beautiful blue eyes," he said.

"Thank you," she said, laughing. "But I'm really tired. I'll see you in the morning."

"You haven't had your drink," he said. "Would you at least care for a glass of wine?"

"All right," she said, thinking that the wine would help her sleep.

While he was pouring the wine, he asked her about the Lindenmayer Award and wanted to know the reason for her visit to Russia. She told him that she had come to visit her grandmother who had unfortunately passed away yesterday. At last, she insisted on retiring for the night. She was so tired she could hardly keep her eyes open.

"Thank you for the lovely wine," she said. As she walked across the kitchen, she felt him watching her. "He's not a bad listener," she thought, stepping into the corridor.

CÓRDOBA, SPAIN

From the balcony of his hotel room in Córdoba, Philip stared at the sunset over this ancient city. He could see the bell tower of the Mezquita. He had just sent Bobby the answer to the Córdoba riddle and a picture of the site, and was expecting confirmation that he had solved it correctly. He should be feeling pleased with himself, but instead he longed for Julian. He even wondered if he should have gone to the United States instead of Córdoba. Several times, he had called Julian and each time Julian had made it very clear that he did not want to talk with him until Philip had told his parents about their relationship.

His cell phone rang and he glanced at it, thinking it would be Bobby but hoping that it was Julian. It was neither. His mother's voice greeted him instead. "Hello, Philip," she said.

"Hello, Mother, lovely to hear from you. Is everything all right?"

Her voice sounded shaky. They had just seen each other. He had not expected her to call. She didn't really like talking on the phone.

"Well, my dear, I'm sure this is just some kind of prank, but it upset me."

"What happened?"

"I got an e-mail from someone—anonymous—I didn't recognize the name—"

"You didn't open it I hope?"

"I did because of the subject heading. It read: *Do you know that your son and Shakespeare have something in common?*"

"And?"

"Well, it's perfectly ridiculous. You'll laugh when I tell you, but when I opened the e-mail, I found Shakespeare's twentieth sonnet. You know the one which begins, 'A woman's face with nature's own hand painted.' The one everyone believes suggests more than any other poem by Shakespeare that he was writing to a man. You're not hiding anything from me, are you?" His mother laughed her trilling laugh, as she always did when she was embarrassed or nervous. He knew that she was expecting him to laugh with her, but he felt unable to. Now was the perfect opportunity to tell her the truth, but he couldn't.

"How odd," he said feeling intensely uncomfortable. "Probably just a crank e-mail. It must be somebody's idea of a joke. I can't imagine who it could be." He talked too fast, as if he could fill the silence with words. He wondered what his mother was thinking.

"Whatever you say, Philip. I just wanted to make sure that everything is all right."

"Of course. You did the right thing by calling me, but don't let it upset you."

"I don't think I'll mention it to your father."

"Right, probably best if you don't."

After she hung up, he felt even more lonely. The sun had dropped so that he could only see a sliver of it. The sky was an odd, almost green color. He thought of Lorca's poem, "Green, how I want you green. Green wind. Green branches." At the same time, he realized that he was hungry. He would go to Plaza de la Corredera, one of his favorite plazas. Built in the seventeenth century, it was lined with bright red-and-green-trimmed apartment buildings, cafés, and shops. He could not understand who could have sent the e-mail to his mother. It seemed unconscionable. He had no enemies that he knew of.

When he reached Plaza de la Corredera, he went into Taberna Salinas. He liked the Old Spanish decor and plant-filled patio. It wasn't too crowded, and it had wireless connection: an ideal spot for dinner while he tried to solve the second riddle. He settled into a corner table by the window and studied the menu. "Looks delicious," he thought. Having ordered a selection of tapas, including the wild asparagus, pork chops, and grilled calamari, he turned on his iPad and read the riddle again.

In the city of C......bridge and its many towers lies in eternal peace the father of Melog, who in search of death backward may have created the first mechanical mind.

"Well, this must be Cambridge," Philip exclaimed. The town was not only famous for its university and great minds but for its abundance of towers. He recalled the fun he'd had as a bell ringer during his student days.

He had fond memories of the years he'd spent in Cambridge, working on his PhD on the cell lineage of *Caenorhabditis elegans*, a worm that many neuroscientists study to understand the development of the nervous system. Recently, *C. elegans*, as the specialists call it, had yielded tantalizing secrets about the process of neuronal death, a topic highly relevant to the understanding of neurodegeneration such as occurs in Alzheimer's disease.

When Philip had first arrived in Cambridge, he'd joined the rowing team, following a Caldwell-Tyson family tradition. While he enjoyed the atmosphere of the rowing crowd, he'd been looking for a new challenge, an activity he'd never tried before. Thomas Warwick, a technician in his lab, told him about the Cambridge University Guild of Change Ringers. Thomas had lived in Cambridge all his life; he'd become a member of the guild when he started working at the university some thirty years before. He told Philip that the guild was formed in 1879 to practice the art of change ringing. The main activity was to ring bells in several churches in Cambridge.

Every Wednesday, Thomas brought *The Ringing World*, the weekly journal for church bell ringers, to the lab. Philip fondly remembered how they would discuss the articles over lunch in the courtyard of Caius College. They also planned their practice sessions together, as they liked sharing their impressions of the different bells afterward.

"It'll be nice to go back to Cambridge," Philip thought. He wondered if Thomas was still working or if he'd retired. "I'll definitely drop by the lab and find out."

He was excited about having deciphered the first half of the clue. As the selection of tapas was being served, he put his iPad on the chair next to him, took a sip of his Alhambra Negra—the caramel-tasting local beer he'd just discovered—and pondered what he would be looking for in Cambridge. "What's the scientific question here?" He tried to concentrate, but the clue for this part of the riddle didn't seem as evident as the one for the city.

In the city of C......bridge and its many towers lies in eternal peace the father of Melog, who in search of death backward may have created the first mechanical mind.

He saw that he needed to separate the clues. "First is '*lies in eternal peace*,' which could have something to do with a cemetery. Then there's '*death backward*.' If I put the letters backward: h-t-a-e-d...no, that doesn't mean anything. Next clue: '*the father of Melog*.' " It meant nothing to him. " '*The first mechanical mind*' has to have something to do with mechanics or physics. Who are the well-known physicists in Cambridge?"

Of course, there had been many, but undoubtedly the greatest was Isaac Newton. While Newton's major work on the law of gravitation, *Philosophiae Naturalis Insignia Mathematica*, was published in 1687, it was still one of the essential texts in astrophysics. Philip recalled that Newton's theory explains how planets are attracted to each other with a force inversely proportional to the square of the distance that separates them.

"Yes, but what do Newton and the laws of mechanics have to do with neuroscience?" he wondered. "Let's go back to the riddle, '*the first mechanical mind*.' What does it really mean? Not mechanics. Not someone who has a mind for mechanics. It's about two things: a father and a mind that is mechanical, meaning not biological, not a living mind, not a brain. So what is a mechanical mind?"

Puzzled, he stopped to sip his beer and nibble on his calamari. "Something like a machine that 'thinks,' a robot, or maybe some sort of a computer or a form of artificial intelligence? But Newton's was a very 'alive' intelligence, certainly not an artificial one. He founded modern astrophysics for God's sake."

He tried to concentrate on Newton and how, in watching an apple fall to the ground, he derived the theory of universal gravitation. "Apple, apple...intelligence...computers. There's something but, no...the Apple computer company was founded in Cupertino, California, not Cambridge!"

Suddenly, he remembered his friend Jimmy Slater, the computer freak at Cambridge. Jimmy had told Philip how Apple got its name and why an apple with a bite in it was chosen as its logo. It was in memory of Alan Turing, the great British mathematician, who committed suicide in 1954 by biting into an apple soaked with potassium cyanide. As a result of his homosexuality, Turing had faced a humiliating trial and chose death instead of prison. He'd never denied his sexual preference, but it was unacceptable in the puritanical society of the 1950s. Philip could only imagine how difficult it must have been sixty years ago to be a homosexual. Once again, his mind wandered to the question of how long he would be able to delay telling his family about Julian.

He sighed and turned on his iPad, initiating a search for Turing, and was soon spellbound by the drama of the mathematician's life. Quickly, he discovered that Turing—considered the father of artificial intelligence—was the author of the theoretical bases that allowed the development of modern computers.

"Excellent," Philip exclaimed when he saw that Turing studied mathematics at King's College, Cambridge. This was the first connection. He read how Turing was a brilliant student, fascinated with the study of probabilities and logics, which brought him, in 1936, to formulate the concept for the Turing machine, which allowed a series of instructions to be formalized into mathematical algorithms to produce a result. Very simply, Turing, for the first time, laid out the principles of computer programming. During the Second World War, he worked at the Ministry of Foreign Affairs to help decipher the secret of Enigma, the code name for the machine the German navy used to communicate with their submarines. Applying his new theory on computability and the principles of algorithms, Turing was able to break the code, an important contribution to the Allied victory in the Battle of the Atlantic. After the war, Turing joined the National Physical Laboratory in London to work on developing computing machines, which could now incorporate the new transistor technology. However, because of his homosexuality, he was soon removed from any sensitive project.

A visionary, he considered it possible that a computing machine could calculate algebra, break codes, handle files, and even play chess. He thought a machine could learn and improve its own programming, and he even imagined a national computing center with remote terminals. In 1948, he joined the University of Manchester, where he participated in designing the first real computer, Mark 1. The Turing machine was considered the first intelligent machine, which was the forerunner of the first computer.

Philip deduced that the Turing machine must be what the riddle meant by "a mechanical mind." So now the riddle began to unfold. If Turing was the "*father of Melog*"—who "*created the first mechanical mind*"—then who on earth was Melog?

Maybe Turing would lead him to Melog. Philip smiled and congratulated himself. He was familiar with the Turing Archives at the Modern Archives

Centre of King's College and was all set for his visit to Cambridge. He clicked off his iPad and placed it again on the chair next to him. He leaned back and breathed deeply. There was a lovely little breeze coming through the courtyard. He ordered another drink.

BOSWELL'S APARTMENT, ZURICH, SWITZERLAND

Standing on the small terrace of his apartment, which looked onto the roofs of Old Town, Boswell held his cell phone away from his ear. "No need to shout," he said. There was a silence on the line. Now he had offended Bobby.

"You don't seem to understand how serious this is," Bobby said. "I do."

He had to hold himself back from saying "I understand it better than you can possibly imagine." He was having a hard time not bursting into laughter. It seemed so funny.

"Tell me again. Slowly. No drama needed, please!"

"Well, several competitors have received serious threats, an iPhone was stolen, and even Philip's family was involved."

"That is strange."

"And Fred asked Sarah to leave Moscow immediately and return to Zurich with the other contestants until we know what is going on."

"Why didn't you consult with me first?" Boswell seemed annoyed.

"Because I couldn't reach you when Sarah called and Fred was in his office. He is very concerned."

"Yes, I imagine he would be. Well, let's sit tight and see what happens next."

"Very well," Bobby said with a wistful tone. "Fred is contacting a PI friend of his to help us with the situation."

"That hardly seems necessary. Got to go. So sorry!" And he hung up.

He could not stop laughing. He really must get ahold of himself. Poor Bobby. He hadn't begun to see what Boswell was capable of. The fun had only started. He couldn't remember the last time he'd been so amused. He was even enjoying Yucun's company more than he had anticipated. Toward the end of their affair in California, he had started to tire of her devotion, but the separation had really helped. He had to admit that he appreciated the way she stared at him as if he were an oracle. He felt sure that she would do whatever he wanted. He almost felt sorry that she had left his apartment to work on her riddle, but it was just as well, because she might have noticed his amusement when Bobby called and wondered at his lack of concern about the contestants' difficulties.

Stepping from the small terrace into his shadowy bedroom, he felt himself in need of a little more cocaine, which was strange because he'd had some not that long ago. Not so strange, he reminded himself. He would need to consume more and more if he wished to maintain this pleasant buzz. He switched on his bedside lamp. He needed to be more careful, he thought, as he opened the drawer to his night table. Yucun could easily have opened the drawer and seen the cocaine and the photograph of Mara beside it. He had kept only one photograph of Mara, a black-and-white one, taken on the morning they had announced to her father that they were planning to get married. Boswell had been working with a renowned neuroanatomist at the University of Johannesburg. Mara worked in her father's diamond business. He remembered how nervous they were when they entered her father's house. Henry McCall had kept them waiting. Even at the time, in the days of his innocence, as Boswell now referred to it, he had felt that the wait was designed to impress upon him the luxuriousness of the mansion where Mara had grown up. Her father wanted him to have plenty of time to admire the living room with its numerous sofas and exquisite paintings and silver. Mara kept jumping up from the sofa where they were seated. Twice she checked herself in the mirror above the marble mantel. When her father finally arrived, he startled them.

He had pretended to be overjoyed at their announcement. Nevertheless, Boswell had felt a distinct cooling in his relations with him. McCall did not mind Boswell as a boyfriend for Mara, but Boswell had felt that McCall didn't think that he was quite up to snuff as a prospective husband.

When he and Mara had left in her beautiful blue Mercedes, driven by her own personal chauffeur, Boswell had been determined to work night and day to become a full professor and prove to her father that he was worthy of Mara. What a fool! Now, looking back, he realized that even if he had become a full professor, McCall would still not have found him up to par. No, what McCall had wanted all along for his daughter was another businessman like himself. And he had gotten exactly what he wanted. Mara had married an immensely rich older man who was in timber. Her father, the bastard, had sent him a newspaper clipping of the wedding with Mara and her husband embracing.

Lying on his bed, in the place that Yucun had just vacated, he told himself that he needed to stop thinking about the past. It was the present he needed to concern himself with.

PONTLEVOY, FRANCE

MAY 3, 2018

As Jean-Pierre drove through the beautiful Loire Valley from Chambord to Pontlevoy, he wondered if he had made the right decision to enter the competition for the Lindenmayer Award. If he were to win, it would indeed give his career a great boost. But his research at the Collège de France was going extremely well and he wasn't sure if his thesis adviser had understood his decision to apply for the award. They thought that if you were working at this academic high-level institution nothing could be better for you.

He was so caught up in his thoughts that he was forgetting to take in the landscape. At this time of year, it was particularly beautiful. Who would have thought someone like him, coming from the small village of Pontlevoy, would end up working in Paris at the Collège de France, or Le Collège, as it was referred to by French intellectuals. It gave him such pleasure to think about this unique institution's remarkable history. The Collège de France was founded in 1530 by King François I. The king was advised by Guillaume Budé, his *maître de librairie* (a kind of scientific adviser), to appoint six royal lecturers, whose mission would be to teach disciplines such as Hebrew, Greek, and mathematics, subjects that were not taught at the Sorbonne. In addition to these cultural and academic purposes, the creation of Le Collège also had a political agenda: It allowed the king to establish a balance of power between Le Collège and the professors at the Sorbonne.

The building in which Le Collège is located today was designed in 1772 by the French architect Jean-François Chalgrin, on the initiative of Louis XV. The list of professors at the Collège de France is a who's who of French scientific, literary, and philosophical achievements. Among them were Jean-François Champollion, who deciphered Egyptian hieroglyphs on the Rosetta stone; Claude Bernard, the founder of experimental medicine; and Henri Bergson, Claude Lévi-Strauss, Roland Barthes, and Michel Foucault, who respectively laid the grounds for modern philosophy, anthropology, and sociology. A unique feature of the Collège de France is that it does not deliver academic diplomas. The lectures given by the professors are open to the public. It is undoubtedly a temple of science and academic excellence.

Jean-Pierre's boss, Jacques Leblond-Vasseur, held the chair of neuropharmacology at Le Collège. He was an outstanding scientist and a wonderful human being, managing to maintain a very personal and warm approach with his collaborators and a sensitivity to their personal development, while encouraging a competitive attitude and desire for excellence. His laboratory, with a few other laboratories in Europe and the United States, was at the forefront of a scientific breakthrough, having discovered new ways in which the cells of the brain communicate with each other. In particular, results in his laboratory had characterized the interaction existing between neurons and glial cells, the other main type of brain cell. The role of glial cells in information processing and cell communication in the brain had only recently been discovered. This breakthrough by his lab and a few other labs opened a new field of neuroscience, now called "neuron-glia interactions."

The term "glia" was proposed in the middle of the nineteenth century by the German neuropathologist Rudolf Virchow, who had identified by using staining techniques cell types that looked quite different from neurons. They seemed to fill in all the spaces not occupied by neurons. From this observation, he deduced that these cells might be some kind of "glue" for the brain, holding neurons together. Over a century later it is now clear that glial cells are everything but inert glue. They do much more than fill the gaps between neurons. In fact, glial cells not only assist neurons in carrying out their job but very recent evidence suggests that they can also participate in the information processing which up to now was thought to be only the turf of neurons.

Jean-Pierre had arrived in Leblond-Vasseur's group at Le Collège at a time when the specific role of glial cells to provide adequate nutrients to neurons had been discovered by a Swiss group led by Jules Maître at the University of Lausanne. Leblond-Vasseur's laboratory was located on the second and third floors of the Bâtiment de Biologie, just behind the main building of Le Collège. Office space was small, but the labs were adequate in size and the equipment was outstanding.

Leblond-Vasseur and Maître were good friends, and they had decided that Jean- Pierre could work on a project run by both labs. At the time, the collaboration had seemed very promising to Jean-Pierre, and indeed that had turned out to be the case. After three years of collaboration, the results, which Jean-Pierre had included in his doctoral thesis, revealed the existence of a new mode of communication between neurons and glial cells. The two research groups, in Paris and Lausanne, had concluded that the field of neuron-glia interaction represented a kind of paradigm shift, which was bringing neuroscience from a neuro-centric approach into a glia-centric one. More and more research suggests that glial cells may be involved in a number of diseases that affect the brain, such as epilepsy, depression, and neurodegenerative diseases, including Alzheimer's.

The emerging role of glial cells in Alzheimer's disease had attracted Jean-Pierre's attention as a possible research topic after his doctorate at Le Collège, and it had also motivated him to apply for the Lindenmayer Award. Recent evidence pointed at a particular type of glial cell, the microglia, as participating in the damaging processes that lead to neurodegeneration such as observed in Alzheimer's disease.

Lately, Jean-Pierre had been discussing with Maître his interest in microglial cells and in the Lindenmayer Award. Maître had recently moved to Paris for a sabbatical. Upon the proposal by Leblond-Vasseur, Maître had been elected by the professors' assembly of Le Collège to the international chair for one academic year. This was quite an honor: The annual chair brings a scholar to Le Collège for a year to give a series of lectures and conduct specialized seminars. The venerable institution imposes certain rites of passage on its professors, even those occupying an annual chair. One of them consists of a gathering in the suite of the head of Le Collège, to which only professors are invited. Usually ten to twenty attend to enjoy the excellent wines that a member of the administration has selected. The atmosphere is relaxed, the participants being comfortably seated in nice art deco leather armchairs, leisurely sipping the delicious wine; a perfect ambiance for scholars to meet in an elegant and informal setting. Informal for all but one person: the professor who has been kindly invited to present a subject for discussion, in general somehow related to his or her work. The challenge is twofold: foremost the style should be unassuming and light, and the content should be deep. No details are necessary and the essence of the question at stake should emerge naturally. The starting point may be, and in fact should be, quite ordinary, yet treatment of the subject should open a discussion on deep topics with far-reaching implications, such as the origin of the universe or the nature of the human mind or other similar topics.

Maître had told Jean-Pierre how much he enjoyed participating in these rare events, where brilliant minds exchange thoughtful comments and arguments with the same ease and seamless execution as professional football players would pass the ball around. But Maître had confided to Jean-Pierre that he had been quite taken aback when one day a senior professor suggested that Maître could give one of these informal presentations on the subject of the workshop that he was about to hold on the role of glial cells in brain function.

Maître had started by providing a simple fact about the brain: It is an incredibly energy-demanding organ. Despite the fact that it constitutes only two percent of the body mass, it uses twenty-five percent of the energy consumed by the entire body. The point seemed to get people's attention.

One of his colleagues asked, "Why does the brain use so much energy and how does energy get to the neurons?"

To address the first part of the question, Maître made an analogy. "Neurons are like batteries," he said, "they have to be charged in order to fire electrical signals. The brain needs to 'burn' glucose with oxygen to produce the needed energy." As to how glucose gets into the brain, well, that's the main job of a type of glial cell, the astrocytes. These star-shaped cells, hence, their name astrocytes ("astro" meaning star in Latin), are the main providers of energy to the neurons. Brain-imaging techniques allow us to visualize how much energy is consumed by neurons in a given brain area. Functional brain imaging has revolutionized our way of studying the brain: Today we can "see" the brain at work.

Maître then brought up another point, which was subtle but with far-reaching implications. No doubt he expected that it would open the discussion to issues of general interest, in particular for the philosophy and literary scholars in the group. "One might think that the brain consumes energy only, or mostly, when certain neurons are engaged in a specific task—for example, commanding a movement—and that the basal activity of the brain is quite low," continued Maître. "But this would be wrong. In fact, basal energy utilization by the brain is very high. The brain can be seen as a car's engine running permanently at six thousand rpms and when a region is engaged in a task it will run up to seven thousand rpms. Thus the question should be: Why is the brain such a glutton for energy even when we are seemingly doing nothing?"

"What if the unconscious, the Freudian unconscious, was at work during these 'inactive' states of the brain?" suggested Pierre Dallemagne, a professor of contemporary French literature and a specialist on Marcel Proust.

"Please, let's be serious," Jean-Louis Marcoux argued forcefully. He was a renowned mathematician, who had lately become interested in building mathematical models of brain function, a field otherwise known as computational neuroscience.

This first exchange had sparked a lively discussion involving several professors. The sound of someone honking behind him brought Jean-Pierre back to the present.

He was driving too slowly, which was completely out of character for him, but he had been so engrossed in his thoughts about the Collège de France that he had not noticed. Glancing at his rearview mirror, he saw that five or six cars were stuck behind him. "So sorry!" he said, speeding up.

When he reached Pontlevoy, he smiled at the sight of the crouching monkey carved in limestone on the cornice of a building on rue des Singes. Everything looked so familiar: the Benedictine abbey and the butcher shop on rue du Colonel Filloux, the village's main street. As his car came to a stop in front of the family farmhouse, the door opened and his mother came running out with her arms open wide. "Jean-Pierre, my boy, it's been so long! How are you? You look so thin—is this how they are feeding you in Paris?" she cried. She hugged him close and he smelled her lavender perfume.

Jean-Pierre knew that his mother was overwhelmed with joy that he was staying at the farm, with his family, overnight. He hadn't been home since Christmas, more than four months ago. Although her eight children were all grown up now, his mother often said, "I'm still a mother hen caring for my chicks." With Jean-Pierre living in Paris, René working in New York, Monique on a mission for Doctors Without Borders in Afghanistan, and Jeanne teaching in Marseille, his mother was happy to still have four of her children living in the Blois region. Paul, Maurice, François, and Marianne were all married with children and Marie loved having her grandchildren stay at the farm. For his mother, family was everything.

"Félicien," she called her husband. "Come quickly. Jean-Pierre has arrived!"

"Maman, attends un peu, calm down. Let me get my luggage out of the trunk. Here are some flowers for the most wonderful *maman* in the world."

As Marie took the beautiful spring bouquet from his outstretched hand, she beamed with pride. Meanwhile, Jean-Pierre watched his father approach them from the farmhouse, noticing how he gazed at her. Félicien Abdoulayé had arrived in Pontlevoy from Sénégal in the late 1970s as a worker on Marie's father's farm. She often joked that Félicien still found her, at sixty-five, as good-looking as the twenty-year-old he met when he started working on the farm, which he now ran. "It was love at first sight," she would boast, "and we were married six months later. I've put on a few pounds, of course, but after all, I've borne eight children and I'm a grandmother of ten."

Félicien and Jean-Pierre sat at the large kitchen table while Marie prepared café au lait in the rustic red bowls Jean-Pierre remembered from his childhood.

"*Alors, mon garçon,*" said Félicien. "What important news did you have to tell us that you traveled all the way from Paris for?"

"Actually one reason is because I am pretty sure that the first part of one of the riddles I am trying to solve revolves around nearby Chambord Castle. And I have also to tell you some big news," said Jean-Pierre, laughing when he noticed his mother's frown, the crinkled lines etched around her rich, amber-colored eyes deepening in concern.

"Don't worry, *Maman*, it is good news. I'm going to defend my doctoral thesis on June second. The timing is perfect: I have submitted my thesis to the jury just before starting the competition to give the jury members a whole month to assess it. I hope you'll be able to come to the Collège de France for that day."

"Of course, we'll be there," Félicien promised immediately. He smiled, so that his round face looked even chubbier and his eyes brightened. He had an unruly thicket of graying hair that his grandchildren liked to touch. "Do you remember, Marie, the first time we saw the Collège de France? It was on our honeymoon."

"Yes, yes, Félicien, but let the boy speak," Marie said.

"Actually, Papa, I will always remember my first visit to Le Collège," said Jean- Pierre with a grin. "I'd arrived in Paris at the Gare de Lyon on the TGV and I'd asked the taxi driver to bring me to the Collège de France. But the driver didn't have a clue. I gave him the address: Place Marcellin Berthelot, but he still had no idea where that was. So finally, desperate to get there on time, I remembered the well-known sports equipment store Au Vieux Campeur and told him Le Collège was across the street."

Félicien and Marie burst out laughing. "Of course, we remember Au Vieux Campeur," said Félicien, looking at Marie with tenderness. "We were on our honeymoon in Paris, we went there to get some camping equipment. Afterward we took a look at Le Collège. Remember, the salesman boasted that Au Vieux Campeur was better known than Le Collège itself."

CAMBRIDGE, UNITED KINGDOM

MAY 4, 2018

Philip had arrived in Cambridge around noon. The Turing Archives would be closed during lunchtime, so he decided to look up Thomas Warwick, the lab technician who had become one of his bell-ringer friends. Walking down the lovely tree-lined avenue toward the entranceway, he wondered again if Thomas had retired; he hoped not. He was looking forward to seeing him and wanted to ask him for advice. He knew that his friend had once faced an even more difficult predicament than he was now facing with Julian. Thomas had been married for many years and had children before he openly acknowledged his sexual preference. Philip thought that perhaps talking with

Thomas would help him get the courage to tell his parents the truth.

As Philip approached the inner courtyard of the college, he could see an elderly man sitting on the bench below the willow tree. This bench had been a favorite of students and staff of Caius College.

As Philip drew closer, he observed that the man was hunched over, his head bowed. His hair was white and he was wearing a pea coat, although it was unusually warm weather for May in England. Philip remembered Thomas as rarely wearing a coat, even in winter. Also, Thomas had been keen on the importance of maintaining good posture. "No," Philip thought. "It can't be him."

At that moment the man stood up slowly and started walking in Philip's direction. Although he saw now that this was definitely his old friend—with his white hair and strong features—his face was altered. It was slack, devoid of his usual focused expression.

"Thomas!" he called, rushing to the elderly man's side. "I was wondering if it was you. It is so nice to see you again!"

Thomas smiled shyly at Philip. His light brown eyes were cloudy, vacant.

"Don't you recognize me, Thomas? It's Philip. We used to ring the bells together as members of the guild."

Thomas's smile widened. He said, "Nice to see you, young man. What a beautiful day. Who would think so during this awful war?"

Tears welled up in Philip's eyes at the realization that Thomas didn't recognize him; clearly, he was suffering from memory loss or some form of dementia. Suddenly the porter's door on the east side of the courtyard opened and Mr. Smith, who had been there for many decades, strode quickly into the courtyard. He was a stout man in his late sixties with a receding hairline and wide smile.

"Hello, Mr. Smith," Philip said, extending his hand. "You probably don't recognize me, but I was once a student here."

"Of course I remember you, Philip. You used to have lunch out here with my friend, Thomas. He talked about you a lot after you left Cambridge." Mr. Smith shook Philip's hand.

"What happened to Thomas?" Philip asked, lowering his voice out of respect. "He doesn't seem to remember me."

"It's very sad. Our friend here was diagnosed with Alzheimer's disease about three years ago, just after his retirement." He wrapped his arm around Thomas's shoulder protectively. "He still has some moments when he knows who or where he is. But more and more frequently he gets confused and drifts into his own world. His companion, Robert, doesn't like for him to be alone, without him. But, once a week, he brings him here so that we can have lunch at the porter's lodge or in the courtyard when the weather is nice. He seems to enjoy these moments; maybe somewhere buried inside he's reminded of happier times when he worked here."

"I can't tell you how sad it makes me to see what's happened," Philip said. He was trying to catch his friend's wandering gaze in the hopes of igniting some memories of their time together—but to no avail. "He used to be filled with such energy and joy."

"I know. It's been very difficult for us, his family and friends, to witness how much this terrible disease has changed him." He turned his attention to Thomas, who had a slightly bemused look on his face. "Come, Thomas, let me take you home to Robert for your afternoon nap." Mr. Smith shook Philip's hand firmly. "It was a pleasure to see you again. I hope you enjoy your visit."

Gently, he led Thomas by the arm toward the porter's lodge.

Philip sat down on the bench. Sorrow washed through him at the sight of his friend shuffling away. But, at the same time, he felt a renewed sense of purpose: He needed to win the competition and head up the institute on Alzheimer's research. He was certain that great things would come from the Lindenmayer initiative.

For now, he had to concentrate on deciphering the riddle. Philip made his way toward King's College and its Modern Archives Centre that held the Turing Archives. Seeing students row on the river reminded him of his days as a student and training with his university's rowing team toward the big event of the season, the annual Oxbridge Boat Race, one of the competitions held between Oxford and Cambridge that takes place over a four-mile stretch on the Thames.

When he reached the archives, he approached the desk clerk, a young woman with an elfin haircut. "Would you be so kind as to direct me to the superintendent of the Turing Archives?"

"Oh, I'm sorry," the woman said, twisting a wisp of her blond hair. "Dr. Mannfield is out of town today. Would you like to leave a message?"

"Actually, it's quite urgent that I talk to him as soon as possible. Will he be back tonight?" Philip smiled.

"I'm afraid not. Dr. Mannfield won't be back until tomorrow afternoon. But maybe I can help you. I could try to reach him on his cell phone. He mentioned that would be all right if something important came up." The woman reached for a list lying in a stack of papers on her desk.

"That would be very helpful, thank you. I should clarify why I'd like to talk to him."

After Philip explained about the Lindenmayer Award, the clerk widened her eyes and started dialing. "That sounds very exciting."

"Yes, it is!"

"Dr. Mannfield," she said, "this is Julie. I'm sorry to disturb you but there's a gentleman here who needs to speak to you urgently. Please call me back when you can. Thank you."

She turned to Philip. "I'm afraid this was only his voice mail. But he usually calls back quickly. If you leave me your number, I'll call you as soon as I hear from him. If you'd like to wait here, there's a coffee bar just down the hall."

"Thank you for being so helpful. Here's my number," Philip said, jotting it down on a scrap of paper she handed him. "I'll see you soon. Would you like me to bring you a coffee?"

"Yes, please, that would be wonderful, black, no sugar. Turn left and walk down the hall. It's at the far end."

When Philip returned to her desk ten minutes later, Julie informed him regretfully that Dr. Mannfield had read about the award, but that the Turing Archives were definitely not part of a clue. She smiled, revealing her straight, shiny teeth. "How about a visit to Turing's former house in the old town of Cambridge? Maybe the clue can be found there?"

Philip thanked her and headed toward the center of town to visit Turing's former home. But there, he also had to face disappointment, as nobody had heard about the award.

Philip decided to take a break and go to a pub for lunch. "What the hell could it be?" He was angry with himself for having followed the wrong lead, but it seemed so logical, at least in terms of the location: C...... bridge.

"Why are there so many dots between the C and bridge," he wondered. He suddenly realized that if the dots were stand-ins for the missing letters, then two of them would have been sufficient for Cambridge. "Why didn't I see that before? I've wasted so much time."

Philip was walking along the busy King's Parade when two tall blond girls nearly bumped into him as they rushed out of a women's clothing store. They were speaking a Slavic-sounding language, Russian, Polish, or Czech. Jan Chopeck, his college roommate, spoke Czech and a few of the words he heard these girls speak sounded familiar. Philip remembered the summer he spent in Prague, with Jan's family, doing an internship at one of the research labs at Charles University. He had particularly fond memories of the evenings when he had walked the streets with Jan, stopping at various bars for a beer. The walk over the Charles Bridge when night had fallen had been breathtaking, with the lights under the edifice's arches turning the Vltava golden and the site of the magnificent Gothic-style Old Town Bridge Tower on the horizon.

Philip stopped short. "The walks in the evening, the beer, Charles Bridge," he said aloud. He retrieved the riddle from his pocket. *"The city of C......bridge and its many towers!* Prague is also known as the City of a Hundred Spires! This could be it!"

He counted the dots for the missing letters: Yes, there were six dots. Grinning, he looked up. There was a man on the other side of the street, leaning against a tree, smoking a cigarette. Something about him caught Philip's attention. He recalled a man, much like this one—wiry, unshaven, in a loose-fitting jacket and jeans—sitting on a bench in the courtyard of Caius College when he'd been talking to Mr. Smith. If he remembered correctly, he'd also noticed him in the hall of the Modern Archives Centre at King's College.

Philip crossed the road and peered straight into the stranger's small, gray eyes as he moved past him, but the man didn't return his attention, nor did he give any sign of recognition. Philip tried to shake off a feeling of uneasiness. Was he being followed? But who would do that and for what purpose? Philip decided to call Bobby to discuss the matter right away.

CHOCOVISION CONVENTION, PRAGUE, CZECH REPUBLIC

2016

The international chocolate convention took place in Prague just a year after Fred had taken over the leadership of the Lindenmayer Corporation. Lindenmayer Chocolate is the oldest division of the corporation and Fred's father and then his brother always made sure that they attended the convention that had made it possible over the decades, well before the age of the Internet and social networks, to connect with other movers and shakers in the chocolate business. Fred would never break with this family tradition and the Prague convention was his first public appearance in the world of the chocolate business as chairman of the board of Lindenmayer Chocolate.

The opening ceremony of the four-day convention was particularly moving, as the organizers had asked for a minute of silence to honor the memory of Fred's brother. He would also be mentioned in many of the speeches in the following days: Hans-Peter Lindenmayer had been a visionary and pioneer in the chocolate world, by introducing, among other firsts, digital marketing and sugarless chocolate.

Fred had taken a few hours off from the convention program to stroll around this intriguing city, which had been shaken up by history so many times over the centuries. He was particularly moved by the Old Jewish Cemetery, which included the souls of some famous Jewish scholars who had lived and died in Prague, but also those of anonymous citizens of the Jewish ghettos. To walk in these spiritually loaded premises made you almost feel like you had been thrown back a few centuries.

Years later Fred would remember this walk very vividly when he decided that one of the riddles of the competition would be set in Prague.

PRAGUE, CZECH REPUBLIC

MAY 4, 2018

Yucun, who was eager to solve the second part of this riddle and move on to the next one before the end of the week, decided to go for a walk in the hope of finding a clue. She would wander through Old Town with its baroque facades, ancient towers, and picturesque squares. The walk would also help get her mind off Jonathan. She found herself thinking more and more about him. When they were apart, she realized how little she really knew about him. She didn't even know if he had any brothers or sisters. All along she had assumed that he was only child, but what if he had siblings? He was so secretive. At first, she had mistaken it for reserve, but now she saw that it was more than that. She had been wondering why

Jonathan had been so insistent about her participating in the competition. Maybe he just saw an opportunity for the two of them to be close to each other, but it was not really happening because she was traveling across Europe. There must have been more to it. It intrigued her that Jonathan mentioned several times that he was very keen for her to win. Why? What would that bring to him?

She had to focus. After grabbing her travel guide on Prague, she put her valuables in the safe and left the hotel. Her walk from the U Zlatého Stromu Hotel on Karlova Street took her past the fourteenth-century Old Town Hall and its medieval Orloj, an astronomical clock—with its intricacies of the clockworks and the blue windows on the tower that open to the procession of the apostles. She proceeded to Kinsky Palace, then up toward the Jewish Museum and the Old Jewish Cemetery. Hungry now, she was hoping to find a Jewish deli in this neighborhood, to eat a pastrami sandwich. As she strolled along the narrow streets of the Jewish Quarter around the cemetery, she found every type of restaurant she could imagine—from Tex-Mex to Lebanese and Chinese to Vietnamese—except, ironically, for the one thing she wanted. Yucun had to give up on pastrami and settle for some dumplings in a small Chinese restaurant.

Once comfortably seated, she rummaged through several pockets of her safari-style camouflage jacket before finding her iPhone with the riddle.

In the city of C......bridge and its many towers lies in eternal peace the father of Melog, who in search of death backward may have created the first mechanical mind.

"Let's see," she thought. "'*Death*,' '*eternal peace*,' two terms pointing to a final resting place. Well, there's the famous cemetery right nearby."

In the index of her guide, Yucun found the page with this description:

Founded in 1478, it is Europe's oldest surviving Jewish cemetery. People had to be buried on top of each other because of lack of space. There are about twelve layers and more than twelve thousand gravestones. One hundred thousand people are thought to have been buried here, the last one being Moses Beck in 1787. The most prominent graves are those of Mordechai Maisel, who built the Maisel Synagogue, and Rabbi Judah Loew ben Bezalel, also known as Rabbi Löw, the creator of the mystical Golem.

Yucun tried to remember where she'd heard the name Rabbi Loew before. She recalled a history book she'd read about the Jewish religion, but the details from it were fuzzy. Yucun closed the guidebook and asked for the check, then decided to go straight to the cemetery.

A few minutes later she reached the Old Jewish Cemetery and made her way through the courtyard just outside the Pinkas Synagogue. This was one of the biggest tourist attractions in Prague, and there were already quite a few people walking between the tombs. She noticed a large group, probably on a guided tour.

As she approached, she saw that the group was clustered around a tomb, listening to a young woman. "This could be Rabbi Loew's tomb," she thought. She drew nearer to be able to read what was written on the tombstone, but she couldn't get close enough without disturbing the group.

However, she was able to hear what the guide was saying in English with only a slight accent.

"Rabbi Judah Loew ben Bezalel was a distinguished Talmudic scholar, philosopher and an expert on the Kabbalah who lived in the sixteenth century and served as a leading rabbi in Prague." The guide continued, "Rabbi Loew is most well known for the story about the Golem, which, according to legend, he created using mystical magical powers. The Golem is a monster made from the mud of the Vltava River and is considered to be the Jewish version of the Frankenstein monster. The story of the Golem dates back to the eighteenth century, when it was first told. Yossel, as the Golem was also called, came to life when the rabbi placed a shem, which is a tablet with a Hebrew inscription, into its mouth. According to the legend, the rabbi did this to defend the Jews of the Prague Ghetto from anti-Semitic attacks. The Habsburg emperor, Rudolf II, was then the ruler over the land, which is now the Czech Republic but which, at that time, was part of the Austrian empire. He invited the rabbi to his court where he became a 'Hofbefreiter Jude,' which means a freed court Jew. His position in the court allowed the rabbi to intercede on behalf of the Jews, who were often being persecuted. Emperor Rudolf was favorable toward the Jewish community; he changed the laws to allow Jews fair trials and removed restrictions on trade. However, he still required them to wear the yellow circle that was the mark of Judaism in Prague. Legend has it that the Golem finally ran amok, and the rabbi was forced to destroy his creation by removing the shem from its mouth. The Golem is supposedly locked in the attic of the Altneuschul, the ancient synagogue, which still stands in Prague."

Fascinated, Yucun thought, "That's quite a story, all the ingredients for a good Hollywood film." But what about the riddle, what did "*death backward*" mean? And who could the father of Melog be?

She wondered what would happen if she inverted part of the riddle. "Let's say for example: '*Melog backward*' and '*in eternal peace.*'" Melog backward—all of a sudden it was obvious—spelled Golem!

She grabbed the note with the riddle and reread it. *In the city of C......bridge and its many towers lies in eternal peace the father of Melog, who in search of death backward may have created the first mechanical mind.* She thought, "If the father of the Golem is Rabbi Loew, he obviously lies here in eternal peace. And '*death backward*' could point to the bringing to life of a dead creature made out of clay. The Golem is often cited as having been the first attempt to create artificial intelligence."

Suddenly, she felt like dancing around the tombs. But she decided it would be more reasonable to look for Lindenmayer's contact without further delay. She hurried to the entrance booth and asked for the person in charge of the cemetery. The lady in the booth introduced herself as Esther Friedman and inquired about Yucun's business. As Yucun explained, the woman grinned. Yucun had found her contact, and gave Esther the solution to the riddle.

"'*In the city of C......bridge and its many towers*' indicates the city of Prague, where the Charles (six dots for missing letters) Bridge is found and which is known for its many towers. '*Lies in eternal peace the father of Melog, who in search of death backward may have created the first mechanical mind*' is the father of Golem (Melog backward) who is Rabbi Loew who lies in eternal peace in Prague's Jewish cemetery. '*Death backward*' refers to the attempt by Rabbi Loew to create intelligent life in the form of the

Golem, which is often considered as the first attempt to create artificial intelligence."

"Congratulations, my dear," said Esther, giving Yucun a big hug.

Yucun was delighted when Esther suggested a cup of tea in her booth. She probably didn't have many visitors who took the time to talk to her, and Yucun was very happy to explain how she had made the connection between the Golem and AI and why it was relevant to Alzheimer's.

"So you see, Esther, what is called artificial intelligence, widely known as AI, is what allows computer programs to learn without being programmed. Such programs can also be taught to recognize patterns in brain activity. Alzheimer's patients who are in the most advanced stages of the disease lose the ability to communicate verbally. Groundbreaking research is being developed in the use of brain-computer interfaces, which can detect patterns of brain activity and translate them into signals, thus providing alternative methods for communicating for impaired patients, and which possibly even hold some potential for rehabilitation."

"Thank you, Yucun. Just imagine what I will be able to tell my grandson Lev, who is also a computer scientist, about my day? This is so special." Esther was talking excitedly now.

*In the city of C...... bridge and its many towers lies in eternal
peace the father of melog, who in search of death backwards
may have created the first mechanical mind.*

PATIO DE LOS NARANJOS, CÓRDOBA, SPAIN

MAY 5, 2018

Sitting on one of the low walls that surround the Al-Mansur Basin in the Patio de los Naranjos, or "courtyard of orange trees," Jean-Pierre tried to concentrate on the riddle displayed on his iPhone.

Federico García Lorca chanted the waters, where the houses of cross and crescent blended, surrounded by the scent of orange blossoms, in a symbol of regenerating life.

He could picture Muslim worshippers, doing their ritual ablutions in the basin, symbolizing their purification, before entering the mosque. Following the conquest of Córdoba, Christians had planted the orange trees from which the courtyard had taken its name. His mind kept switching from the first half of the riddle, which pointed to a monument, to the second half, which seemed to relate to a disease or medical issue particular to Córdoba. Where to begin? Why not Arabic medicine? The great Averroes came to mind. It was extraordinary to think that he was a doctor and philosopher in the twelfth century. It was not an exaggeration to say that Averroes had laid the groundwork for modern medicine both as a science and as an art. He seemed so modern. Perhaps the riddle was embedded in one of his texts. Frère Lucien, Jean-Pierre's philosophy teacher at the Petit Seminaire, a religious school that prepared boys for priesthood, had to admit, despite his reservations about Averroe's theses on the compatibility of religion and philosophy, that Averroe's *Colliget*, the book of universal medicine published in 1162, contained remarkable insights into physiology, anatomy, and the origins of diseases. Frère Lucien used to say that if Averroes and other famous Arabic doctors lived today they probably would have a paper appearing every month in *Nature* or *The Lancet*. They did not experience the anguish of today's scientists to publish or perish. Scientific competition was not an issue.

Since he was young, Jean-Pierre had been fascinated by the lives of Arabic doctors and thinkers. Their refined culture and knowledge of medicine and science seemed so advanced compared with the dark Middles Ages that reigned over western Europe, where people were persecuted and burned at the stake for their beliefs and where the Christian church explained the order of nature by invoking God. By contrast, the great Arabic thinkers and scientists had tried to come up with a scientific explanation for natural phenomena.

He looked at the second half of the riddle again. *Where the houses of cross and crescent blended.* The past tense obviously indicated that these structures had been erected in the past, probably during the Middle Ages. The cross clearly pointed to Christianity while the crescent referred to Islam. Christians and Muslims had fought over this Iberic land.

The sound of a child splashing water made him look up. A boy shrieked with delight as he played with water in a basin, but a woman, probably his mother, took him by the hand and dragged him away until they disappeared behind the orange trees. Something about the scene was familiar. He remembered his school trip to Sicily. He wondered what had triggered the memory and then he realized it was the pervasive smell of orange blossoms.

Such a wonderful scent, he thought. Fascinating to think that this sensuous, olfactory memory should override his analytical musings about the beginnings of medicine, as riveting as he had found them. A few thousand odorant particles swept across the garden by a gentle breeze were able to activate an electrical storm in the neurons of his olfactory system, generating impulses that traveled at more than two hundred miles per hour from his nose to the olfactory cortex in his brain. Extraordinary that this part of his brain was able to recognize this particular odor out of the thousands to which he had been exposed since birth. He had no doubt that this smell was associated with the pink blossoms of the orange trees that he could see in the distance.

He remembered all at once why the olfactory experience had imprinted itself in his brain with such precision. It had happened on a school trip to Sicily, so many years ago, in 2005, if he remembered correctly. They had visited the Duomo di Monreale, just above the city of Palermo, on the slope of Monte Caputo, overlooking the fertile valley called La Conca d'Oro, the golden shell, famous for its orange, olive, and almond trees. In 1174, King William II had started the construction of the cathedral of Monreale, one of the greatest examples of Norman architecture. The nave was designed like an Italian basilica but the triple-apse choir was similar to churches found in Syria. The cathedral was known mostly for its mosaics and, in particular, for the mosaic representing a very large half-length figure of Christ.

When he saw the Duomo of Monreale for the first time, Jean-Pierre had been very impressed with this mosaic. It had been both an aesthetic and a mystical experience. He had never felt so close to God. Yet, when he came out of the Duomo and stood on the terrace of the little café across the square, he couldn't help noticing the three girls sitting at one of the tables. They were laughing. Three beauties. They looked so happy.

Frère Lucien suggested they have a drink before returning to Palermo. He pointed to a vacant table near the girls. "This is my lucky day," Jean-Pierre thought. "Now I'll get to see the beauties up close." As he drew closer to the girls, a sweet scent enveloped him and he imagined that it was one of the girl's perfume. But when he sat down, he noticed the blossoms on the orange tree hanging over the girls' table and realized that the scent was coming from its blossoms.

The girls were speaking Italian but he couldn't understand what they were saying, probably because they were using a Sicilian dialect. He managed to figure out their names. Isabella was the tall, blond, almost Scandinavian-looking girl, while Maria was Mediterranean with dark eyes and hair. Giuseppina had red hair and a pale complexion. She had freckles and looked as if she came from Scotland. In these three girls, you could almost see the melting pot of Sicily. Sicily was a crossroads between Europe and Africa, between Normans and Arabs.

It seemed appropriate that in this place Jean-Pierre should have reconsidered his vocation as a priest. "Yes," he thought, "I love God, but if I devote my life to Him, what of the Isabellas and the Marias and the Giuseppinas of this world? My body is reacting to the sight of their skin, breasts, beautiful legs, and the sound of their voices, everything I'm not supposed to be enticed by." This was a defining moment in his life. He had decided then that he would not become a priest. He would leave the seminary as soon as he received his baccalaureate.

His musings had brought him rather far afield. Obviously, the symbol of regeneration was key to solving the riddle. Arabic medicine had not yielded the answer. Olfactory neurons, those very neurons that were being activated by the orange blossoms, are regenerated throughout life and this is true from fish to man. Until recently, however, it was thought that olfactory neurons were the only neurons in the nervous system to regenerate. Now we know that the adult brain is capable of producing new neurons throughout life and these are not limited to olfactory neurons.

He remembered when he was a teacher's assistant at the École Polytechnique, near Paris, how surprised the students were when he outlined the steps involved in neurogenesis. He had explained that the adult brain has stem cells that can be identified as different types of cells; one lineage produces neurons while another produces cell that are important for brain function, such as glial cells. He thought of one of his colleagues, who spent days and nights trying to purify a factor, "the factor" that would turn stem cells into neurons. He'd spent countless hours endeavoring to find the "serum of life." Jean-Pierre tried to imagine taking stem cells from a brain and transforming them into neurons in an incubator and then putting them back into the brain to replace neurons that were degenerating as a consequence of Alzheimer's or Parkinson's, for example. If one could do this, one could transplant neurons back into the brain and replace those that were dead. Recovery of brain functions would then occur as a natural result of this procedure. A Nobel Prize in Medicine had recently been awarded for the discovery of a combination of factors that enabled one to produce neurons and other cells from stem cells.

Enough musing, Jean-Pierre said to himself. There was something odd about the design of this mosque-cathedral. The cathedral appeared superimposed upon the mosque. Jean-Pierre was puzzled. He entered the building. As he walked through the arches and down the corridors of the mosque, he could see a structure taking shape in the distance. The structure seemed out of character with the Islamic architecture. It turned out to be the transept of the cathedral. It was like a new but foreign body that had been grafted to an older one. As Jean-Pierre walked down the main aisle of the transept, he suddenly felt weak. He sat down in one of the pews. "Graft. Graft. Of course, a symbol for regenerating life!"

The riddle said "*symbol of regenerating life.*" This could refer to a cure for a disease through regeneration. Yes, grafting stem cells differentiated into neurons to cure for example Parkinson's or Alzheimer's disease. And the Córdoba cathedral is a symbol of "the graft" of a church onto a mosque. "Fantastic! I think I may have found it." In his enthusiasm, he spoke aloud, startling a little old lady who was praying in one of the pews. "I'm so sorry!" he said to her before rushing out of the cathedral. He must find the curator of the cathedral. In the garden of orange trees, he found a gardener, who told him that the curator's name was Maria de la Vega and that she could be found inside. He pointed to an open door. "Third room to your right."

Jean-Pierre ran to the door and with the briefest of knocks entered Maria's office.

"You must be one of Mr. Lindenmayer's competitors." Maria smiled. "You seem in a hurry to give me the answer to the riddle."

"I'm so sorry, madam, but yes, I'm very excited."

"So what is the answer?"

"'*Federico García Lorca chanted the waters*' refers to the Guadalquivir and Córdoba. '*Where the houses of cross and crescent blended, surrounded by the scent of orange blossoms, in a symbol of regenerating life*' indicates the Mezquite, a cathedral within the ancient mosque which symbolizes the graft of new neurons in an ailing brain. It is the symbol for a procedure that can regenerate life."

"Excellent," she said. "You are..."

"Jean-Pierre Abdoulayé from France. I apologize for not introducing myself sooner," he extended his hand, apologetically.

"It is a pleasure to meet you." Maria shook his hand. "Now, let's ask someone to take a picture of us."

*Federico García Lorca chanted the waters, where the houses
of cross and crescent blended surrounded by the scent of orange
blossoms, in a symbol of regenerating life.*

BLOIS, FRANCE

MAY 5, 2018

"I can't believe I'm actually drinking this coffee," Edoardo said to Benedetta. He looked down at the murky brown beverage with disgust. "If only Europeans could understand that we Italians know what real coffee is. All it takes is a good espresso machine!"

"It's not that bad," she said. "You exaggerate."

"It's like water."

"You're looking awfully pleased with yourself, despite the bad coffee."

"I'm beginning to think that there are distinct advantages to receiving threats." He was referring to Benedetta insisting on accompanying him to Chambord.

"My own personal bodyguard. They're not usually so attractive."

"Don't let it go to your head," she said.

It was almost three o'clock, and sunlight filtered through the leaves of the plane trees that surrounded the terrace of the Hôtel le Médicis. They had arrived in Blois the day before, after a two-hour drive from Paris. He'd chosen this hotel for its location on Allée de François I; Edoardo viewed this as a sign, as François I had built the castle of Chambord.

Edoardo was quite superstitious, believing that there were no coincidences in life. It was certainly a sign that there was a connection between the name of the hotel and its setting: Catherine de' Médicis had been François I's daughter-in-law, the wife of his son, Henri II. Saint-Dyé-sur-Loire was the village closest to the Chambord region. But Edoardo's guidebook hadn't indicated any hotels there, so he had settled for Blois and the hotel located on a street named after Chambord's first owner.

On the table before him lay the riddle that had brought him here.

The jewel of François I, King of France, harbors the secret of life recognized by a noble Francis four centuries later.

"I hope I'm not mistaken about François's jewel," Edoardo said to Benedetta. "I have to figure out what kind of secret this castle hides. A *'secret of life'*—but where to start?"

They had already been to the castle and walked around the grounds extensively, but he hadn't found a clue to the secret of life. He'd bought quite a few books on the castle, and they hadn't revealed anything that could help him solve the riddle, either.

"We should go on a tour," she suggested, not for the first time.

"No, no," he said, leafing through a guidebook. "It goes against my principles."

She laughed.

"What would my family think?" he added.

"They don't have to know."

Edoardo chuckled as he thought about what his family would say if they knew he was considering taking a tour. The education he'd received from his typical haute bourgeoisie Milano family had insisted that as part of his cultural upbringing, he should be informed about Europe's most significant monuments, and when visiting such monuments, he should do it at his own pace and never dream of joining a tour, where he'd be herded around like cattle by a guide who was less educated than he.

Edoardo felt he should resume reading the books he'd bought and try to find clues that might make reference to a secret.

He read aloud to Benedetta: "The Chambord castle is an emblematic piece of architecture for the early

French Renaissance. It's situated in the Loire region, southwest of Paris, in a large wooded property of about 5,500 hectares. Today, it is the largest wooded park in Europe. With its 440 rooms, 365 fireplaces, 84 staircases, and enough stables to accommodate 1,200 horses, the château of Chambord is the largest of its kind in the Loire Valley. The park where the castle stands is surrounded by a wall that is 22 miles in perimeter. There were 1,800 workers who took part in the construction of Chambord, which began in 1519, as a project of King François I of France, and lasted for more than thirty years. The project was finished under the reign of King Henri II—"

"There's a tour at four," Benedetta interrupted.

He continued to read: "At first sight, the castle looks medieval, with a donjon inside a rectangular four-towered surrounding wall. But Chambord definitely was designed in the Renaissance style. Four rectangular vaulted halls on each floor form a cross-shaped structure, meeting in the center with a spectacular double-helix openwork staircase, where people can ascend and descend simultaneously without meeting. This main staircase and the subsidiary ones are crowned with lanterns."

Ignoring Benedetta's yawns, he mused, "That's all very nice. But what about the architect?"

Edoardo was more interested in people than buildings, and he continued reading: "The archives offer no conclusive information about the architect's identity. But an analysis of the structure has revealed an extremely close tie to some of Domenico da Cortona's other projects. Cortona was an Italian architect, who is widely credited with the design of Chambord. The French master mason Pierre Nepveu, from Amboise, probably oversaw the construction of the castle; it was often the case, at the time, that the design and the construction were executed by two different professionals. The architecture of the castle was profoundly influenced by Leonardo da Vinci, who was a friend and the official architect of King François I. Even though he died in 1519, some months before construction began, the famous double-helix staircase is related to a project design by Leonardo, which consisted of four distinct superimposed flights of stairs. It is therefore possible that the Leonardo da Vinci staircase design, which may have been conceived for Chambord, was then simplified by the master masons when construction started. Even though the castle of Chambord fulfilled François I's dream, the king only spent a few weeks there and left the castle without inhabitants or furniture."

Edoardo thought, "Typical of kings. They build castles they don't even have time to inhabit!"

Edoardo read aloud, "'The castle became state property in 1932 and it welcomes around 800,000 visitors a year.' And I'm one of them!" He put the guidebook down.

"Come on," Benedetta said. "Let's go, we want to be on time for the tour at four."

Standing at the foot of the marble staircase, surrounded by tourists, Edoardo felt ridiculous. Benedetta kept smiling at him, knowing exactly what he was thinking.

"Ladies and gentlemen," Roger, the elderly tour guide began, "François I had these stairs built in a double helix, so that people ascending them could not be seen by people descending them and vice versa. Does the architectural structure of these stairs remind you of something? Anybody? No? Look carefully."

Edoardo narrowed his eyes to look at them more carefully.

"I call them the DNA stairs," Roger continued. "Some twenty years ago an American scientist, John Perkins, came on this tour with his wife. As we were getting to the stairs, this scientist told us that these stairs resembled the double helix of the DNA molecule, a major scientific discovery by Jim Watson and Francis Crick. They received the Nobel Prize in 1962 for their discovery of the structure of DNA, which they declared 'the secret of life.'"

Edoardo's heart skipped a beat; he felt his blood racing through his veins. He gripped Benedetta's arm. He was almost certain to have found the solution to the second part of the riddle. "Could it be this simple?" he wondered. "I need to find the contact person for the award. Maybe it's our tour guide?"

"What?" Benedetta asked.

"In a minute," he said.

He couldn't very well interrupt Roger's presentation. He'd have to wait.

Roger was recounting a discussion that had taken place twenty years ago at this exact spot, when after he had said, "If Watson and Crick had seen these stairs before, they might have discovered the double helix much earlier," a man in the crowd had cried out. "I'm John Perkins, retired professor of molecular biology at Harvard. I used to work with Jim Watson on DNA research. I could give a quick overview of what DNA is. But it'll take some time, and I'm sure our guide would like to finish the visit."

Roger said, "Actually, the tour finishes here at the stairs. I'm happy to learn about this discovery. Whoever is interested can sit down with me on the stairs." Quite a few people followed his example. When everybody was settled, Professor Perkins began. He told the audience about a scene, vividly described by Watson in his famous book *The Double Helix*. The scene occurred in the late afternoon in 1953, when Crick stepped into the Eagle Pub in Cambridge and proclaimed, "We have found the secret of life."

"Indeed," the professor said, "Watson and Crick had figured out the molecular structure of DNA, the molecule that contains the genetic code of every living organism. They'd also described the mechanism by which this molecule could somehow replicate and allow the faithful transmission of the genetic material from generation to generation."

He scrutinized the audience through his thick, round glasses. "Is everyone following?"

When he observed several people nodding, he continued. "In their famous article, published in the April 25, 1953, issue of the scientific journal *Nature*, Watson and Crick concluded with typical British understatement: 'It has not escaped our notice that the specific pairing we have postulated immediately suggests a possible copying mechanism for the genetic material.'

"Four molecules, also known as bases, make up the DNA alphabet: A for adenine, T for thymine, G for guanine, and C for cytosine," Professor Perkins went on. "The stroke of genius was the realization by Watson and Crick that the A–T and G–C molecules could pair up, and in fact constitute the steps on a twisting ladder of DNA, the now-famous DNA double helix."

There was a short silence after Perkins finished talking. But soon after, a vigorous applause broke out and several people from the audience came over to thank him.

Edoardo was losing patience, at Roger's retelling of the professor's speech. All he wanted to do was get a picture and send a message to Bobby. But Roger wasn't finished with his story.

"And that's how Professor Perkins told us about DNA and the double helix," he said to the group. "What a great day it was. He even sent me a postcard from California after that. Now, ladies and gentlemen, for those of you who are interested, we can take the stairs up to look at—"

"Excuse me, sir," Edoardo interrupted. "I'm very sorry to disturb you, but I would like to take a picture of you and me in front of these stairs, if you don't mind." Having made his way through the crowd, he now stood beside Roger. Lowering his voice, he asked, "Are you the contact for the Lindenmayer Award?"

"Yes, that would be me," Roger answered, smiling.

Edoardo turned to Benedetta and asked her to take the photograph of him and Roger.

Edoardo and Roger stood at the bottom of the stairs. "I hope you will send me a copy, monsieur. Where are you from?" Roger asked.

"I'm sorry. I haven't introduced myself," Edoardo said. "I'm Edoardo Gardelli and I'm from Italy, but work in the States. This is Benedetta, my fiancée."

"Nice to meet you," Roger said.

"Please make sure you have the staircase in the picture," Edoardo said to Benedetta.

She had to take several photographs before he was satisfied.

"Unfortunately, we have to go now," he said to Roger. "But I'm very grateful to you, monsieur, for the eye-opening tour of the château. You can't imagine how much it means to me," Edoardo said with a big smile on his face.

As he and Benedetta walked back toward the parking lot, Edoardo said, "I can't believe all I needed to do was go on a guided tour!"

"What did I tell you," Benedetta said. "Who knows how long you would have taken if I hadn't accompanied you? In the future, you better follow my every suggestion."

He was laughing now, getting into his rental car. He took out his iPhone and typed a message for Bobby: *"The jewel of François I" is the castle of Chambord. "The secret of life" is the DNA molecule, which is made of two strands organized in a double helix like the famous staircase in the castle; "noble Francis" is Francis Crick, who received the Nobel Prize with James Watson for the discovery of the DNA structure."*

A few seconds later he received a message from Bobby confirming that he had the right answer. He turned to Benedetta to give her a high five.

"And now, *amore mio*, I'm going to take you to a fancy restaurant to celebrate!"

"That sounds perfect, but tell me, Edoardo, I'm wondering, how can a riddle about DNA be relevant to Alzheimer's? I thought the award and the riddles were all about Alzheimer's disease."

"You're absolutely right," Edoardo confirmed, "genetics and DNA are very relevant, because certain forms of Alzheimer's disease are hereditary. This means that people can inherit genes that can either cause or predispose for Alzheimer's. The familial forms of Alzheimer's are relatively rare, only in two to three percent of the cases. They are due to a mutation in certain genes, which invariably will result in Alzheimer's in the patients who inherited these mutated genes. There is also another genetic issue. Indeed, people can inherit a particular form of the gene that encodes APOE, short for apolipoprotein, that confers vulnerability to Alzheimer's to fifteen percent of the population. This form is called APOE4."

"That is pretty scary," Benedetta replied, "because there is a two percent chance for you to inherit the familial form of Alzheimer's, but there is also a fifteen percent chance that you inherit the APOE something protein, that predisposes you for the disease."

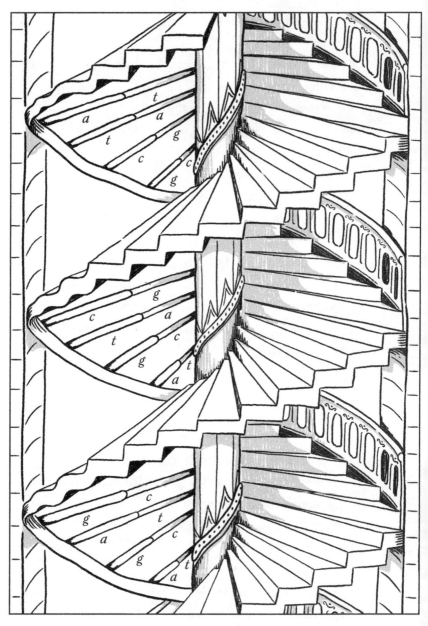

*The jewel of François I, King of France, harbors the secret of life
recognized by a noble Francis four centuries later.*

"Yes, and this raises quite a complicated ethical issue," Edoardo said. "You can be tested to see if you are a carrier of the bad form of **APOE**, **APOE4**, but in the end it doesn't help you at all because there is no known cure for the disease."

He heard a text message come in and he took out his phone. The message started with capital letters: *DANGER AWAITS.* He was about to turn off his phone when Benedetta grabbed it from him. She had noticed the change in his expression.

"What does that mean? Who the hell sends you a message like that?"

"Benedetta, let me explain," Edoardo said, pulling the car to the side of the road.

LINDENMAYER CORPORATE HEADQUARTERS, ZURICH, SWITZERLAND

MAY 6, 2018

Bobby threw one dart after the next with such rapidity that poor Oban could not keep up. He flew valiantly from his master to the chair by the board, jumping up to pull the dart from the board and then flying back to his master. At last, Oban stopped and looked up at Bobby, wagging his tail.

"I'm sorry, old chap," Bobby said. "I am upset by the man next door."

He wondered where Boswell could be. Boswell had told him he was just stepping out but it had been close to two hours since he left. Fred was en route to the office but Bobby wanted to get Boswell up to speed. This time Boswell couldn't complain about his overreacting. Poor

Edoardo, he must have felt terrible when he received yet another threatening message. Why was he particularly targeted? Maybe because he had already solved two riddles? But Yucun was working on her third, and she had not received any threats. This was very strange indeed. Bobby noticed that Oban was standing by the door with his tail raised. What did he hear? Could it finally be Boswell? He thought he heard someone slip into the office next door. Bobby rushed out with Oban barking at his heels. Without knocking, he opened the door to Boswell's office. Boswell slammed his desk drawer closed and then stood behind his desk. His lips quivered.

"I'm so sorry," Bobby said, "I forgot to knock. It's kind of an emergency."

"Kind of?"

The man had an unpleasant way of repeating one's words. "No, really. It's become a really worrying situation."

"Really?" Boswell said, in an almost sarcastic tone. "How? What is the latest?"

"Edoardo has received yet another threatening message. He has just solved his second riddle, like Yucun. But the strange thing is, that she is the only one who doesn't seem to be targeted with threats, I really wonder—"

Boswell interrupted him rudely. "I'm sure there is nothing to it. And as you said yourself, the PI will certainly come up with a logical explanation, probably having to do with the contestants' past or something."

The man is infuriating, Bobby thought, he never shows any emotion or empathy. He doesn't seem worried at all.

"What do you think is going on?" Boswell asked, as if Bobby would know.

"No idea, but it's obvious that someone is trying to ruin the contest or put an end to it."

"But why? What could their purpose be?" Boswell turned to the window as if he could find the answer there. The sound of a car driving across the gravel reached them. It was probably Fred. "Have you informed Fred?" Boswell asked Bobby, still without turning to look at him.

"Yes, he's called an emergency meeting. He canceled his golf round."

"Oh dear!"

"He's been talking to a PI who is a former police investigator. He has started to look into things."

They could hear Fred coming down the corridor. With Oban at their heels, the two men left Boswell's office for Fred's. Fred sat behind his desk while Boswell and Bobby took the chairs opposite.

"So what is the latest news?" Fred asked Bobby.

Bobby explained what had happened in Blois. "It seems that Edoardo is the main target of the threats.

But the good news is that he has just solved his second riddle. So Edoardo and Yucun are definitely ahead of the others with two riddles solved each."

"And has Yucun received any threats?" Fred asked, as Bobby was about to raise that issue.

"No, and that is the point that puzzles me most," Bobby commented.

Fred seemed to be lost in his thoughts, running his fingers over his mustache. Bobby and Boswell sat silently, waiting for him to speak.

"He is such a nice man," Bobby thought. As a business tycoon, Fred had the reputation for being tough and decisive, but his employees discovered soon enough that he was a kind, trustworthy man who was fair in his appraisal of situations. Fred always made time to meet with his employees and listen to their suggestions or complaints. He believed more in discussion and negotiation than in authoritarian decision-making. He could talk to anybody and be genuinely interested in the other person's views and opinions—whether it was a CEO at a black-tie event or a line worker in a plant. Fred didn't have any enemies as far as Bobby knew; wisely, most of his business associates preferred to be friends with him.

Boswell was his opposite, though. Bobby had noticed that Boswell's demeanor was quite different when he was in his boss's presence. He adopted a humble attitude and even his posture was different. He sat with his shoulders hunched. As a rule, there were very few people Bobby disliked, but Boswell was definitely one of them. It was instinctive, exactly like two dogs that did not like each other's smell. "You show good judgment," Bobby thought, seeing Oban flop next to Fred's chair.

Fred reached down and caressed the top of Oban's head.

"It seems as if someone is doing everything possible to make life difficult for our contestants," Fred finally said. "It can hardly be a coincidence. Someone is trying to sabotage the competition."

Bobby turned to Boswell, waiting for him to comment, but Boswell didn't flinch. Then Boswell's phone started ringing.

"I'm so sorry," Boswell said. "I'll be right back." He stepped into the corridor, closing the door behind him.

Fred turned to Bobby. "I'm very appreciative of the way you've handled these problems so far. I know you've taken on a lot."

"You're welcome. I've been trying to figure out who would sabotage you. What reason could he or she have? Do you think it might be someone at a competing neuroscience institute working on Alzheimer's research?"

"Well, it's hard to imagine, but not impossible. One thing is certain: I plan to get to the bottom of this and my dear friend Marco Comina, the PI, is going to help us. With his many years as a police investigator, he's just the person for this job."

"That's excellent," Bobby declared, much relieved not be alone in this. "We need all the help we can get."

"I'm going to call Marco right now to organize our meeting with the contestants tomorrow," Fred said, glancing at his watch.

"What a relief," said Bobby.

The door opened and Boswell reappeared. "Did I miss anything important?" he asked.

"Bobby will tell you," Fred replied, picking up his phone.

LINDENMAYER RESIDENCE, KÜSNACHT, SWITZERLAND

MAY 6, 2018

Standing in front of a window in the living room, Fred dialed Marco Comina's phone number. Dark clouds were accumulating over the lake; a storm was moving in and the atmosphere seemed charged with electricity. Fred felt like an overcharged battery. He was restless, with anxiety pressing down on his chest. He couldn't pinpoint the exact source of his feelings today. Could it be just because of the weather, or was it something more threatening that was nagging him?

"Hello?" he heard Comina saying. "Anyone there?"

"I'm so sorry, Marco, Fred here. My thoughts were somewhere else."

Marco asked him if everything was all right, and Fred confessed that he was wondering, at this stage, if the idea of a competition had been the right way to identify a director for the Lindenmayer Institute. He admitted to Marco how tired he was and how he was toying with the idea of dropping the award altogether.

"Yes, I understand your worries," Marco said. "So far the incidents are not too serious, nothing life-threatening, but they are disruptive for the contest and they are creating an atmosphere of uneasiness."

"Yes, so what do we do next?" Fred asked. Marco could sense the stress and anxiety in Fred's voice.

"For one, don't give into blackmail and do keep the contest going. We will figure out how to handle all this. Trust me." Marco was trying to sound reassuring.

After thanking Marco, Fred put down the receiver and looked at his watch. It was 11:30 a.m. and Meg would be joining him soon for lunch. His eyes were drawn back to the lake. It was now almost completely dark. A ray of light illuminated the far rim. Fred heard the door open and turned around to see Meg, who was walking in slowly, with obvious hesitation, a blank look on her face. She stopped in the middle of the room, frowning, as if not knowing what to do next. Fred approached her and gently took hold of her arm, guiding her toward her favorite armchair by the window. He leaned down toward her.

"How are you feeling, darling?" he asked.

She glanced up at him, glassy-eyed, and asked, "Do we know each other?"

Tears burned Fred's eyes. He took her face between his hands with a soft touch, explaining who he was, and that she was at home. He pointed toward the lake where the thunderstorm had broken out and heavy rain was lashing the windows.

Meg raised her eyes but didn't seem to register the rain or the thunder. She seemed to be focusing inward, as if lost in her own world. Fred let go of her face and sat down in the armchair next to her, stroking her hand. In such moments he couldn't help wondering if she was conscious of her illness. She had to be, because she still had lucid moments, blocks of time when she seemed to be in touch with reality.

When the diagnosis had been made, Max Fernshaw—Meg's neurologist—had told her everything that was presently known about Alzheimer's. She'd asked many questions, but after that day she never wanted to broach the topic of her illness again. Fred had been worried about her attitude, her seeming denial, but Max had explained that every patient had his or her very personal way of dealing with such devastating news. Fred assumed that when she was in a "disconnected" state like today, she certainly wasn't aware of her illness and its consequences. But if, at other times, she was cognizant that something was wrong, it was certainly an immense tragedy for her to keep all of her anxiety and fears to herself.

Why were her beautiful emerald green eyes so distant and empty today? Their daughter, Barbara, had inherited those exceptional eyes.

Fred was overwhelmed by a terrible anguish, one with which he'd wrestled before but chosen to bury until he could face it head-on. Could their children have inherited their mother's disease? Could Meg's Alzheimer's be the genetically transmitted form? That would be another tragedy for their family. Fred felt an urge to call Max and question him: Was it possible to tell which form of Alzheimer's Meg was suffering from? If it was the genetically transmitted form, what were the chances that Barbara or Steven would also develop Alzheimer's disease?

Fred noticed that Meg had dozed off and rushed to his office to make the call.

Max picked up the phone after the second ring, sounding startled. Fred realized it was the middle of the night in California and apologized, offering to call back at another time.

"That's all right, my friend. What's going on?"

Fred burst forth about his concerns for his children.

"Don't worry. Less than three percent of Alzheimer's disease cases are familial." Max was a living encyclopedia, at least for neurology and psychiatry. He knew everything. "These familial cases are due to mutations in a few genes that cause the accumulation of abnormal proteins, in particular, the one you know well because we talked about it a lot: beta-amyloid. These genetic abnormalities concern the early form of Alzheimer's disease, the one that manifests itself around the age of fifty."

"Is it the form that Auguste, Alois Alzheimer's patient, had?" Fred asked as he remembered one of the numerous conversations he'd had with Max.

"It probably was that form," Max said. "Auguste was only fifty when she presented the clinical symptoms. Alzheimer related these symptoms to his findings at Auguste's autopsy where he could describe the histological features that are the hallmark of Alzheimer's disease, namely the presence of amyloid deposits and of neurofribillary tangles in the brain."

Fred listened to Max's explanations with great concentration. He wanted to make sure he didn't miss anything important.

"You can relax—I mean it. The chance that either of your children will develop Alzheimer's disease is very low."

But Fred was still uneasy about the genetics and asked Max if they could check whether Meg carried one of those genes.

"That wouldn't help us with Meg's treatment since as you know there are no cures that will address abnormalities associated with the genes that cause Alzheimer's disease. And, if you were to test your children and find that they actually carried the gene, it would generate a tremendous anxiety in your family, without providing any solution," Max said firmly. "There are ongoing ethical debates on whether or not one should test people for genes for diseases for which there are no treatments. But my position is clear, Fred. I don't do those tests."

Agitated, Fred said, "I totally disagree. I want to know the truth. It's my right."

Max said calmly, "Then, my dear friend, you have to find another neurologist to run the test. I will not do it."

Fred exhaled and stayed silent.

Max continued, "I want, however, to qualify my position regarding what we call the sporadic form of Alzheimer's disease, meaning the form of Alzheimer's disease that is not familial and which seems to be the case for Meg. This form may be associated with a gene which doesn't necessarily cause the disease but predisposes one for the emergence of the symptoms, a gene that encodes for a protein that carries cholesterol in the blood. As I told you in our previous conversations, the protein is called apolipoprotein E or APOE. As you may remember, the unlucky cases express APOE4."

"Yes," Fred said. "What does that mean for Barbara and Steven?"

"Okay. So, only fifteen percent of the population will express this form of the APOE gene, which, on a statistical basis, seems to be associated with a higher incidence of Alzheimer's disease. I underline the term 'statistical.' If you have APOE4 in your genes, that doesn't necessarily mean that you'll develop Alzheimer's. It just means that, statistically, out of a large number of individuals, those who express APOE4 have a higher incidence of the disease. So even if you were to do this APOE test, it wouldn't bring us much information."

Fred found the neurologist's explanation very clear and calming. "Thanks, Max. I appreciate your patience with me," he said. "I suppose it's best, then, to bypass testing my children."

"Absolutely. As I said, no good can come of it."

After hanging up, Fred returned to the living room where he found Meg still in her armchair. She seemed to be asleep. In her lap he found some family pictures that she must have taken down from the mantel. She was looking at family pictures more and more often, as if she were trying to rebuild in her mind the memories she was losing. He gently lifted the three frames out of her lap to put them back with the others. One of them caught his attention: It showed Barbara in front of the Schönbrunn Palace outside Vienna. They had taken her there to celebrate her tenth birthday, so it must have been about thirty years ago. He remembered how she had been proud to be taken on a trip alone with her parents, leaving Steven with their grandparents in Zurich.

A knock on the door pulled him out of reminiscences. "Come in," Fred said, turning toward the door. It was Boswell.

"Fred, I wanted to let you know that all the contestants are on their way back to Zurich for the briefing with Comina tomorrow."

IN THE CAR, ZURICH, SWITZERLAND

MAY 7, 2018

Fred had stopped his car at the traffic light near the Opernhaus on the Seestrasse, the road that runs along the lake from the center of Zurich toward Küsnacht. As the light turned green and he started to accelerate, he saw a car coming from the opposite direction driving too rapidly. "Another irresponsible driver who is going to get caught by the radar," he thought. But as the car passed him, he could have sworn he recognized the BMW. Something about the vehicle bothered him, but he couldn't figure out what. He turned toward Marco Comina in the passenger seat—who was typing notes into his laptop—and decided that, since he couldn't pinpoint the source of his uneasiness, he would keep his thoughts to himself.

The detective said, "I'm completing the list of the different issues we'll need to address with the contestants today. We may need more than one day to figure out the best strategy to protect them from further interferences and threats."

"Don't worry," Fred said. "I've told them not to make any plans for the next couple of days and asked them all to stay in Zurich until further notice. Until we have a better idea about how the investigation is progressing, I prefer that they stay here where you can keep an eye on them."

Fred pulled into his driveway.

Ida opened the front door. Fred greeted her warmly as always. After he introduced her to Comina, Ida informed them that Boswell had called and left a message. He had told her that he forgot some documents at the office and would be back as soon as possible.

Fred frowned at this inconvenience. It wasn't like Jonathan to be forgetful. But then he turned toward his friend. "I'll be with you in a minute, Marco. I'm just going to say hello to Meg. Ida will show you into my office and offer you a drink. The contestants won't be arriving until two."

After a working lunch in his office, Fred and Comina joined the contestants in the living room. Fred was perturbed by Boswell's continued absence. It was really very strange that he should be so late. What if something had happened to him? Fortunately, Bobby had arrived punctually, as usual, and had ushered the contestants into the living room. Fred shook everybody's hands and introduced them to Comina. Then the five scientists sat on the cream-colored settees around a coffee table. Sarah and Philip looked exhausted and stressed out, Fred thought. Jean-Pierre sat nervously on the edge of his chair, as if he were ready to leap off of it. Only Edoardo looked fresh and pink, his usual self. Yucun always looked serious, and today her expression was particularly grave.

Outside, the view showed the still-snow-covered mountains lining Lake Zurich, which was a deep cobalt color.

Fred sat in his favorite armchair by the fireplace and began by reiterating how sorry he was about having had to call them back to Zurich for this meeting.

"I'll make sure to resolve the matter as quickly as possible and send you off again on your riddle-chasing around Europe," he said jovially, noticing how all five contestants were looking at him with a focused expectation in their eyes. "First of all, you have to know that with Marco's help we'll hopefully put an end, once and for all, to the threats you have been receiving. Marco is not only a dear friend, he is also a very experienced PI. He used to be the director of the Zurich criminal police department before joining a large PI firm when he retired."

"Very impressive," Edoardo said with a quiet clap of his hand.

"*C'est bien!*" Jean-Pierre exclaimed.

Pleased with their response, Fred said, "Marco will brief you on what information we've been able to gather so far, and he'll explain the security measures that will be taken to guarantee your safety."

Marco thanked Fred for his kind words and turned toward the contestants. "I'm very happy to meet you all. It's good to have the opportunity to discuss the incidents with you directly. You'll also be interviewed individually. I'm convinced that by telling me what happened, you'll remember certain aspects of the experience that might have been forgotten otherwise. At this point, unfortunately, we have very little information about the reason for the threats or who is making them. I've been researching all kinds of groups and individuals who could be connected to Fred's family, his business, or the competition in any possible way. We need to understand why someone would want to work against the Lindenmayer Award. I'm sure you must have questions. Yes?"

Philip was the first to ask, "Is there anything we can do to protect ourselves?"

"Yes. I was coming to that." Fred took over from Marco. "Your security is what's most important to us. As you know, we have contacted the Swiss embassies in the countries you are bound to visit, and they in turn have informed the respective national police forces about our problems. As a first measure, we'll give you a list with the names and contact details of the heads of security in all the embassies. You can get in touch with them at any time to discuss your concerns." Fred paused, looking at them. "I cannot stand the atmosphere of insecurity and threat that these incidents, although still relatively minor, create for the contest. What could happen next? I don't want you to be in danger."

The discussion continued for a couple of hours. Finally, Fred suggested breaking up for the day so that everybody could get some rest at the Hotel Sonne in Küsnacht, where they were staying. The next day would be spent on detailed security measures, and Marco and one of his colleagues, a police psychologist, would do some role-playing to show the candidates how to deal with unexpected or threatening situations, like talking to an anonymous caller on the phone or being stalked in the street.

Fred was pleased to see that the five scientists looked more relaxed than when they'd arrived. Edoardo was joking with Philip and Jean-Pierre was engaged in a lighthearted discussion with Sarah. Only Yucun stood apart. She was the first to say good night to Fred: polite, professional, and inscrutable as always.

After Comina and the contestants had left, Fred wondered again what had happened to Boswell. He walked over to a window in the living room and stared out. Directly below, he saw Boswell and Yucun talking. Yucun placed her hand on Boswell's arm. Boswell glanced furtively around as if to make sure no one was nearby then bent over and kissed her on the lips.

Fred had had no idea that a romantic relationship was blossoming between them. He wasn't sure what to make of it, certainly not a good idea. However, this still didn't explain Boswell's lateness. Boswell had also seemed restless lately. On two separate occasions, when Fred went to look for him in his office, he was not there.

Hearing Boswell's familiar footsteps, Fred turned and said, "What happened to you?"

"I'm so very sorry," Boswell said. "I got a flat tire on my way here."

"That's unfortunate, but why didn't you call?"

"It took longer than I thought."

"Why don't we take a stroll along the lake?" Fred suggested. "I've been meaning to talk with you."

Boswell turned pale, as if he feared being repri-manded, or worse, as if he feared being dismissed.

"Please don't misunderstand me," Fred said. "I don't mean anything dire. I just thought it might be helpful for us to talk."

They walked in silence for a while. The sun was setting over Lake Zurich. A ship blew its horn as it set off from the harbor. "Jonathan, I must admit I'm a bit worried about you. You haven't been yourself lately. If there's anything I can do to help, please don't hesitate to ask me. You seem very restless. Perhaps the job is getting boring for you? I've always known you were overqualified for it, and sometimes, I've even wondered why you stayed on with me, but I've grown so used to your help that I did not want to ask for selfish reasons."

"Thank you, Fred," Boswell said, sheepishly. "I apologize again for being so late today. As for the job, I really do like working for you."

"No need to apologize. I just want to know if there's something I can help you with."

"I appreciate your concern, but there's nothing to worry about. I've had a lot on my mind."

"I can imagine," Fred said. "Perhaps you have met someone?"

"Oh no," Jonathan said. "It's probably just the stress of having to deal with the threats against the contestants. I think it's taken more of a toll than I realized."

"Ah," Fred said, thinking that Jonathan's statement didn't sound very heartfelt, but it was probably because he was uncomfortable with Fred for having alluded to a possible relationship with a woman. Fred had always attributed Jonathan's reserve to shyness, but it was perhaps more than that: a deep insecurity, a self-consciousness that must be very trying.

"I know what you mean," Fred said. "Sometimes I can't sleep at night because I worry so much about the competition. And now I'm even concerned about the contestants' safety." He paused and waited for Boswell to say something more. But his assistant had stopped and was gazing out at the lake, a vague, almost wistful, expression on his face.

"I'm sorry you missed the meeting," Fred continued.

Boswell finally turned his attention back on the conversation and smiled. "I saw the contestants on their way out and they seemed reassured. I'm sure they're glad that Comina is handling the situation."

"Yes, that was my impression too. Oh, I forgot to tell you, just before the contestants arrived, Bobby told me about the state of the riddles. It seems that Yucun and Edoardo are doing very well. They've taken the lead."

"That's great!" Jonathan now seemed genuinely happy. "I'm glad to hear something positive after the last few days. Of course, with three weeks to go the other contestants still have a chance to catch up."

"Absolutely," Fred said. "I must admit, though, that I have a soft spot for Yucun—even though she's much more reserved than the others. I was very impressed by her intelligence and quick mind when I first met her." Fred sincerely believed what he was saying, but he was also hoping to give Jonathan another chance to confide in him. But Jonathan only said, "It was the same for me when I first read her application." His eyes brightened behind his small, round glasses. "Her scientific record is quite extraordinary."

"I'm excited to see who the winner will be. After all, he or she will be the scientist I'll be working closely with over the next few years," Fred said, realizing that Jonathan clearly wasn't ready to confide in him yet. There was no point in trying to rush him.

"Well, another few weeks of patience, Fred. Despite all the tension, at least the riddle part of the competition is still fun."

"You're probably right." Fred tried to sound confident. "I'm going to walk a bit farther, but you go home. It was a long and stressful day."

As Fred looked at Jonathan walking back up to the house, he decided that he was too tired to continue his walk and sat down on the "love bench," as Meg and he called it. It was a lovely, ancient bench of sculpted wood that had been given to Fred's grandparents as a wedding present by a friend who was a well-known craftsman in the Engadin valley. Often after dinner he and Meg would come down to the lake and sit on the bench to discuss their day and how happy they were to finally be in Switzerland after all those years in Colorado. Little did they know that soon after their return an emotional tsunami would hit them in the form of an Alzheimer's diagnosis for Meg. But they continued to spend time after dinner on their bench and talked a lot about their years together and how they met. They were both very conscious of the fact that one day Meg would start forgetting many things that they had shared and so their time together here was like writing a diary. One of Fred's favorite stories was the one of their first date, which always made them giggle when they reminisced about it.

N°316,
ASPEN, COLORADO

_____

_____

_____

_____

_____

1967

Fred had been standing at the bar for more than
thirty minutes waiting for Meg to arrive. He had arrived early to make sure that they would have the table
he particularly liked. It was a corner table with a lovely
dark red velvet covered bench with old pictures and
mirrors hanging on the walls around it. The bench reminded Fred of his grandparents' chalet in Sils Maria
in the Swiss Alps. He had very fond memories of vacations with his brother and their cousins at this typical
Engadiner chalet. In the kitchen a bench ran along two
sides of the old carved wooden table, and the cousins
always fought over which of them was allowed to sit
on the bench. He could almost hear his grandmother's

voice as she ordered the children around in the kitchen while baking Fred's favorite nut cake with honey, which was one of the culinary trademarks of the canton of Graubünden.

His eyes shifted from the table to the front door. Every time it opened, his heart missed a beat: What if Meg had decided not to show up? Last time they had met was the previous week for a lunch with their boss, the director of operations for the Aspen resort. They had disagreed on almost all the issues that had been discussed. This had put their burgeoning relationship on trial, even though they really felt very much attracted to each other. They were both working as employees of the Tourist Office, and they had been put in charge of the program for a group of European travel agents visiting Aspen for the first time. They never seemed to agree on anything concerning the program they were supposed to design for that visit. After the third, fruitless meeting they still hadn't agreed on a program. At that point Fred had decided, as he now remembered shamefully, that as the more senior employee, he was going to tell Meg that he was in charge and that he was going to finalize the program with or without her approval. He had added that she was new to the job and definitely lacked experience in the hospitality business. Meg had left the room feeling insulted and put down.

As the door had closed on her, Fred had felt devastated. Never in his life had he talked in such a condescending way to anyone, let alone a kind and lovely young woman. He had behaved like the typical alpha male that he so much disliked. Why had he behaved in such an appalling way? He was wondering if it was his insecurity about Meg's interest in him that made him feel so irritated? For the first time in his life he was overwhelmed by a feeling he wasn't familiar with. Was hc falling in love seriously this time? He'd had many flirtations and had fallen in love before, but this was definitely something different. He felt very protective of Meg and at the same time he was intimidated by her easy, natural way of interacting with people. And she also came across as being very clever. Not in the sense that she would try to impress with her knowledge, but her whole being seemed to be shaped by a rare emotional intelligence. Fred suspected that she already had him figured out and it made him feel uneasy, even more so as he had few clues about Meg, her personality or her feelings. He had to decide what his next move would be to get to know her better.

Fred had called her the next day to apologize and invite her for dinner at his favorite steak house, N°316. Meg had been very kind on the phone and took his apologies gracefully. This was three days ago and now Fred was getting really nervous about how tonight's dinner was going to turn out. He was considering what he would say to her when she finally got there. He looked at his watch, only five minutes to go until eight o'clock. He was wondering if she would be on time.

"Hi there, I'm sure you were wondering if I would arrive on time!" Meg came up to him from behind, startling him.

Fred turned around and almost hit her with his head. "So sorry, I didn't expect you . . . that is to say . . . where did you come from?"

"From home," replied Meg, laughing, "but I'm sure you meant which door did I use."

"Yes, because I was looking at the entrance door but I didn't see you come in." Fred looked puzzled.

"No, I came through the employee's entrance. I have a friend working here and I came in with her."

"That explains it!" Fred laughed and asked if she cared for a predinner drink.

"I would prefer not. I can't take alcohol on an empty stomach, and I wouldn't want you to see me dancing on the table before dinner," she explained with a twinkle in her eyes.

"Well, maybe I would enjoy it, I'm sure you're a great dancer." Fred was very appreciative of her good sense of humor. "But if you're hungry, we better order dinner." Fred took her arm and guided her toward their table.

Meg was impressed with the place, which was one of the high-end restaurants in Aspen. "This is beautiful, but I don't want you to spend all your money on a dinner to apologize," she commented as the waiter was handing them the menus.

"Don't worry, it is my pleasure, and it will make me feel better after having been so rude with you at our last meeting. You look very nice, by the way."

"Thank you." Meg started to feel quite shy. "My friend Annie loaned me the outfit for the evening. I didn't really have anything to wear to such an elegant place."

"Let's order!" Fred tried to lighten the atmosphere and help Meg relax.

As Fred called the waiter, Meg wondered who this guy from Switzerland really was. He was more than the eye could see. Even though he dressed and behaved in a modest manner, everything seemed to come naturally to him. He must be from a well-to-do family, Meg thought. This kind of smooth easiness was not part of her world. Her parents were farmers and theirs was a hardship life. Meg had been lucky to earn a fellowship to attend college, but she was working during summer and winter breaks to make ends meet, since her fellowship just barely covered her tuition fees and board.

She realized that Fred was looking at her with his raised glass: "A toast to the most stubborn but also the most lovely new colleague this year!" His smile went straight to her heart and she also raised her glass: "And to the nicest Swiss boss ever!" Their eyes met over their glasses and somehow they both knew at that moment that this was the beginning of something very special.

After dinner and a lively discussion about their work and their lives, they took a walk around the resort. They were talking about why they both aspired to build their lives and careers in the mountains of Colorado, when they came to the end of the snow-covered path that had taken them quite far out from the resort. Fred put an arm around Meg's shoulders and pointed to the moon. It was coming up big and red over the mountain range.

"How beautiful, the moon seems to reflect in your eyes." Fred was pulling her into his arms.

"Wait," Meg put a hand up to Fred's cheek, and drew closer to him to murmur into his ear, "the moon is telling me that you will probably kiss me now."

"The moon is so right." Fred took her chin and softly put his lips to hers.

Meg felt her legs go all wobbly and she couldn't believe how Fred made her feel. Never had a man shown her such tenderness. She buried her face into his neck. No words were necessary, Fred simply held on to her while looking at the moon. This is perfection, he thought, I will never let her go.

HOTEL SONNE, KÜSNACHT, SWITZERLAND

MAY 7, 2018

When Sarah arrived at the hotel at seven after the meeting with Marco Comina, she collapsed into a warm bath and was drifting to sleep when the phone rang.

"Hello, Sarah, it's Michael. How are you?"

"Oh...hi! I was falling asleep in my bath. How are you?"

"Great and I have good news. I was in Bern all day for the conference but guess what? I'm back in Zurich. Are you up for dinner tonight?"

Taken by surprise, Sarah blurted, "Yes, Michael, hmm...Sure."

"Great. I'll pick you up at eight. And dress casually!"

"Okay. See you later." She hung up, still not quite sure what to do and decided to stay a bit longer in her bath.

Just before eight o'clock, she looked at herself in the mirror, and after a satisfactory glance, grabbed her coat and stepped out of the room. Michael had called two minutes earlier to let her know he was downstairs.

When the elevator reached the lobby, she wasn't sure she could step out. She felt paralyzed by shyness, as if her feet were glued to the floor.

"Hello, princess, your carriage is waiting. Would you like to step out of the elevator?" He was laughing and reached for her arm.

"It's nice to see you," she managed to say.

"And you too. I've been looking forward to this evening." He kissed her cheeks. "Shall we go?"

"Sure," she said, regaining her composure. "Where are you taking me?"

"You'll see. It's a surprise." He was holding the car door open for her.

After a thirty-minute drive, he stopped the car in front of a beautiful old house, overgrown with ivy.

"This is not a restaurant," she remarked, as they stepped out of the car.

"Well, it's a private restaurant. It's called Les Saules and the chef's name is Michael."

Sarah stared at him, then smiled.

"Welcome to my family's home. I hope you like my cooking!" He took her hand and guided her inside the house.

The entrance hall opened onto a big living room that gave onto a terrace. As they stepped out, she took in the beautiful old trees in the garden and, farther down, a little pebble beach that skirted the lake. "It's magnificent. What a beautiful home!"

"I love it," he said simply. "I have lived here ever since I was born. My grandparents gave the house to my father when my mother was pregnant with me, their first grandchild. My grandparents always said this house was made for family life and many children."

"How many siblings do you have?" she asked, a bit envious, as she was an only child.

"I have a brother and two sisters, but at the moment we all live abroad. Will you accompany me to the kitchen so that I can put the finishing touches on our dinner?"

"Can I help? But I must tell you that I'm not much of a cook."

"That's okay, you can be my assistant and do all the hard work. How about that?" With a hand on her back, he guided her into the kitchen.

After dinner, Sarah and Michael settled into the old-fashioned wood lounge chairs on the terrace.

"I hope we will be able to fly back to Moscow to-gether," he said. "When do you think your meetings will be over?"

"Actually, I'm not going back to Moscow."

"What? Why not?"

"My stay in Moscow had nothing to do with the competition. I only was there to visit my grandmother who was dying."

"I'm sorry, Sarah. I just assumed you were also there for the competition because Mr. Lindenmayer had asked us to help you leave the country safely."

"Well, the competition had already been launched when I heard about my grandmother. I decided I would rather lose a few days in the contest than not see my grandmother one last time."

He took one of her hands into his. "So, with the problem of the anonymous message, and being called back to Zurich, you were not even able to see her?"

"Sadly she had already passed away by the time I arrived in Moscow."

"Well, where will you be going next then?"

"I have no idea. After coming back to Zurich with you, I went to Prague to solve a riddle and that is the only one I have figured out so far." She tried not to sound discouraged. "I came back this morning for the meeting with Fred and the PI, but I need to deal with the next riddle."

"Why don't we have a look together," he suggested. "We have all night and I must tell you that as a boy I was quite good at solving riddles. Do you have it with you?"

"Of course," she said, taking her iPhone out of her bag and handing it to him.

Michael read aloud: *"On the mountain road, in the city where Nations meet, Hans handed him the key to the vociferous unknown.* Quite challenging," he said, "but let's think about it." He got up and started pacing. "Now let's see, what we can make out of—*'where Nations meet'*—it could have something to do with the United Nations or some other international organization."

"Well, there are quite a number of cities in Europe with UN or international organizations: Geneva, Strasbourg, Brussels, or Vienna—too many places to choose from."

"Yes, but I think we can exclude Brussels, Strasbourg, and Vienna, as there are no mountains around these cities. This leaves Geneva."

"Okay, Geneva it is," she said. "I have always wanted to go there. Now to the scientific clues: What is meant by *'the vociferous unknown'*?"

"I'm not sure." He stopped pacing and sat opposite Sarah. "But let's see about the other words: *'Hans'* and *'the key.'* Hans is a Germanic first name . . . This could be a hint that the rest of the sentence relates to the German language? The word '*unknown*' could be translated into German as *unbekannt* or *unbewusst...*"

"What fast thinking! And I always thought diplomats turned their tongues three times in their mouth before speaking."

"Well, we must think fast if you want to win the award, but you're right; in diplomacy, every situation needs to be considered in order to make sure that you are making the right decision. Now back to our Germanic *unbewusst*—"

"Wait a minute," she interjected. "Isn't *unbewusst* what Freud called the unconscious?"

He looked puzzled. "What about Freud? I don't get it."

"Of course, don't you see?" She was getting excited. "It could very well be about Freud. My cousin Katia is a psychoanalyst and she often talks to me about Freud. There was a famous case about Little Hans, who was still a child when his father asked Freud to analyze him, and then—"

Michael raised his eyebrows.

"You do know who Little Hans was," she said. "Don't you, Michael?"

"No, how should I know about Little Hans?" He looked at her as if she was telling him some fairy tale. "Is Little Hans maybe the one from Hansel and Gretel, who is almost eaten by the witch?"

"What?" She hesitated. "Who are Hansel and Gretel?" Suddenly she remembered. "Oh, you mean the fairy tale!" She laughed. "No, it is not about Hansel and Gretel, but you do have a very imaginative mind. I meant Freud's Little Hans, one of his most famous cases."

He chuckled. "Of course, now I understand, and—" He stopped abruptly as if some sudden thought had silenced him. He became quite serious. "Sarah, listen, I think you're onto something." He was clearly eager to explain his idea. "Hans and the unconscious... but then it should be Vienna, not Geneva. Freud lived in Vienna, not in Geneva."

"Yes, you are right, too bad. We thought we had it. Let's see... I could call Katia and ask her about Freud and Geneva."

"Yes, you do that. In the meantime, I'm going to call my uncle Théodore whose wife was a psychoanalyst in Geneva. I'll just go to the kitchen to check on something."

A little while later, as he walked back out to the terrace, he heard her say goodbye to her cousin. Sarah was looking perplexed.

"Katia told me the whole story of Little Hans's psychoanalysis." She took Michael's hand and pulled him down into the lounge chair next to hers.

"So what about it?" he asked, pleased with this physical contact. "Has she solved the riddle for you?"

"Not exactly, but I hope that Freud's treatment of him will help us move toward the solution to the riddle, although she couldn't say anything about Freud and Geneva."

"Ah, but I know about a Little Hans in Geneva." He looked very pleased with himself. "My uncle Théodore told me that when Little Hans was an adult, he moved to Geneva to become the director of the Grand Théâtre, the Geneva opera house."

"That's extraordinary. Did your uncle say anything else about him?"

"Oh yes. He even remembers him: Herbert Graf, which was Little Hans's real name, was a good friend of my uncle Théodore's father."

"Why don't we rush to Geneva? That is, if you don't have any other plans," she added blushing.

"No, I don't. But if I had, I would change them," he replied. "I'm sure we can stay with my uncle. Since his wife died, he lives alone in a big house that must have at least ten bedrooms!"

"That would be really nice, and I would love to visit the city. I have never been there."

"We'll do whatever you want, Sarah, but now you better tell me about Little Hans and Freud."

"Sure, but it's a long story. Are you positive you want to hear about it now?" She was looking at her watch. "It is almost eleven o'clock and I have a nine o'clock meeting at Fred's, but we could leave late in the afternoon for Geneva."

"You're right, the story of Little Hans can wait. Let's get some sleep. I'll drive you back to your hotel." He got up and offered her his hand to help her out of her chair, but when she stood up, she could not resist wrapping her arms around him.

ON THE TRAIN TO GENEVA, SWITZERLAND

Sarah and Michael were seated next to each other on the intercity train from Zurich to Geneva, Michael farther from the window. The direct route did not include any of the magnificent views of the Alps Sarah had hoped for, but this would force her to concentrate on the riddle. She wondered if she had made the right decision by agreeing to have Michael accompany her to Geneva.

"You look very serious," Michael said. "What are you thinking about?"

"Oh nothing, just the riddle and Little Hans," she said looking at the riddle on her iPhone.

"You still have to tell me about Little Hans and Freud," Michael said, reaching for her phone. "Let me have a look at the riddle again."

Sarah obliged. "Little Hans is one of the most important cases in the history of psychoanalysis. It's the first report about a psychoanalytical treatment of a phobia in a young child. Sigmund Freud published the case in 1909 in a paper entitled 'Analysis of a Phobia in a Five-Year-Old Boy.' His parents were longtime friends of Freud. Max Graf, Hans's father, was an author, critic, and musicologist. Hans's godfather was Gustav Mahler, the famous composer, who was also an acquaintance of Freud's. Freud chose to call his young patient 'Little Hans' in reference to the Kluge Hans, a horse that had the reputation for being extremely intelligent and even capable of doing some simple arithmetic. At the time, everyone in Vienna knew about Kluge Hans."

"Okay, wait!" Michael raised his hand. "That already sounds too complicated for me. What does a horse named Kluge Hans have to do with anything?"

"Sorry," she said. "I got ahead of myself. Little Hans is the first case that provided Freud with the key to understanding the links between the sexual development in children and the origin of neurosis, in this particular case, phobia. He actually psychoanalyzed Hans indirectly. It was the boy's father who regularly reported the observations to Freud, who then advised the father about the understanding and interpretation of Hans's symptoms. Freud only saw the boy once during the entire time Hans was 'in therapy.' Still the case was extremely instructive in helping Freud formulate several concepts of psychoanalysis." She exhaled deeply. "Are you following so far?"

"Yep," Michael said with a grin. He tapped the side of his head. "So far, so good, but what about the Kluge Hans?"

"I was getting to that. The boy's first symptom was an overwhelming fear of being trampled in the street by a horse. The trigger occurred suddenly in 1908 when Hans and his nanny were walking through the Stadtpark in the center of Vienna. Without warning, Hans started to cry, asking to go back home to his mother right away. At the time, he was almost five years old and had been a normal, happy child. The next day, his mother took him to Schönbrunn Palace, the imperial summer residence outside the city, which is surrounded by a large park. Hans started crying, and his mother could see he was very frightened. On their way home, he told her that he was afraid of being bitten by a horse." Sarah looked at Michael who seemed to be listening attentively. "Are you sure you're really interested in hearing all about Hans's therapy?"

"Absolutely, although," he lowered his voice, "I'd rather be kissing you. But we do need to solve this riddle, so I should learn more about this case."

"How do you expect me to concentrate if you talk to me about kissing?" She leaned over to give him a quick peck on the lips.

"That wasn't much of a kiss." He looked at her forlornly. "But go on with the case."

"Okay, try to focus!" she said, with a light slap on his hand. "So, Hans's fear of horses took on other forms; he became afraid that they would fall while carrying heavy loads, and of them having black stains around their mouths. Particular circumstances would trigger panic to the point that Hans would refuse to leave home. One of his worst fears was that of horses falling over and moving their legs in the air with great noise. Interestingly, Hans compared this position of being on the back with the four legs in the air as the one that he would adopt when he had an urge to pee."

"This is getting too strange."

Sarah took a breath. "The main point is that, according to Freud and his theory about infant sexuality, Hans was experiencing anxieties related to the fear of being castrated, the infamous castration complex. Another unacceptable impulse was Hans's desire to replace his father as his mother's sexual mate, which would also imply the death of his father, or the Oedipus complex."

"Ah, we're finally getting to the interesting part," Michael said. "Is there more to come about sexuality?"

"You're incorrigible. Not everything in Freud's theory is about little boys wanting to have sex with their mothers."

"I'm sure it isn't, but that's what most people know about Freud."

Of course Michael was right, as she herself hadn't known much about the psychoanalytical theory before asking Katia about it.

"Should I finish?"

"Yes, please," he said with a clap of his hands.

"This case was the first to provide clinical support for Freud. He thought that Hans's fear was probably the result of several factors, including the birth of a little sister and emotional conflicts over masturbation. He considered the anxiety as having originated from the incomplete repression and other defense mechanisms being used to fight off the impulses involved in Hans's sexual development. But the basic idea of Freud's theory is that children can't become conscious of these desires, which are unacceptable to them. Little Hans, and most young children, have several anxieties, which actually manifest themselves almost physically with symptoms for which there is no reason and turn their anxieties into acceptable objects. For Little Hans, it was horses, which became the object that allowed his anxiety to somehow materialize and become a symptom that could be identified. These inexplicable and unbearable fears are defined as phobias."

"We're getting into phobias now? So, Dr. Sarah, I have to confess that I've had one of my own for many years: It's a phobia of women," Michael said with twinkle in his eye.

"I'm sure you are a hopeless case. It must be because they all fall for you, no matter how you behave," she teased. "Is that correct?"

"That would be correct, yes. But now I'm really worried because I'm falling in love and I'm not sure what to do about this new symptom."

This was the first time Michael had mentioned love, a huge declaration downplayed, perhaps, by their banter. Happiness welled inside of Sarah.

"The best remedy, of course, is to engage in a curative kissing season and stop listening to what she is telling you about Dr. Sigmund," she asserted, intent on keeping up the light banter, which precluded talking about anything more serious. "But we don't know where this would take us, and we're supposed to be behaving on the train. Seriously, though, I can stop my lecture if you're fed up with it."

"No, I want to hear it all, till the bitter end, even if all I'm thinking of are your kisses." He smiled at her longingly. "Sorry, I mean your riddle."

"Then, of course, I must go on," she said in a mock-serious voice. "Freud believed this case provided strong support for the theory of infant sexuality which he'd written about a few years earlier and published in 1905 in a book entitled *Three Essays on the Theory of Sexuality*. It was heavily criticized by his contemporaries and was condemned as abominably immoral. He was described as 'having an obscene mind.' The idea of children having sexual desires was sufficient to shock the rigid and conservative Viennese society, which denied children's sexuality and glorified their innocence. Again, Freud was labeled as 'pansexualist' with an obscene mind or, at best, a Viennese libertarian."

"But does anyone know if Freud's analysis cured Hans?" Michael asked.

"You're hooked, aren't you?" Sarah said, smiling. "The answer is, actually, yes. In his description of the case, Freud indicates that he told Hans's father what he could do about his son's problem. Graf was to tell his son that all this business of horses was foolishness and nothing else. He should also tell Hans that it was normal that he loved his mother and that he wanted to be close to her in bed. The strategy was to tell Hans the truth about some facts, like the development of his sexual impulses. The aim was to make him acknowledge the fact that horses were just an image standing in place of some of his desires. This approach had a remarkably positive effect and, within a few weeks, Little Hans had been liberated from his phobia. In 1922, Freud wrote a short conclusion to the case study, in which he reported that Little Hans was now a healthy young man of nineteen, who no longer suffered from neurotic behavior."

"Wow, you're a fountain of information!"

"Yes, this was quite the extensive lecture," Sarah said apologetically. "I hope I haven't bored you too much."

"Absolutely not," Michael assured her. And with these words, he grabbed her by the waist and pulled her toward him, covering her lips with his.

Once he set her free, Sarah noticed an elderly couple smiling in their direction. "Now, back to business," he said matter-of-factly. "My turn to share what I learned about Herbert Graf's life and what happened to him in Geneva."

"Yes, please." She straightened her shirt, which had ridden up so that her belly peaked through near her waist. "I'm sure that should help us get a clearer idea of what is meant in the riddle."

"This story about Herbert Graf is really puzzling. He was a very successful opera producer who set up several operas in Germany, Poland, and Austria. In 1936, at the age of thirty-three, he moved to the United States, where he worked as a producer at the New York Metropolitan Opera until 1960. From 1960 to 1962, he was director of the Zurich opera, and in 1963 he was appointed to the Grand Théâtre in Geneva, where he died in 1973."

"What did he die from?"

"He died of what he had feared most as a little boy. One day, while surveying some work at the Grand Théâtre, he fell into the orchestra pit and landed on his back, his legs and arms shaking and moving in long convulsions, just like the falling horses that were at the center of his childhood phobias. Apparently, he died of the consequences of this fall."

"That's ironic!" she exclaimed. "His phobia of horses, and their falling over, followed him in a twist of fate to the day of his death. I wonder what Freud would have made of that?"

"We'll never know. But I think we've spent enough time on the good doctor. Let's focus on Geneva. Would you like me to tell you about my memories of the city?"

MILAN, ITALY

MAY 8, 2018

Edoardo was leaning back in a comfortable leather armchair in his father's study. He loved this dark room, with its imposing cedar furniture. It always reminded him of the days when he was a boy and his father would call him into his office for a "man-to-man talk"—which was code for "Don't tell your mother." Over the years, they had discussed many issues, ranging from a bad joke young Edoardo had played on his primary-school teacher, to, in later years, women and sex, once he'd reached adolescence.

He chuckled as he remembered this conversation about sex education very well. He was a bit embarrassed, and so was his father, and they had both stood by the window while talking, looking toward the Conservatorio Giuseppe Verdi across the piazza. He was reminiscing over his weekly piano lessons and the memorable soccer games with his cousin on the piazza. He had fond memories of the lively family house this had once been. Indeed, his father's brother and sister lived on the other floors with their families, in the building that had been designed by his grandfather, a famous architect. During summer break and on weekends, the three families often stayed at Villa Fiorentina, the family's estate in Stresa, on Lake Maggiore with views of the Borromean Islands surrounded by mountains.

Edoardo checked his watch and saw that he had some time left before dinner to work on his next riddle. Although he has already solved two, this next one seemed particularly challenging. He still hadn't figured out the first part of the riddle. Where would it take him next? He wondered if he had made a mistake by entering the contest. When he'd seen the award announcement in the newsletter of the Society for Neuroscience, he thought it might be fun to take some time off from hard science and do something completely different. He had craved something out of the ordinary, and the competition seemed a perfect opportunity. Up to now he had been following the well-defined career of an ambitious young scientist.

But even though he was excited to be a contestant—
and thrilled at the prospect of spending more time
with Benedetta—Edoardo already missed his lab at
the Salk Institute and his work at the bench. He loved
his life in San Diego, where he had moved from Rome
just a year ago. What he particularly appreciated in
Southern California was its slower pace: golf, surfing,
beach parties. He was also very fond of his boss, Professor Judy Blomstein. He'd had a job interview with
Professor Blomstein at an annual meeting of the Society for Neuroscience in Washington, DC, in 2016. She
was on the faculty of the University of California San
Diego and had a research position at the Salk Institute
in La Jolla, close to the UCSD campus. She'd offered
him a position in her lab at Salk; happily, he had also
been accepted in the PhD program in neurosciences
at UCSD. Edoardo suspected that her recommendation had helped him get selected as a candidate for
the award.

He remembered a conversation he'd had with his
uncle Luigi when he'd told him about his job at the
Salk Institute. As soon as he'd received the offer, Edoardo had rushed to his uncle's office to share the news.
Luigi Gardelli was one of Italy's most prominent architects and designers. Edoardo loved the atmosphere
of the sober office filled with the drawings of Luigi's
designs. Located on the ground floor of a building on

Via Conservatorio, designed by the architect Emilio Gardelli—Edoardo's grandfather and Luigi's father—the office looked onto Piazza della Passione and the Conservatorio.

"So, you're going to work at the Salk. Lucky you!" The ever elegant and gracious Luigi had clapped his hands and thrown back his head in a delighted laugh. "My dear Edoardo, the Salk Institute is one of the great architectural marvels of the twentieth century. I saw the original plans that Louis Kahn drew—must have been 1958. We were in Chicago, for a gathering in honor of Mies van der Rohe."

Luigi was very fond of the United States and proud of having a few of the lamps and other pieces of furniture he'd designed exhibited at the Museum of Modern Art in New York. He was a friend and great admirer of Kahn, the American architect who had captured the vision of Salk, the discoverer of the polio vaccine, to design an exceptional scientific institute close to the University of California San Diego.

"You must be quite good at what you do," said Luigi, faking a surprised expression. "Well, after all, you *are* a Gardelli. But it's too bad you won't be carrying on with the family tradition in architecture."

"You know, Zio Luigi," Edoardo said with a smile, "neuroscience is not too far from our family tradition. I'll be studying the architecture of the brain."

"Granted, but architecture is about creation. Neuroscience is about observation and description. When I finish a building, I know I have created something that didn't exist before."

"Zio, I can assure you that nothing is more rewarding and exciting than finding one of the brain's secrets; it's as if you're discovering nature. Yes, it's true that this 'secret' has always existed. But, by revealing it, you're creating it in a way."

"Umm." Luigi paused. "You may have a point."

Edoardo wasn't surprised when his uncle looked at his watch, and then stood up. "I have to go now," Luigi said, "an interview with *Architectural Digest*. It's a bore, of course, I hate these rituals. But you know, it's one of the things a man in my position is obligated to do."

Edoardo smiled. He didn't believe a word of Luigi's complaint. He knew his uncle too well: Luigi loved to be the center of attention.

"Let's continue our conversation tomorrow at the golf club at Villa d'Este," Luigi suggested. "I have a tee-off time at three. Will you join me?"

"With great pleasure, Zio." Edoardo looked forward to it. He hadn't played golf with his uncle in a long time.

"By the way, if your pipettes, microscopes, and little rodents don't take up too much of your time, you'll get in a lot of golfing in San Diego," Luigi said, as he put on his jacket. "The Salk is next to Torrey Pines Golf Course." He winked at his nephew.

"I know," Edoardo said, smiling. "Why do you think I accepted the position there?"

"Well done. First things first!" Luigi chuckled as he rushed out of the office.

As it turned out, Edoardo had immediately loved his work environment at the Salk Institute on a breathtaking hilltop overlooking the Pacific Ocean. His laboratory, with walls built of glass panes so that the space was flooded with sunlight, was a peaceful but productive place. Salk's vision had been to create an institute where biologists could conduct groundbreaking research in an environment that would facilitate collaboration and foster reflection about the impact of biological research on humanity. Nuclear physics research and the Manhattan Project, which ended with the use of the nuclear bomb, still haunted him and other concerned scientists. Such a disaster should never happen in the field of biology. The Salk Institute was to be the place where scientific excellence would serve the good of mankind, particularly in developing treatments for diseases. The motto of the institute is "Hope lies in dreams, in imagination and in the courage of those who dare to make dreams into reality."

GENEVA, SWITZERLAND

After arriving in Geneva, Sarah and Michael took a cab directly to his uncle Théodore's home in Cologny. The village, a very upscale residential area, was situated on the left bank of Lake Léman—often wrongly called Lake Geneva—not far from the center of town. As they were being driven, Michael told Sarah that Théodore, despite his wealth, was a rather thrifty Calvinist. He'd suggested Michael take public transportation rather than a taxi from the train station.

"He insisted that they charge too much," Michael said. "He believes they're for those 'nouveaux riches in international finance.' He's a scion from a centuries old

family and can't stand what he calls this new generation of rich, pretentious financial raiders."

"So I suppose we'll get into trouble if he finds out
the truth?"

Michael grinned when he confessed that he hoped
Théodore didn't question their mode of transportation.

Looking out the window at the beautiful country-
side with its mountains in the distance and its vineyards, Sarah felt anxious at the thought of going to
Michael's uncle's upscale home. On the one or two occasions she had entered a rich person's home, she had
felt uncomfortable and out of place. Of course, they
had a purpose. Tomorrow, they would visit Geneva's
Grand Théâtre with the hope of finding the solution to
the riddle.

"Are you all right?" Michael asked.

"Just a little weary," she said, squeezing his hand.

The cab stopped and after Michael had paid, they
walked up the long pathway to his uncle's sprawling
home.

When the door swung open, Michael's eighty-five-
year-old uncle stood before them. He had a glistening
bald head and a wide smile.

"Welcome," he exclaimed, extending his hand
to shake Sarah's. Then he grabbed his nephew and
engulfed him in a bear hug; he appeared spry and

quick-witted as he joked about the fact he "caught them riding in style."

Yvonne, a slender middle-aged woman in a dark cotton dress, scurried down the stairs. She nodded to Michael and Sarah, and Théodore asked her to show them to their rooms. Winking at Michael, he said, "I instructed Yvonne to prepare the yellow and the red rooms. But, of course, you are adults. So feel free to make your own sleeping arrangements."

With a laugh, Michael kissed his uncle's cheek and thanked him for his hospitality.

Michael took Sarah around the estate for a tour before dinner. She was enchanted with the beauty of the rose garden and the lush orchard with a goldfish pond. The property was extensive, including two hills covered with vineyards and, most surprising of all, a museum located at the bottom of the estate.

Michael explained that the museum hosted one of the world's largest collections of ancient books and manuscripts, which his uncle had collected over the last fifty years. It included a rare copy of the Gutenberg Bible, as well as some Egyptian papyri and an original copy of *Paradise Lost* by John Milton. The exhibits were usually open to the public, but this week the museum was closed so that a new exhibit could be installed. Uncle Théodore insisted that he would take them on a tour himself.

At dinner that evening, Théodore enlightened Sarah about his and Michael's family, the Eschlers, boasting that they would celebrate their five hundredth anniversary as citizens of Zurich the following year. Despite the fact that he'd moved to Geneva after the war, he still felt very connected to his Zurich roots.

Sarah found Théodore to be sweet and felt at ease in his presence.

"Tell me about your hopes and dreams," he said with a wink and a smile. When she explained about the Lindenmayer Award, he leaned across the table and peered at her with interest. "This sounds fascinating. What an exciting opportunity!"

Before retiring for the evening, Théodore asked Michael and Sarah about their plans for the next day.

Michael said, "We plan to go to the Grand Théâtre with the hope of finding the solution to the riddle there. Afterward, we'll have lunch in Old Town and do some sightseeing in the afternoon."

"Well," Théodore said, "that's quite a busy schedule. But if you think you'll be home for dinner, why don't you invite some cousins or friends you'd like to see?"

"Thank you very much, uncle. I'd love to invite Jacques and Caroline, as well as my old friend Antoine whom I haven't seen in at least two years."

"Wonderful, wonderful. At my age, it's such a treat to have company. Many of my friends have passed away and, as Michael may have told you," he addressed Sarah, "my children and grandchildren all live abroad."

Michael bid his uncle good night, and Sarah kissed the old man on the cheek. Théodore blushed with happiness.

Sarah and Michael had just closed the door to their bedroom when Sarah's cell started ringing. She pulled it out of her bag. "Hello?" she said. It was Bobby. "Sarah, I'm so sorry to bother you, but I wanted to let you know that several contestants have received new threats."

"Oh no," Sarah exclaimed.

"I just thought you should know so that you can be on the alert. Please call us immediately if you have any concerns."

"I will," she said. "Thanks for calling."

"Who was that?" Michael asked Sarah. "I couldn't help hearing. What threats?"

And Sarah explained what Bobby had told her.

MILAN, ITALY

Sitting with Benedetta in the café of the Piccolo Teatro near the Duomo, Edoardo thought that he should be happy. He was spending some moments with his girlfriend, enjoying an *aperitivo*.

If only he didn't have to worry about the text and photograph of Giovanna. He had been so disappointed when Bobby called and told him that the lead Comina was following about drug dealers from Bulgaria unfortunately turned out to be false. Indeed, Comina was working hard to come up with a solution, but they thought Edoardo should know that there was the distinct possibility that this group—whoever they were—would send the photograph of him and Giovanna to Benedetta. It might be best to tell Benedetta exactly what had happened.

He had resolved to tell her that very morning, but when they had sat down for the *aperitivo*, he didn't have the courage. Instead Edoardo reached across the table to take hold of her hand. "*Amore*, I cannot tell you how happy I am to be here with you and..."

His cell phone rang. He thought it must be Bobby or Fred.

Benedetta's eyes registered annoyance at this interruption.

Smiling at her sheepishly, he picked it up. "Hello, this is Edoardo." There was silence on the other end.

"Hello?" Again, silence.

"Hello, can you hear me?" Edoardo was about to put the phone down when he heard a muffled voice. "Is this Edoardo Gardelli?"

"Yes, who is this?" he said, getting impatient.

"You don't know me, but I know you," said the voice, menacingly.

"Is this your idea of a joke?" Edoardo shrugged, trying to appear nonchalant for Benedetta's sake.

"We are very disappointed that you did not follow our excellent advice. There will be consequences."

"Consequences?"

"You will see, all in good time. We don't want to destroy the suspense. Danger awaits you. You should have listened. Goodbye, Mr. Gardelli." Edoardo heard a click and the line went dead.

Benedetta was staring at him, her green eyes darkening with concern. "What was that about?"

Edoardo tried to keep his voice steady. "Someone just told me to drop out of the competition, otherwise my life could be in danger."

"What?"

"It's no big deal. I don't want you to worry."

"What do you mean this is no big deal! This happened before. Do you remember Chambord when you received a phone call?"

He took both of her hands in his. "There've been several attempts to make the contestants give up. Remember, that's why Fred called us all back to Zurich, to discuss the matter with the private investigator he hired. The Zurich police department was also informed. Fred can't understand what would motivate anyone to try to call off the competition."

"And you kept me out of this?" Benedetta asked, frowning. "After all I am a police profiler. Maybe I could be of some help."

"Yes, I'm sorry. I thought it best. I knew you were busy with your work in Milan."

"I could have helped, at least with some advice," she snapped.

"*Amore*, please let's not fight. Let's try to enjoy the little time we have together."

Glaring at him in disbelief, she said, "You mean you're just going to ignore that call?"

"No, of course not. I'm going to let Fred and the PI know about it. And then we'll take it from there." Edoardo rose from his chair and pulled her toward him into an embrace.

"You can't ignore this," she said. "We need to get to the bottom of these threats."

He tried to inject a little levity into their conversation, but he could see that it had absolutely no effect on Benedetta.

GENEVA, SWITZERLAND

When Sarah and Michael arrived at the Grand Théâtre at nine thirty, they saw that the doors to the administration office didn't open until ten.

"Oh dear." Sarah was unable to hide her disappointment.

"It's not the end of the world," Michael said, putting his arm around her. "Why don't we visit the Parc des Bastions? It's very close by, and then we'll come back."

"All right," she said, looking wistfully at the Grand Théâtre.

Michael explained to Sarah that the Parc des Bastions was one of Geneva's landmarks because of the famous Monument International de la Réformation, more commonly known as Mur des Réformateurs. This monument was built along the old city walls, which date from the sixteenth century, and stretches for a hundred meters, with statues of the pioneers and protectors of the Protestant Reformation on the front of the wall.

During the Reformation, Geneva was the center of Calvinism and the monument honors Jean Calvin with a statue, along with the bearded, robed figures of Théodore de Bèze, Guillaume Farel, and John Knox— three other leaders of the movement. On the wall is the engraved motto of Geneva: Post Tenebras Lux— after the darkness, the light. The monument was inaugurated in 1909 for the four-hundredth anniversary of the birth of Calvin and the three-hundred-and-fiftieth anniversary of the foundation of the Académie de Genève, now the University of Geneva. When the citizens of Geneva adopted the Reform on May 21, 1536, they also acknowledged that education was a major feature of the movement and decided to build a school and a university that their children would be able to attend.

By the time Michael enlightened Sarah about the history of the Reform movement in Geneva, it was past ten o'clock. They crossed the Place de Neuve—the historic square considered to be the cultural epicenter of Geneva—toward the Grand Théâtre. At the porter's lodge, they asked for Mademoiselle Henriette who, according to Uncle Théodore, must have known Herbert Graf.

Sarah was growing excited at the thought that Henriette might be the keeper of the clue.

"Madame, monsieur? How can help you?" Mademoiselle Henriette inquired. She arrived so silently they hadn't heard her.

"Hello, I'm Michael Eschler and this is Sarah Majewski. We'd like to ask you about Herbert Graf, if you don't mind. And also, we'd like to know if you are aware of the Lindenmayer Award?"

"Lindenmayer? No, that doesn't ring a bell. Is it an opera award? No? Then I'm sorry. I've never heard of it."

Michael and Sarah exchanged a disappointed look.

"But you also wanted to ask me about Herbert Graf. What is it you would like to know?" asked Mademoiselle Henriette kindly.

"Are there any places in Geneva that could be related to his life here in the city?" Sarah gazed at Mademoiselle Henriette, hopefully.

"The only place I can think of would be his home at the rue Calvin, number 6, if I remember correctly."

"I know where that is," Michael said. "Thanks so much, mademoiselle, for your help."

Michael shook Sarah's hand and guided her toward the door.

"The rue Calvin is just a few minutes from here," he told Sarah. "Maybe we'll find some clue there."

While they were walking uphill toward Old Town, Michael recited what he recalled about the history of the buildings they passed. When they arrived at the address, Michael noticed a bronze plaque reading "P & de S Banquiers Privés," the name of a private bank. He rang the bell, which was soon answered by a buzzing sound; he pushed the heavy wooden door open. They walked through the paved courtyard and announced themselves at the reception desk in the entrance hall of this former stately home from the eighteenth century.

A receptionist with a practiced smile and a soft voice asked if they had an appointment. As this was not the case, she inquired if they would like to meet with one of their wealth managers.

"May I ask who the senior partner of the bank is?"

"Certainly, sir. It's Monsieur Thierry Picot."

Michael clamped his hand to his mouth to stop laughter from escaping. "Sorry for that," he apologized to the receptionist. "I didn't mean any disrespect."

Sarah looked at him, wondering what was so funny.

To the receptionist he said, "Would you let Mr. Picot know that Michael Eschler would like to see him, please?"

She nodded and turned to the phone.

In a low voice, Michael said to Sarah, "Thierry Picot was a good friend of mine, years ago, at university. He was a militant for the Marxist-Leninist Party in Geneva, even though he came from an old banking family."

Within minutes, a portly man in a black suit and burgundy tie strode into the room. He had a rosy complexion and sparkling eyes.

"Michael, *mon cher ami, quelle surprise*," he exclaimed, exuberantly. "What are you doing here?"

"It's a long story, Thierry," Michael said, reaching for his friend's hand and shaking it hardily. "First let me introduce you to Sarah Majewski."

"I'm delighted to meet you, Sarah," Thierry said. "Please, come to my office and tell me all about your business here." He took Sarah by the elbow and escorted her to the grand central stairs.

That evening, Uncle Théodore was hosting a dinner for Sarah and Michael and some of Michael's cousins and friends. He was dressed in his navy linen suit and bow tie, looking delighted in the company of such vibrant youth. He asked Sarah if they'd been able to find some clue for the riddle at the Grand Théâtre. While Michael filled the others in on the award, Sarah explained to Théodore how they'd ended up in a bank and met Thierry Picot, one of Michael's friends, who had never heard of the Lindenmayer Award.

"Thierry is now a banker?" Théodore asked. He bellowed with laughter.

"Thierry who?" Caroline asked. She was a few years younger than Michael, with a wide mouth, dark eyes and hair, and a long, straight nose.

"But Thierry Picot, of course," Michael informed her. "Can you believe it?"

Caroline exclaimed gleefully, "Thierry? Your Thierry from university?" Michael nodded and she, too, burst out laughing.

"So, what are you going to do now?" Théodore asked Sarah, kindly.

"I'm not sure. We've solved the second part of the riddle. Hans is most likely Freud's young patient, Herbert Graf. It says '*Hans handed him the key to the vociferous unknown.*' I would say that the *vociferous unknown* probably refers to the unconscious, therefore to psychoanalysis."

"That sounds very plausible. Let's see, would you remind me of the first part of the riddle, please?"

Sarah quoted the riddle: "*On the mountain road, in the city where Nations meet, Hans handed him the key to the vociferous unknown.*"

"So what made you think Geneva was the right place?" Théodore asked.

"It may have been my mistake," Michael replied. "We tried to figure out what location would fit the description '*the city where Nations meet*,' as well as the riddle's conclusion, '*on the mountain road*.'"

Grinning, Théodore said, "What if I told you about my trip to Vienna a few years ago with my beloved wife, Diane, who, as you know, was a psychoanalyst?"

Sarah saw that Théodore looked quite pleased with himself. Everyone's attention was focused on the old man.

"Of course she wanted to visit Freud's former home, which is now a museum. And do you know the address of the Freud Museum? It's on Berggasse!" He paused, as if waiting for the others to register the significance of his remarks. "Just in case you don't know, in German *Berg* means—"

"Yes, of course, it means mountain!" Sarah exclaimed. She jumped up from her chair and rushed to Théodore's side to embrace him. "You're a genius!" She laughed while he hugged her back.

"It's amazing what you have to do these days to get a beautiful woman's attention," he said with a satisfied smile. "Well, my dear, all you have to do now is book a flight to Vienna!"

ZURICHHORN PARK, ZURICH, SWITZERLAND

MAY 9, 2018

After jogging around the park, Yucun had been happy to lie on a nice patch of grass and wait for Jonathan, but an hour had passed and he still hadn't arrived. It was cooler now and she felt a chill penetrate to her bones. What could have happened to him? He was usually so punctual. She checked her phone again to see if he had called but there were no messages. In the cool evening air, a flowery scent filled her with nostalgia. She looked around and discovered a flower bed directly behind her. She spotted lilies of the valley. Their sweet smell brought back her mother's scent. She remembered her mother's soft cheek when she had last kissed her goodbye. She felt a wave of sadness realizing how much she missed her parents and her sister, Mei.

When she was still living in Shanghai, she used to work as a volunteer in the institution where her sister spent her days. Mei had become mentally disabled after meningitis, which was not diagnosed in time to stave off the side effects. Yucun was born two years after Mei's illness. Although China still had a one-child policy, which in those days was strictly enforced, her parents were allowed to have a second child, since their first one had become disabled. They knew that it was not out of compassion that such an exception was applied; it was because the state and the party wanted "normal" children for the future workforce.

Her parents had suffered so much during the Cultural Revolution. They'd had an extremely difficult life during this chaotic, violent ten years, and the consequences on their health had been devastating. Her mother, who'd been a lovely young woman—with a flawless complexion and elegant bone structure—had grown old prematurely and was suffering from regular spells of rheumatism and arthritis, which for a painter was an agonizing ailment. Before the revolution, she'd been a successful artist with regular commissions from party leaders, nationally recognized for her exquisite landscapes. Yucun's father, a renowned art historian at the University of Shanghai, had been sent to work as a street cleaner during this time and had developed emphysema. He'd been reinstated at the university after the revolution. But by then, he'd become a broken man, physically and mentally, and soon afterward, he'd been offered the chance of an early retirement.

Yucun hoped that her success would mitigate her parents' suffering. If she won, it would give her the career boost she'd been hoping for and she would get international recognition for her scientific achievements. It would also compensate for the four-year separation from her parents. Though her parents had encouraged her to go abroad, she knew that her departure had caused them unhappiness. She still remembered their last meeting. When they had said goodbye on that hot, humid summer day in Shanghai, they had known that they would not see one another for many years. Yucun was thirty when she left China for the first time in her life. She'd received a postdoctoral fellowship from the Rockefeller Foundation to join a neurophysiology laboratory at UCLA to work on a project exploring the molecular mechanisms of memory. She felt wonderfully carefree, since for the first time in her student life, she would not have to work in order to pay for her studies.

Despite the loneliness she felt, leaving China had turned out to be a positive experience for Yucun: the easy lifestyle, the fascinating work, the endless stream of sunny days in California. And then, of course, meeting Jonathan, the affair that followed, and now, best of all, the serendipitous luck of their both ending up in Switzerland—and the rekindling of their relationship.

Wiping the tears from her eyes, she was about to get up and return to her hotel when she spotted Jonathan hurrying along the path. Panting, he ran up to her. "I'm so sorry, I'm late," he said. "We had an emergency meeting with Fred. Then I had some unexpected business to attend to. I came as soon as I could."

"Is everything all right?" she said, getting up from the grass. Again, she felt a chill.

"Hopefully, but Fred and the PI are intensifying their search for the culprits."

"How come?"

They now stood opposite each other. She could see that he was sweating.

"It seems that someone is really intent on disrupting the contest. As you know, each of the contestants has suffered some kind of setback: threatening messages, problems with their iPhones or their iPads. And Fred is getting very upset about it."

"That's terrible," she said. "I guess I've been very lucky."

"Yes, you have," he said, smiling oddly.

"I suppose that's why I'm ahead of everyone with only two more riddles to solve."

"Not just luck, my dear. You mustn't forget you're brilliant..." He did not complete his sentence. He drew her behind a bush.

"How odd," she thought. "Who is he hiding from?" Through the branches of the bush, she discerned a dog she thought she recognized: Oban, Bobby's dog.

"Why are we hiding?" she asked.

"I didn't want him to see us."

"Why not?"

"We don't want him to get the wrong idea."

"About what?"

"Well, my dear, I didn't think it was necessary to share with Fred and Bobby the exact nature of our relationship. If we had told them, then the other contestants would also find out and they might think that you had an unfair advantage by being connected so intimately with someone on the award team."

Before Yucun had time to ponder this information, he suggested that they go home and have dinner. "I have just the place in mind," he said, stepping from behind the bushes. In the distance, Yucun caught sight of Bobby and Oban.

BOSWELL'S APARTMENT, ZURICH, SWITZERLAND

The whole day, Boswell had felt invincible, able to deal with any liability, the master of his own destiny. But now he felt anxious and could not stop pacing. His apartment felt small, cramped, as if he were in a cage. He questioned his latest decisions. Perhaps he should not have hired Cuno Milic to sabotage the competition. Perhaps he would have done better to deal with the contestants on his own and facilitate Yucun's victory. He could still help Yucun, but now that he had hired someone, he was running more risks. This feeling of anxiety, as if he were walking a tightrope, was bringing back feelings he'd had years ago when he was dating Mara and also indulging in cocaine. After he and Mara had told her father their intentions to get married, he had entered a very difficult period. He had felt increasingly insecure about his ability to satisfy her father's expectations. Nothing he did seemed to satisfy the man. At the same time, Jonathan's own father was fired from his job through no fault of his own. In retrospect, this had impacted Jonathan as a young man. He had been shaken to see that his father, who had worked for thirty years for the same company, could be so summarily dispatched simply because the company had to cut back.

Jonathan remembered in detail the first time he decided to tamper with the data of his research. He could still see the spot appearing on his computer screen after fiddling with Photoshop. He was analyzing the presence of a protein in the blood of patients who presented early signs of memory loss. He'd had some very promising initial results showing the presence of a protein in blood samples of patients who had subsequently developed Alzheimer's disease. This was a major finding: This protein would be a marker for the diagnosis of Alzheimer's in the earliest stages and hopefully identify patients who could benefit from novel treatments that would be developed. The discovery could be published in a top scientific journal making his research very visible, exactly what he needed to achieve a permanent position at the university. However, he had been unable to reproduce these encouraging preliminary data. The goddamn protein would not appear on the screen after the analytical procedures that he did on the blood of additional patients. He had seen it a few times, so it must be true. The fact that he could not reproduce the initial data must be due to some technical problem. So why not "help" the analytical technique with some creative interventions with Photoshop? The protein must be there. All that was needed was to "facilitate" its appearance. Using this rationale, Jonathan went back and forth, back and forth, wondering whether or not to add the spot, until he thought he would go completely mad. In the end, he had fudged the data.

The first time had been the most difficult. After that, he kept telling himself that whether he fudged one or two or three data, it didn't really make much difference.

He wondered now, too, if Yucun had sensed something amiss earlier that evening in the park. It was very bad timing, Bobby showing up with Oban. Boswell wanted to keep his relationship with Yucun absolutely secret. It seemed unlikely that she would guess his true motive for her to participate in the contest. What had made him uneasy was the fact that she had turned down his invitation to stay the night. She had never done that before, but perhaps she was still miffed at his being late for their appointment. He didn't feel at all tired. Perhaps he should take a walk along the lake. It might calm him. Exercise was always an excellent way of dealing with anxiety. He must resist the urge for more cocaine. He had to admit that it was becoming more and more difficult.

BENEDETTA'S APARTMENT, MILAN, ITALY

MAY 9, 2018

Lying in bed after a wonderful night of lovemaking, Edoardo was just thinking that he couldn't remember feeling so relaxed when Benedetta came running into the room. She looked upset. He was about to ask her what had happened when she threw an envelope onto the bed, spilling several photographs of him with Giovanna, who was leaning over and about to kiss his lips.

"That's not all," she said. "Look inside the envelope."

With trembling hands, he opened the envelope and found a message constructed out of newspaper clippings. He read, "Edoardo does not care if something happens to you."

"I can't believe that you would do something like this," she said.

"Of course I wouldn't. It's not what you think."

"How do you explain it?" Benedetta insisted.

"I should have told you."

"Yes, Edoardo, you should have told me what?"

"What I mean is that they sent me this photograph before."

"What do you mean?" Benedetta sounded really angry now.

"I never found the right time to tell you," Edoardo said apologetically.

"So you admit that you know this woman, Edoardo?"

"She used to be my teacher."

"Oh my God! And you probably expect me to believe that there is nothing going on between you?"

"Yes," he said.

She picked up the photograph and peered at it. "You seem quite happy to be kissed!"

He stood, wondering how he could convince her. It was an impossible situation. "Look, I'm telling you the truth, I swear. I was attracted to my teacher as a student, but this was many years ago. I had a crush on her. She sent me an e-mail a couple of months ago when she read about the award and the contestants. She asked me to give a talk to her students if I was in

Italy sometime during the competition. After my lecture, she walked over and kissed me and someone—a man with a scar who had been following me—took a photograph."

"You must have given her some encouragement."

"Benedetta, I love you. I didn't do anything beyond this kiss!"

"Enough! I'm not going to listen to another word. It's just too hard to believe. This is too much!"

She grabbed her coat and handbag and stormed out of the room. Everything had gone terribly wrong.

LINDENMAYER CORPORATE HEADQUARTERS, ZURICH, SWITZERLAND

MAY 9, 2018

It was hard to believe, Boswell thought, that only nine days had passed since the launch of the competition. The last couple of days had been very hectic, and increasingly he had the feeling of not being in control. He, who was punctual to a fault, had been late on several occasions, and each time, his lateness had resulted in unforeseen consequences. Just when he was starting to grow tired of Yucun's devotion, she had shown that she was quite independent, turning down his offer to spend the night. Now Fred knew about his relationship with Yucun. As Boswell had bent over to kiss Yucun, he had sensed someone watching him, but when he looked up at the window the curtain fell back into place. He had pretended not to understand Fred's insinuations about his relationship with Yucun.

Even though it was extremely unlikely Fred would think it odd that only Yucun had been spared from threats and connect this fact with Boswell's predilection for her, Boswell had taken the precaution of sparing Sarah as well as Yucun in the latest difficulties he had set up for the contestants. How he wished he could have observed Edoardo's expression when he received the text with photographs of Giovanna. Boswell laughed. He could not stop. It seemed funnier than the incident warranted.

Comina was the only person who worried Boswell. He was a professional and therefore Boswell would have to be careful. It didn't take Comina long to figure out that the Bulgarian lead was not the right one. Shaking hands, Boswell had felt Comina taking his measure.

Looking out the window, Boswell noticed a particular angle of the light as raindrops started falling, which reminded him of the last time he had seen Mara. They had met in the garden of her father's house. She had known as soon as he appeared that something was terribly wrong. He was very pale and shaking. For a while they had walked in the garden without talking. He had his arm around her waist and she looked particularly beautiful. She was wearing a white dress that stood out against the green of the bushes. He kept thinking that this was the last time he would see her. Perhaps the last time he would talk with her. He did not know how to begin.

He kept visualizing the meeting he'd had with James Hewitt-Palmer, the dean of the University of Johannesburg Medical School, only a few hours earlier. He remembered the exact tone of the dean's voice as he had said, "I regret to inform you that the Johannesburg University Hospital has decided to dismiss you as a consequence of the findings by the Ethics Committee, that has determined that the results of your latest publications were falsified." He then handed the letter of dismissal to Jonathan. "Such a shame," Hewitt-Palmer added. "You're a damn good scientist with so much potential."

Jonathan could feel the letter in his pocket. He couldn't bear waiting any longer. He stopped beneath a purple jacaranda. He took both of Mara's hands in his. He felt some drops of water on his: It had started raining. "I'm so sorry, Mara. What I have to tell you is bound to be very hurtful—"

"What is it?" She had looked up at him with such trust.

He could not find the words to explain what he had done. The rain was now hitting the soil hard. "I changed some data—and now I have been dismissed—"

"What?" she said, horrified.

"I did it for you."

"For me? I don't understand."

"Yes, for you. I wanted to—" He could not explain that he had tampered with the data so that he could get high-visibility articles and tenure faster, thereby securing her father's acquiescence to their marriage. Saying something against her father would only make Jonathan look even more of a cad. How could she respect someone who had lied and tampered the results of his experiments? At that same moment, they heard her father calling for her from his bedroom terrace. Jonathan had turned away, and, ignoring Mara's calls, he had raced through the garden in the pouring rain toward the gate.

The knocking on the door to his office grew more peremptory. He had no idea how long someone had been banging. It could only be that annoying Bobby, no doubt. He either came in without knocking or he practically broke down the door. Let's just hope he had remembered not to bring his awful dog.

"Come in," Boswell managed to say at last.

LINDENMAYER RESIDENCE, KÜSNACHT, SWITZERLAND

MAY 9, 2018

Sitting at his desk, Fred was trying to focus on what Edoardo was telling him over the phone, but he felt tired and old.

"That's all I know, Fred," Edoardo said.

"Edoardo, I'm going to call Comina and ask him to look into it. Why don't we talk later," Fred suggested.

"Okay," Edoardo replied.

"I feel so badly for you and the other contestants. I never imagined this turning into such a stressful competition."

"Don't worry, Fred," Edoardo said. "We're still really into the competition and the riddle-solving hasn't lost its appeal. I can't wait to figure out the next one."

"I'm glad to hear that," Fred said.

"There is something else I wanted to ask you, Fred," Edoardo said. "Benedetta is a police profiler, as you may know, and she would be happy to help us on the case. She'd like to start working up a profile of the person who sent the pictures."

"Good idea," Fred said. "Why don't you ask Bobby to call Benedetta? I'd be delighted to have another professional working on the case."

"Sure, Fred, and I imagine that between Comina, the police, and Benedetta, someone is bound to come up with something."

"Thanks, Edoardo. That would be really helpful. Talk to you later." Fred hung up.

He felt terrible at the thought of what poor Edoardo must have gone through.

"If I'd known there would be so many problems," he thought, "I don't think I would have launched this competition." He was trying not to feel defeated, but it was difficult not to think that he was fighting a losing battle. Only the thought of Meg and his plan for a new research institute gave him hope.

"You need to fight back," he thought, surveying the room, his gaze landing on the Matisse. "You need to make sure that your project succeeds. You owe it not just to Meg but to the patients and their families. You can't abandon their hopes because of a bunch of criminals." Fred got up and stared through the window, where he saw Meg walking, arm in arm, with dear Boswell. He was coming to rely on him more and more. Looking back, he was glad that he had ignored his initial misgivings. Everyone should be allowed a second chance. The knowledge that Meg was in Boswell's capable hands allowed him to take a few hours off. After closing the door to his office, he felt pleased at having succeeded in changing his mind-set and he now looked forward to the prospect of meeting his friends for their weekly golf foursome.

On his way to the first tee of the golf club in Zumikon, Fred tried to concentrate on the spectacular view and forget the travails of the award. The course was quite challenging, hilly with some very scenic holes. His grandfather had been one of the founders of the club in 1930. He remembered his father saying that the club insisted on hiring former officers of the British army, preferably of Scottish origin, to work as secretaries.

"They invented the damned game," he would say. "They have the right attitude and authority to guard us against all the business and vulgarity that is invading what should remain a gentleman's sport."

His father had been very appreciative of the discreet manner in which the golf club in Zumikon was run. It reminded him of the golf club at Muirfield, near Gullane, the home of the Honourable Company of Edinburgh Golfers. His father had been accepted as an overseas member of the HCEG thanks to some acquaintances he had made while doing an internship at the Royal Bank of Scotland in Edinburgh, when he was just out of university. To this day, there are only about seventy overseas members of what is rightly considered the oldest and most exclusive golf club in the world. The HCEG was established in 1744, ten years before the better-known and today exceedingly visible St Andrews Golf Club. Members of the HCEG played initially at Leith on a nine-hole course, but by the end of the eighteenth century moved to Musselburgh, until the Muirfield links were opened in 1891. Members of the HCEG share a passion for golf, good company, food, wine, and whiskey, but they are very much averse to bragging and any allusion to business. Muirfield is a marvelous example of a links course, the terms "links" meaning that the stretch of land onto which the course is designed links the sand and shores to the mainland. It is regularly home to the British Open and has been the theater of memorable and dramatic final rounds of the most prestigious golf tournaments. Its values are authentic and traditions are highly valued. Muirfield and the HCEG are simply unique. As Meg used to define Muirfield, it was a club where you could take your dogs but not your wife. This would drive Fred crazy because it was absolutely untrue. Granted that HCEG had been a club for men only, like many others around the world, but things have changed, and now membership is open to women.

A defining tradition in the life of the HCEG is "the dinner." It takes place every five or six weeks. Dress code is formal: black tie and kilt for those who own one and care to wear it. The evening begins at seven with drinks, whiskey or gin and tonic are de rigueur. The next hour is dedicated to organizing matches between members until the next dinner to be convened a few weeks later. There is only one format for the matches: match-play foursomes over thirty-six holes. At eight sharp, the steward announces, very formally, "Dinner is served." At the end of the dinner, celebrated by a toast to the Queen, a long recitation begins, during which a member of each foursome formally requests permission from the captain to play against another team. Once all the matches have been announced to the captain and members have made bets on their favorite team, a couple of hours have gone by and a few bottles of red wine and whiskey have been consumed. Everyone goes home in a rather jolly mood.

Fred had come to know Muirfield when his father brought him there to play the annual "fathers versus sons" tournament. Sons between the ages of eighteen and thirty and their fathers are invited to play over the weekend. It is also a very friendly social event, which provides the opportunity for members to get to know potential future members. Fred had eventually been accepted during his forties as an overseas member just like his father. Since he had moved back to Switzerland, he had tried to play at Muirfield more frequently. Gareth Cochran usually caddied for him during his matches; like many of the caddies, he lived in nearby Gullane.

One day Fred had asked him about his son, Bobby. Gareth was very proud of Bobby. He had graduated with a degree in computer science from the University of Leeds and was hired right after his graduation by a small start-up in Edinburgh.

"He is not doing too well," Gareth said, his usual smile vanishing. "He's been laid off. Some kind of merger, and he's sacked after working so hard for five years. No recognition!" Fred had asked to meet Gareth's son and a few weeks later Bobby was working as an IT manager for the Lindenmayer Corporation in Zurich.

VIENNA, AUSTRIA

MAY 10, 2018

Sitting in the historic Café Sperl, near the museum quarter, Sarah thought how friendly people were in this city. She felt pleased when the word *gemütlich* came to her. She hadn't forgotten all the German she had learned in school. She could still picture her German teacher, who wore thick glasses that made her eyes look huge, explaining that the exact meaning of *gemütlich* was difficult to convey but could best be translated as "relaxed" or "easygoing."

If only Michael were sitting opposite her. It was too bad that he had been unable to accompany her. He would have loved this delicious Sacher Torte. She had noticed that he had such a sweet tooth. He would also have enjoyed hearing the guide's explanation of the history of the café. Standing in one corner surrounded by a small group of tourists, the guide announced in a very dramatic tone, "Let me tell you about the Sacher Torte. This world-famous cake was created by Franz Sacher, a baker from Vienna, in 1832 for the Duke Klemens von Metternich, who was an Austrian statesman and perhaps the most important diplomat of his era."

As Sarah listened to the guide's account, she became aware that a young woman with bright red hair kept looking in her direction. The woman looked vaguely familiar, but Sarah couldn't think where she had seen her before.

The guide's voice became increasingly dramatic, as if demanding her audience's attention. "The cake consists of two chocolate biscuit layers separated by apricot jam and glazed with chocolate. There are two official recipes, and two Viennese pastry shops, Sacher and Demel, got into legal fights about which of them was allowed to sell their cake as the 'original' Sacher Torte. In the nineteenth century already, this famous cake had been at the heart of an argument over which ingredients should be used for a true Sacher Torte. It seems that the people in Vienna took their baking so seriously that the Congress of Vienna had to rule on the matter." Here, the guide laughed.

At the same moment, Sarah realized that the young woman with red hair now stood by her table. "Excuse me, miss," the woman said. "I wonder if I could ask you a few questions. I'm writing a piece for *Kurier*, a Vienna newspaper, on tourists visiting the city."

"Well, I'm happy to talk with you for a few minutes, but I have to go to the Freud Museum."

"A good choice," the woman said. "It's such an interesting museum."

"I expect so."

"This is your first visit to Vienna?" the woman asked, then proceeded to ask Sarah a series of questions: the length of her stay, where she was from, and why she had chosen Vienna.

For some reason, Sarah felt reluctant to tell the woman about her involvement in the contest.

While she answered the woman's questions, Sarah's attention kept drifting to the guide's explanations: the culinary controversy involving the Wiener schnitzel, a Viennese-style veal fillet, one of the most famous traditional dishes. "It is actually a northern Italian specialty," the guide explained. "And no one is sure how the recipe got to Vienna. It could have found its way here in the fifteenth or sixteenth century, but according to another theory the schnitzel was introduced by Field Marshal Radetzky in 1857. The dispute over the dish's origins continues to this day between people from Vienna, who insist on calling it Wiener schnitzel and people from Milan who insist on calling it cotoletta alla milanese. The schnitzel is prepared from a thinly sliced piece of veal flank, which has to be tenderized with a steak hammer. It is then dipped into flour, eggs, and bread crumbs before being fried in butter or olive oil. It was originally a dish reserved for feasts, and in the seventeenth and eighteenth centuries, gold dust was mixed into the bread crumbs to create an extra-golden, appetizing color. Nowadays, it has become one of the most popular meals among Austrians and there is even a fast-food chain serving only schnitzels."

When Sarah turned to look at the journalist again, she found that the woman had gone. However, she had left a note. Sarah idly lifted it from the table, thinking that it was probably just a thank you or a note indicating why the woman had vanished so abruptly.

As she unfolded the note, her hands started to tremble. She recognized the gray paper, the typewritten letters. *You chose to ignore our first warning. This is your second and final notice. If you do not give up the contest something terrible will happen to you.*

She tried not to panic, but she felt faint.

She reached for her cell phone, pressed the 1 key, and after two rings Bobby's voice came on.

"I don't think I can continue with the contest," she said.

"Why? What happened? You sound upset."

"I received a note threatening that something terrible could happen to me."

"When? How? Where are you?"

She explained what had just occurred.

"Listen, I'm going to call Comina," Bobby said. "Then I'll call you right back. You stay put. Nothing can happen to you while you're in the café."

As Sarah waited for Bobby's call, she glanced around the café and suddenly remembered where she had seen the young journalist with red hair. They had crossed paths in the hallway of her hotel.

LINDENMAYER CORPORATE HEADQUARTERS, ZURICH, SWITZERLAND

MAY 10, 2018

Everything was going according to plan, Boswell thought, pacing in his office. No one would suspect the car accident Philip's partner, Julian, had suffered in California was related to the competition. They certainly couldn't accuse him. He was in Switzerland. It almost certainly meant that Philip would withdraw. At the very least, it would mean that Philip would have to interrupt his search to fly to Los Angeles. Boswell couldn't help smiling at his success. Now, if he could just handle Comina, all would be well! He should be arriving any minute.

Hearing a knock at the door, he thought it was Comina, but it was Bobby.

"I have some very bad news," Bobby said, panting.

The poor man, Boswell thought, really should diet. He seemed to have put on more weight.

"Oh." Boswell did his best to adopt a tone of alarm and surprise.

Bobby then proceeded to describe in excruciating detail the unfortunate circumstances of the accident. Boswell had to commend himself for his self-control. He wanted so badly to tell him to get to the point. All he wanted to know was if Philip had withdrawn from the competition.

"They're not sure Julian will live," Bobby said.

"Terrible," Boswell said, then seeing that he had not adopted the necessary degree of concern, he added, "It's hard to believe."

"I'll say it's hard to believe. We've had such bad luck that it makes you wonder—"

"Wonder?" Boswell felt his mood change in an instant, though he realized the next moment that Bobby's remark was quite innocent and devoid of any subtle intent.

"Philip was so upset. He wanted to quit immediately."

"It's probably best for all concerned," Boswell said. Boswell was about to make up some excuse to get rid of the man when the door opened to reveal Comina.

"I'm sorry," Comina said. "Perhaps I'm catching you at a bad time? I was with Fred and he told me to knock on your door."

"I was about to call you," Bobby said.

"Quite fortuitous," Boswell said. "Your visit, I mean." Boswell wondered how much of the conversation Comina had overheard.

In any case, Bobby filled him in.

"Please do sit down." Boswell gestured to a capacious armchair, but Comina walked over to the window instead.

"I wonder if I might ask you a few questions?" he said to Boswell.

"Of course, it would be my pleasure to assist in any way I can," Boswell said. "You may leave, Bobby, unless you are also wanted for questioning." He stared quizzically at Comina.

"No, that's quite all right. Bobby and I have already spoken."

As soon as Bobby had stepped out, Comina swiveled from the window. "I'm puzzled by the motives of the person or persons who are attempting to disrupt this contest and I thought you might be able to help me."

"Me?" Boswell placed his hand on his chest in a gesture of surprise. "Why me?"

"Well, for one, you have known Fred for quite some time and you are probably the best informed about his friends and acquaintances or people who would like to harm him, particularly now that his wife is no longer able to help us."

"I see. I see. Meg's condition is quite disheartening."

"What I cannot understand is how it would be advantageous for someone—for anyone—to derail the contest. What is to be gained from it?"

"Oh, I don't know," Boswell said. "I really don't."

"It cannot be for monetary gain. The only reason I can come up with is that someone has a perverse need to make poor Fred suffer. Whoever he or she is must be a complete freak—unnatural, perverted. I don't use the word 'evil' easily, but in this case it seems warranted." Comina punctuated each word by slamming his fist on Boswell's desk.

Boswell had the uncomfortable feeling that these words were directed toward him. For a moment, he wondered if Comina had figured everything out, but then he told himself that he was being ridiculous. Slowly, he bent over and picked up several objects Comina had sent flying to the floor, among them one of Yucun's origami. He was about to slip it into a drawer when Comina asked him what he was holding.

"Origami," Boswell explained.

"You are full of surprises, Boswell," he said. "I would never have pictured you doing origami in your spare time."

Boswell didn't respond, thinking it was probably better not to disabuse of the notion.

"Well," Comina said. "If anything comes to mind later, do let me know."

"Of course," Boswell said. "Certainly, I will make it a point to think of every person Fred knows." He then gently closed the door after Comina.

VIENNA, AUSTRIA

Though Sarah had felt reassured after speaking with Comina and later with two security men from the Swiss embassy, she could not shake the feeling that she was being followed as she made her way to the Freud Museum. In front of the Kunsthistorisches Museum, a man seemed to peer over the top of his newspaper. "He was just admiring you," she could hear Michael say. Passing through the Hofburg grounds, she kept glancing over her shoulder. Once it was just a little girl running after a red ball. Another time, it was jogger.

From the Sigmund Freud Park, she took Währinger Strasse to the famous Berggasse, where the Freud family had lived from September 1891 to June 1938 when they were forced to leave and live in exile in London. At the museum she was told by the woman selling tickets that the curator, Dr. Magda Müller, was in a meeting.

"Would it be possible to see her after my visit?" Sarah asked in her soft voice.

"You have to make an appointment," the woman said, in a peremptory tone. She was dressed all in black except for a fake red rose pinned to her breast pocket. "She is very busy."

"Mr. Lindenmayer wanted me to contact her."

"Lindenmayer?"

"Lindenmayer," she said.

"Wait over there," she pointed to a bench in the entrance.

Sitting on the bench, Sarah wondered if there was some kind of mistake. Perhaps this was not the right place after all, or perhaps someone was trying to make her think it was not the right place.

There was nothing she could do until Dr. Müller came out of her meeting. While she waited she might as well read about her cousin Katia's hero, Dr. Freud, in the leaflet she had taken at the entrance. Most of the biographical details she was familiar with. He was the father of psychoanalysis and had developed techniques in the treatment of psychological and emotional disorders. He was born on May 6, 1856, in Freiberg, Moravia, now Pribor in the Czech Republic. He had graduated from the Medical School of the University of Vienna. In September 1891, he moved to Berggasse 19 in Vienna where he had worked for the next forty-seven years.

From time to time, Sarah looked up to see if the door to the conference room had opened, or she glanced at the lady who had spoken to her in such an unfriendly fashion. She read that Freud had first used the term "psychoanalysis" in his paper "The Aetiology of Hysteria." In 1902 he had begun a weekly discussion on psychoanalysis with some like-minded colleagues. In 1908, the group started to call itself the Vienna Psychoanalytic Society. Two years later, the International Psychoanalytical Association was set up in Nuremberg. The Swiss psychologist Carl Jung had become its first president. On March 12, 1938, German troops marched into Austria and on June 4, with the help and support of numerous international personalities, including Princess Marie Bonaparte, a former patient and now a fellow psychoanalyst, Freud was allowed to immigrate with his family to London. He died on September 23, 1939.

Sitting on the uncomfortable bench, Sarah thought how sad it was that Freud had died in exile. She needed to stretch her legs, but she was afraid of missing Dr. Müller. She still decided to take a quick peak at the various rooms. As she walked through the consulting room and into the study, she noticed that Freud's work and items from his life were arranged chronologically and displayed in glasses cases. Leaning over to take a better look at a first edition, she caught sight of a woman peering over her shoulder. The woman's hair was wrapped in a kerchief. When she first entered the room, Sarah had mistaken her for a cleaning woman, but she recognized the red-haired woman who had addressed her in the café. The woman muttered in English, "You stupid girl. You did not listen." By the time Sarah had registered what she had just heard and turned around, the woman had disappeared.

Turning from the glass case, Sarah ran out of the room after her, trying to find her.

"Running in the museum is forbidden," called out a security guard.

Sarah couldn't see the woman anywhere. As she called Bobby, to brief him about the incident, she collided with someone, another woman.

"What is going on?" A name tag pinned to the woman's dress indicated that she was Dr. Müller.

"I'm so sorry," Sarah said, breathlessly. "I didn't mean to cause a disturbance. I'm one of the contestants from the Lindenmayer Award."

"I told her to wait on the bench," the woman dressed in black said.

"I waited but then I thought I would take a peek at the museum," Sarah said.

"I told her you were in a meeting," the woman said, touching her red rose.

"Yes, yes, Frau Lotte. Come with me, Sarah. You look quite pale. Let us go to my office." She held Sarah's arm and guided her to her office, where a large black cat sat in one chair. "I hope you don't mind cats," Dr. Müller said.

"Oh no, I love them." Sarah went to the cat and caressed it. "My grandmother had a black cat."

"I think you have something to tell me," Dr. Müller said. "The solution to the riddle?"

"'*On the mountain road*' refers to Berggasse where Freud had his practice. '*In the city where Nations meet*' is Vienna, the site of several UN organizations. '*Hans handed him the key to the vociferous unknown*' is a reference to Little Hans, one of the founding cases of psychoanalysis, which helped Freud in his understanding of the unconscious—'unknown' in German is *unbewusst*, which has since been translated as 'unconscious.'"

"Excellent," Dr. Müller said. "Let's take the picture then."

As Sarah walked back to her hotel after that eventful afternoon, she wondered what the relationship between

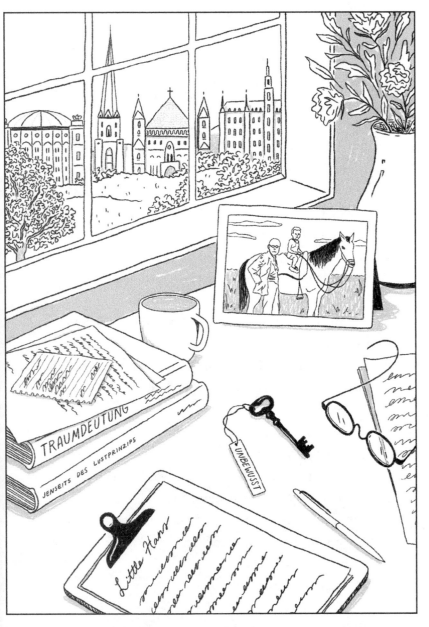

On the mountain road, in the city where Nations meet,
Hans handed him the key to the vociferous unknown.

psychoanalysis and Alzheimer's disease could be. She really needed to understand, her thoughts seemed to be in a state of great confusion. First there had been the false lead to Geneva, where Little Hans had been the director of the opera house, and now that she had finally solved the riddle correctly, she really needed some clarification. Suddenly she knew who could explain it to her, Katia of course who had first introduced her to Freud and Little Hans. She grabbed her cell phone from her coat pocket and looked for Katia's number. As it was ringing, she suddenly remembered the time difference with New York where Katia lived.

"Hello? Sarah is that you?" Katia didn't seem to be asleep.

Sarah checked her watch. No, it was just past five in Vienna, so it was late morning in New York.

"Sarah? Are you there?"

"Yes, Katia, so sorry, I was afraid I would disturb you, how are you?"

"Doing great, thanks. And you? Still running around Europe for the competition?"

"Yes, I'm in Vienna right now and I need you to fill me in on the connection between Alzheimer's and psychoanalysis."

There was a moment of silence on the other end.

"That's not a question I get every day" Katia replied. "You always did like to test my brain."

"Well, this time there is no competition, as I literally know nothing about psychoanalysis," Sarah commented humbly. "Please share your great mind with me on this."

"Great, for once I'll have the upper hand!" exclaimed Katia happily. "This is how I would explain it. Psychoanalysis is based on the notion that unconscious memories exist and that they can unexpectedly emerge into daily life. As you know Alzheimer's patients, particularly in advanced states, present major cognitive impairments and memory losses. These impairments contribute to creating a loss of identity, which can cause a state of anxiety, anger, and confusion. By engaging in reminiscence sessions inspired by psychoanalysis, often using drawings or photographs provided by relatives, patients can somehow reconnect with some familiar aspects of their life. This approach can provide a possibility of establishing a contact with the patient, who can then have, even if ever so briefly, the feeling of having reacquired an identity. I would add that psychoanalysis could also be of benefit for the caregivers of Alzheimer's patients, and help them establish a contact with the patient, who is unable to consciously produce the symbolic representations and meaning of words. Although psychoanalysis can certainly not be called a therapy for Alzheimer's, it is probable that if a psychoanalytical context is offered to patients and caregivers, it may result in an appeasing effect on their anxieties and fears."

As Sarah tried to process everything Katia had explained, there was an exclamation on the other side of the line.

"Oh no, it is almost lunchtime! I'm so sorry Sarah, I need to pick up Johnny at day care. Let's talk later."

KLOTEN AIRPORT, ZURICH, SWITZERLAND

_____

_____

_____

_____

_____

MAY 11, 2018

As soon as Yucun entered the arrival hallway, she spotted Boswell. He was dressed in a navy blue suit and appeared to have come from a meeting of some kind. He was peering down at his iPhone and frowning. She was so glad to see him. During the entire flight from Paris, after solving the Chambord riddle, she had pictured this moment. Before the plane started its descent, she had spent considerable time in the bathroom, to the annoyance of the other passengers, who knocked several times. She had been determined to look her very best: makeup perfectly applied, hair gleaming, and breath fresh. She was wearing a new dress—white with tiny blue flowers.

She hurried over to Jonathan, observing with some amusement but also disappointment that he continued to stare at his phone. She threw her arms around him, almost knocking his phone out of his hands.

"What the—" He looked up annoyed, but then he saw that it was Yucun and he smiled. "You surprised me."

"What are you looking at?" she said, teasingly.

"Nothing. It's just for work."

"And I thought you would be pining for me."

"Naturally." He took her by the arm. "You look very pleased with yourself."

"I'm just so happy to see you." She smiled up at him.

"It wouldn't have anything to do with the contest— and the fact that you have solved the fourth riddle? I think we should celebrate. Let's go to Pavillion at Baur Au Lac."

"Really?" She laughed.

"Why not?"

She held his arm tightly all the way to his car, a sleek black BMW with seats that smelled deliciously of leather. She sank into the seat.

"This is really nice," she said, as he merged onto the highway.

"Glad to oblige," he said in his usual ironic tone.

"I have something to tell you."

"You sound very serious."

"I've decided to quit," Yucun said.

"What?" He looked perplexed.

"The contest. I just have a really bad feeling about the whole thing, and I was so frightened by all the threats the other contestants received. You don't know what it's like to be threatened. My parents constantly felt threatened, and although I never experienced it personally, I can't deal with even the suggestion of a threat."

"Don't be ridiculous," he said, speeding up and passing a car.

"That seems a bit harsh."

"You have nothing to fear."

"How do you know? They could be following us right now." She turned to look out the back window.

"I assure you, my dear, these threats present absolutely no danger. Look, has anyone been hurt?" he asked, intentionally neglecting to mention Philip's boyfriend's accident.

"Not yet."

"You're not to quit the contest. I forbid it."

"Why does it mean so much to you?"

"I want you to succeed. I don't want some silly threat to prevent you from winning. You know what they say, 'Behind every great woman is a man.'"

"Hmm." She smiled. It was very endearing how seriously he took her career. She hadn't met many men like Jonathan, who were genuinely invested in their girlfriend's or wife's career. Usually, it was the opposite. They felt threatened by their success and intelligence.

"Now that we've resolved that," he said, adjusting his glasses, "shall we swing by your hotel so that you can change?"

"I just bought this dress! Don't you like it?"

"It's just that, well, don't take this the wrong way, but it looks a bit young."

She flushed with embarrassment and pursed her lips. This was not what she had pictured at all. "Are you saying that I'm old?"

"I'm sorry. I shouldn't have said that."

"No, you shouldn't have."

"Will you forgive me?"

He looked so penitent that she decided it was silly to allow one remark to ruin the whole evening. "Very well, but just remember I'm only thirty-three, not exactly middle-aged."

"Of course, my dear, and you don't look it at all, barely twenty—in fact, I'm surprised that you don't get carded."

BOSWELL'S APARTMENT, ZURICH, SWITZERLAND

MAY 11, 2018

Boswell listened to the soft sound of Yucun's breathing. She had just fallen asleep. He had nearly blown it, he thought, remembering the scene in the car. He had hardly been able to believe what he was hearing when she announced that she was thinking of quitting the contest, and then, like a fool, he had made that stupid comment about her dress! He'd had to spend the whole evening trying to get back in her good graces. He was confident that he had succeeded. She had not hesitated to sleep over at his apartment. On the contrary, it was she who had suggested they skip dessert so that they could return to his apartment. Then she had thrown herself at him, as if she hadn't seen him in months. It seemed to work rather well for them to be apart for a few days.

Seeing Yucun in that white dress had reminded him of Mara, and for a moment, he could not contain his disappointment. He would never again experience the intense feelings he'd had for Mara. It was impossible. Waiting for Yucun at the airport terminal, he had also been annoyed to find a message from Comina requesting the pleasure of his company tomorrow. Comina wanted to ask him a few questions, again.

Comina made him uneasy. Just thinking of him made him feel the need for more cocaine. He tiptoed into the bathroom and snorted some of the white powder. Then he padded over to the balcony. He stared up at the sky and the stars. Suddenly, they seemed so bright and more beautiful than he had ever seen before, which was strange because he usually felt that the sky above Switzerland was disappointing in comparison with the sky above South Africa. Everything looked so small here.

He just couldn't get over how wonderful he felt! It was the most delicious feeling. Too bad one couldn't feel like this all the time. He literally felt as if he could fly over the balcony and across the water like a big black bird. Comina probably just wanted to ask him some boring questions about Fred and whether he had come up with anyone who might have a grudge against his boss. The irony of Comina asking him about the threat was really quite amusing. And, just for the record, Boswell didn't have anything against Fred. He was almost sorry that getting back at the young scientists involved ruining Fred's contest. The truth was that he could not stand them. He could not bear to watch them succeed where he had failed. He could only stand it if Yucun won thanks to the help he was planning to offer her.

VIENNA, AUSTRIA

_____

_____

_____

_____

_____

MAY 12, 2018, 10:00 P.M.

Edoardo was trying to enjoy his after-dinner coffee on the terrace of the majestic Hotel Sacher in Vienna. He had just solved the fourth riddle. But the truth was that he had never felt so alone. He didn't blame Benedetta for being upset about the pictures. Right now, he had to resist the urge to call and share with her this wonderful book he was reading.

Although he was not particularly keen on psychoanalysis—he found it too "unscientific"—Edoardo was immersed in a book about a dialogue between neuroscience and psychoanalysis coauthored by Pedro Maguilones, a leading neuroscientist, and François Debussy, a prominent psychoanalyst. As stated by the authors, this endeavor could be compared to intercourse attempted between a polar bear and a whale. Yet Maguilones and Debussy rather convincingly proposed that the very nature of neuronal plasticity, namely the mechanisms through which life events leave a trace in the neuronal circuits, could provide a common conceptual framework to engage neuroscience and psychoanalysis into a fruitful exchange.

Food for thought, Edoardo pondered. But now he needed to concentrate on the last riddle. How many, if any, of the other four were ahead of him? It was rather unsettling not to know where the others stood. At any rate, the sooner he solved the last riddle, the better. But of course he would have to figure out where—what city in which country—the first part of the riddle would take him.

Edoardo decided to take a short walk before going to bed. Stepping out of the hotel onto Philharmoniker Strasse, he looked at the imposing Staatsoper, the Renaissance Revival opera house, across the street—a reconstruction of the magnificent nineteenth-century edifice that had been destroyed by Allied bombs during World War II. His walk through the historic center of the city took him to Albertinaplatz. He passed the Albertina museum, which housed an impressive collection that included works by Dürer, Raphael, Rubens, Goya, Klimt, and Picasso. It was a lovely spring night, and he strolled down Goethegasse along Burggarten, one of the gardens of the Hofburg, the former residence of the Austrian emperors.

Suddenly Edoardo was enveloped by a sweet flowery scent. It reminded him of Benedetta's perfume and he missed her so much that he could not resist calling her. He longed to hear her voice. He reached for his phone in his pocket and called. It rang three times, but on the fourth she picked up.

"*Ciao amore mio,*" he said happily.

"Don't call me that."

"Benedetta, I called to tell you how much I miss you and how beautiful the stars are in the Vienna sky tonight."

"How romantic! Is that your favorite line?" Her tone was unmistakably sarcastic.

"I miss you too," he replied to lighten the tone.

"I've got to go," Benedetta said.

"Wait. Guess where I am walking? Down a little street called Goethegasse. Do you remember that funny story about my friend John Morris who had signed up for a course on Goethe at John Hopkins?"

"Yes. He's the one living in New York now. After the first lecture, he went to see the professor and asked if this wasn't supposed to be a course on 'goath.' John had no clue about German and couldn't know how you pronounced the writer's name."

"It doesn't sound that funny now, but if you knew John, you'd understand. Anyway, what I wanted to tell you is—"

Suddenly a pair of powerful hands gripped Edoardo from behind and shoved him against the park's wall. He gasped, the wind knocked out of him. They punched him in the back. They punched him again. He cried out.

"Edoardo? Can you hear me?" Benedetta shouted. "This isn't a joke is it? Please don't do this."

"Let me...go...What do you want...Stop it!" He cried out in pain and confusion as the blows kept coming: to his gut, his chest, and, finally, his head. Everything went dark.

MILAN, ITALY

_____

_____

_____

_____

_____

MAY 12, 2018, 10:15 P.M.

On Benedetta's end, the phone went dead. She called back several times only to reach his voice mail. Panic swept over her. Her heart was thumping and her hands moist. What should she do? Edoardo was in Austria and she in Italy. Who could she call, the police in Vienna? And tell them what? That she was on the phone with her boyfriend and that they were cut off and that she believed something terrible had happened to him?

She remembered what Edoardo had told her about emergency situations the evening of that threatening call. There was a number and e-mail address in Zurich for Bobby, the Webmaster working on the Lindenmayer project. But of course, she didn't have the contact information. What about calling Marco Comina?

"Yes, that's a good idea," she coaxed herself. "But where did I put his number?" She checked her cell phone but hadn't entered his number. She felt helpless, ineffective, emotions that were uncharacteristic of her. She was used to being in control. Somebody must be able to help her locate Comina's contact details in Zurich.

LINDENMAYER CORPORATE HEADQUARTERS, ZURICH, SWITZERLAND

Bobby grabbed a handful of darts. He threw one, then another. He often played darts when he had to think something through. By keeping his mind in what he referred to as "default mode," he had the impression that his brain, like a computer churning data, would find the solution. He was still reeling from Benedetta's call. What if something terrible had happened to Edoardo? He might be badly hurt, or worse. Whoever was behind these acts was becoming increasingly careless and violent. To think that Edoardo had been on the phone with Benedetta. She had actually heard him call for help. The worst had been having to tell Fred. He had been so distraught.

Bobby threw a few more darts. The routine had the advantage of pleasing Oban. He had named his dog after the single malt he favored despite the fact that he felt he had betrayed his origins in doing so. He should have picked the name of one of the East Lothian single malts near Gullane, but he found these malts too clean and much preferred the Islay taste.

Not bad. Four darts had hit the board right at the center. "Go. Fetch," Bobby instructed Oban.

Usually, Oban raced across the room, jumped onto a small chair next to the dart board, and bit the darts, which he would then bring back to Bobby. This time, however, there was no sign of the dog. "Come on, Oban. Get going," Bobby said, adopting an angry tone for the dog's benefit. Still Oban did not come. Glancing over his shoulder, Bobby saw that the dog was chewing something. He was always chewing paper. "Stop," Bobby said. "Drop it." The dog was chewing a small white bag. "What are you eating, you rascal? Give it to me." Bobby tried to pull it from the dog's mouth. It was then he realized that the bag contained white powder. Cocaine. He'd seen some at parties and, once, he had tried it but didn't care much for it. The bag had been punctured. Maybe by Oban's teeth, and from where the dog was lying, a trail of white powder could be traced to the door.

ZURICH, SWITZERLAND

MAY 12, 2018, 11:00 P.M.

Sitting in his car, Boswell was panting, sweating, and trembling. He was having a hard time focusing. He was in desperate need of cocaine. It was all because of that imbecile, Bobby. Boswell had reminded him several times to knock before entering, no matter how urgent his business. But Bobby had come running into his office to tell him about Edoardo. In his haste to hide the cocaine, Boswell had put it in a stupid place on a low shelf.

He dialed his dealer's number again. "What the fuck's taking so long?" He slammed his fist against the dashboard. He must stay in control. If he didn't, all would be lost. Why was he sitting in the dark? He turned on an inside light. A mistake. He now saw his face reflected in the glass. When had he grown so old? He was increasingly bald. Cutting his hair extra short would no longer do the trick. He was shaking. He could not prevent his body from trembling. He hugged himself. How had he allowed himself to become so dependent on the stuff? It wasn't as if he didn't know how it worked. He knew perfectly well that cocaine played a trick on the neurons that contain the neurotransmitter dopamine. After many years of cocaine, his neurons must be completely desensitized and in need of ever higher doses. The proof was how he was reacting to not having any cocaine.

The phone rang. "About time," he said, picking up. "I need it now." He started the car and, driving very fast, he took Museumstrasse to get to Klingenstrasse.

Soon he would have the feeling he needed. Everything would seem possible; the night would be darker and the stars brighter. He thought of Yucun. She must have arrived in Vienna by now. He would never forget the look of horror she had given him when he'd hinted that he could give her the solution to the last riddle she had to solve. Her firm refusal to listen to him had made him absolutely furious. What was she fussing about, trying to stay honest to the end of the contest? Her attitude was destroying his hope of becoming her scientific partner at the new Lindenmayer Institute. She had to win! And getting the information hadn't been easy. It had required hours of eavesdropping on his part. He'd had to leave his door open. Of course, Bobby thought he was becoming friendly. What a fool! Although he didn't need to eavesdrop anymore, he reasoned that it was better for him not to disillusion Bobby about their growing closeness. He had even consented to playing a game of darts with Bobby, what a bore!

MILAN, ITALY

———————————
———————————
———————————
———————————
———————————

MAY 13, 2018, 3:00 A.M.

In her dream, Benedetta heard bells ringing for her wedding. As she walked through the streets to the church, the sound of the bells became increasingly unpleasant, jangling in her ear. She awakened, startled. It wasn't bells; it was her cell phone. She switched on her bedside lamp, expecting to see her cell by the base of the lamp but it was not there. It kept ringing. She jumped out of bed and looked on the floor. There it was. It had fallen into one of her slippers, still ringing.

"Hello, this is Benedetta."

"It's Marco. They've found Edoardo. He's at the University Hospital. He's in surgery."

"Oh my God! What happened? Is he badly hurt? Will he be all right?"

"Yes, yes, nothing life-threatening, but they broke his jaw and he has a few cuts and bruises. He'll be okay."

Marco's voice was very calm, but Benedetta was not reassured. She had to see Edoardo for herself.

"Thanks so much for calling, Marco," she said, and then, after a pause, "By the way, how did the hospital know who to get in touch with?"

"I thought you might ask me that. Edoardo had Bobby's phone number on him. And, fortunately, Bobby was still in his office when the hospital called. Fred called me right away and suggested I check with you first before contacting his family."

"I think it's best to wait. Edoardo's parents are on a trip in South America, but I will call his sisters in the morning. I'll fly to Vienna as soon as I can, on the next available flight out of Milan. Thanks again, Marco. As soon as I get there, I'll call you with news of Edoardo."

Benedetta hung up and started shaking. It was from the shock, she knew, but she could not help trembling. She hated to think of Edoardo in pain. If she were with him, it wouldn't be so bad. She decided to go to the kitchen and make herself some herbal tea.

UNIVERSITY HOSPITAL, VIENNA, AUSTRIA

MAY 13, 2018, 5:00 A.M.

The voices seemed to come from far away, as if Edoardo were at the end of a very long tunnel. Gradually, he drew closer to the light. Now he could distinguish shapes. Two people, wearing white coats, were leaning over him. The odors were familiar. He recognized Betadine, a disinfectant his mother used to apply when he scraped his knee.

"Mr. Gardelli? Can you hear me? You are in the hospital."

He opened his mouth to speak, but there was no sound.

Someone took his hand. A face peered down at him. Her hair was pulled back and she had large eyes.

"If you cannot speak, don't worry. Just nod to indicate that you understand what I'm saying. Okay?"

Edoardo nodded.

"I'm Dr. Ilse Kamper and this is a nurse, Trudy. You are in the intensive care unit at University Hospital in Vienna."

Edoardo nodded again.

"You were brought in a few hours ago. An elderly couple found you lying unconscious in a dark side street. Actually, their dog found you. It looks as if you were involved in some kind of fight, or perhaps you were mugged."

Edoardo thought, "I can't remember anything. If only I could talk."

"I know you are trying to talk but you've been heavily sedated. You had surgery."

He would have smiled if it hadn't involved a lot of pain. He wouldn't be entirely reassured until he saw his face for himself.

"I spoke with Mr. Lindenmayer in Zurich and I've also been in touch with your fiancée. She will be arriving in Vienna today."

"Benedetta," he thought, feeling his eyes close.

"We'll let you sleep, now. Trudy will be checking on you regularly and I will see you in the morning."

"If there is anything you need, just press the red button," Trudy said, placing it by his right hand.

UNIVERSITY HOSPITAL, VIENNA, AUSTRIA

With Benedetta sitting on his bed, Edoardo thought the hospital room looked much friendlier. He could hardly bear to see her leave the room for a minute. She was trying to cheer him up as she knew how frustrated he must be after what Dr. Kamper had told him a few moments ago.

"I will not allow you to leave the hospital until May 20," she had said. No amount of cajoling would persuade Dr. Kamper to release him sooner. Edoardo realized that this would jeopardize his chances to win the competition since it meant he could not travel, but at least he wanted to try and solve the first part of the last riddle from his hospital bed.

He wanted to explain this plan of his to Benedetta, but when he tried to speak the words came out garbled.

"You are not supposed to speak yet, *amore*. You just had surgery for a broken jaw," Benedetta said, passing him a notepad and pen.

How could she speak so calmly? Hastily, he wrote what he had tried to say. Then he passed her the note and gazed at her reaction.

She laughed and tapped him lightly on the shoulder. He winced with pain and she apologized. "I'm so sorry, *amore*. Of course we can try, but you realize that if you figure out the city, you won't be able to travel there."

He nodded, and then he wrote, "Let's look at the riddle."

"Why don't I read it aloud," she suggested and he nodded again. *"Most serene, she lies in the arms of the sea: witness to glorious centuries, she hides in one of her many shapes the site of memory."*

"How can a city be serene?" Benedetta asked. "I think we should just forget the award and plan a romantic weekend as soon as you are out of the hospital. We could go to Venice. My parents will be away so we will have the house to ourselves."

As soon as Benedetta had uttered the word "Venice," Edoardo grew agitated and grabbed the notepad. He knew the answer. Venice was frequently referred to as "the Serenissima," or, serene in Italian. Frantically, he wrote in the notepad.

"I can't read it," she said. "Like most doctors, you have terrible handwriting."

"Was she doing it on purpose?" he wondered, re-writing the note using print instead of cursive. I HAVE SOLVED THE RIDDLE. THE SERENE CITY MUST BE THE SERENISSIMA, VENICE OF COURSE. LET'S GO THERE ASAP. I <u>MUST</u> LEAVE THE HOSPITAL TOMORROW.

Benedetta looked at him tenderly and explained that this was not going to happen. "You do realize," she explained, "that your jaw is broken in several places with an open wound and there is a major risk of infection. Like it or not you are stuck in bed with an arterial line delivering high doses of antibiotics for at least a week. I know this is very disappointing for you, but your health comes first," she said bending down and kissing him tenderly on his forehead.

FREUD MUSEUM, VIENNA, AUSTRIA

MAY 14, 2018, 6:00 P.M.

As Yucun hurried through the streets of Vienna to the Freud Museum, it started to rain, not just a light rain that could be ignored but a heavy rain that whipped people's umbrellas out of their hands. Several lay on the ground. She could not help thinking that the weather was not auspicious. She almost expected something bad to happen to her on the way to the museum. There you go being superstitious again, she could hear Boswell saying, using the ironic tone he often adopted with her.

When she arrived at the museum, instead of proceeding inside, however, she stopped for a moment to enjoy her feeling of accomplishment. She was sure that she had solved the second part of her last riddle and must therefore be the winner of the contest. She just needed the confirmation now. She was still feeling very uncomfortable about Jonathan insisting on giving her the solution to her last riddle. She couldn't stand the idea of cheating, something that resonated with injustice and the suffering that her family had been subjected to during the Cultural Revolution. Her parents had had to fight against injustice most of their lives, to open opportunities for her education, and to care for her disabled sister. She could picture Mei's vacant but sweet smile, and her parents, who were getting old. There might not be many more opportunities for her to make them proud and for them to bask in her success.

Just at that moment, she saw Dr. Müller and her assistant locking the door to the museum. "Excuse me," she said. "I'm sorry I'm late, but I'm one of the contestants for the Lindenmayer Award and I have the answer to the riddle."

"You're all wet. Please come in. Frau Lotte, do you have a minute? I just need you to take a photograph."

"I suppose," the assistant said.

Yucun felt that the assistant was annoyed at not being able to leave immediately. She seemed to stare suspiciously at Yucun. When Yucun entered the museum, she almost cried out upon seeing a large black cat.

"She's perfectly harmless," Dr. Müller said.

Yucun didn't reply, but she was thinking that this was another bad omen.

"Well," Dr. Müller said, and for a moment, Yucun felt confused, but then she remembered that she hadn't given Dr. Müller the answer to the riddle. Even when she realized that she hadn't given the answer, she felt unable to speak.

"Is this going to take much longer?" the assistant asked. "My mother is waiting. She's very old and she gets anxious when I don't get home on time."

"So sorry," Yucun said, and then she proceeded to give the answer.

"Excellent," Dr. Müller said, then asked the assistant to take the photograph of the two of them.

After exiting the museum, Dr. Müller offered Yucun a lift to her hotel, but Yucun declined her kind offer and set off once again through the wet streets of Vienna. She needed time to enjoy that moment of deep satisfaction of being the winner of the contest. Just before leaving the museum, she had sent Bobby the solution to her last riddle. And she was now waiting for his answer, confirming her victory.

LINDENMAYER CORPORATE HEADQUARTERS, ZURICH, SWITZERLAND

MAY 14, 2018, 6:30 P.M.

Bobby had been very preoccupied since Oban had found the bag of cocaine. Of course, he had mentioned the discovery to Fred, but his boss had been distracted by the violent attack on Edoardo. They had all been very upset and worried about Edoardo. But once the news had arrived that he was safely out of surgery, Bobby started thinking about the bag of cocaine again. He knew very little about the substance so he had looked it up. He read that the drug interferes with mechanisms that underlie the communication between neurons that use dopamine as a neurotransmitter. Not really understanding what this meant, he'd had to read further. Apparently, neurons communicate with each other by using chemicals called neurotransmitters, which are released at the level of the synapses. Dopamine is one of the transmitters used by neurons that are involved in the mechanisms of reward. Indeed, all addictive compounds, whether cocaine, heroin, nicotine, or even alcohol, activate these reward neuronal pathways that use dopamine as their transmitter. The way it works is that cocaine "plays a trick" on the neurons that contain dopamine. Normally once dopamine is released by a neuron it is rapidly cleared from the synapse and recaptured into the neuron that released it. It's as if the dopamine neuron says to itself, "Hey, it was hard to produce dopamine, so let's save whatever is not used." If cocaine is present, it blocks the reuptake of dopamine into the neuron. This means that much more dopamine will remain in the synapse. What's wrong with that? More dopamine means more reward, right? The problem is that the excess dopamine, which is caused by the regular intake of cocaine, changes the way neurons respond to dopamine itself. Little by little, the neurons on which dopamine acts become less responsive to its action. It's a kind of desensitization. This means that in order to feel the same effects caused by cocaine, a consumer needs to regularly increase the intake of the drug. Cocaine is not only bad for the brain, it's also bad for the wallet, as one needs to buy more and more cocaine to satisfy one's needs.

This last bit of information Bobby had found particularly fascinating. The user of cocaine would therefore have to be someone who had money at his or her disposal unless he or she was a criminal. He also read that if cocaine is not provided in sufficient amounts, dopamine neurons will function in an abnormal manner, resulting in a condition known as "withdrawal syndrome," a series of physical conditions characterized by extreme agitation, increased heart rate, general discomfort.

It was while reading this paragraph that he recalled Boswell's strange behavior the evening Oban had found the cocaine. When Bobby left the office that evening he had noticed Boswell's black car in the parking lot. The light was on in the car and he could see Boswell clearly. Boswell appeared to be having an argument. He saw him slam the dashboard then hug himself. He was trembling.

It was only now, however, that Bobby realized that Boswell had probably been suffering from withdrawal symptoms that evening.

Suddenly, a message from Yucun appeared on Bobby's screen, interrupting his recollection. A sense of elation overtook him as he read the message and realized that the contest had ended happily. He immediately called his boss.

"Fred, it's so exciting, we have a winner, it's Yucun!" he yelled into his phone. "How would you like to proceed?"

"Fantastic news!" Fred said. "I can't believe the contest is finally over. What a relief!"

"Yes, you have your first director for the Lindenmayer Institute," Bobby said.

"Please send a message to all the contestants advising them that the contest is over, that Yucun has won, and that they should all reconvene in Zurich on May 16 for a debriefing," Fred said joyfully.

"I will," Bobby said, and then he added, though he wished he did not have to diminish Fred's joy, "There's another small matter that I wouldn't bring up now but it might be important."

"Yes, yes, of course. Don't hesitate. What is it? Nothing can destroy my good mood."

"Well, this is very awkward, but as you probably recall I mentioned to you that Oban found a bag of cocaine in the office. I now believe that it belonged to Boswell."

There was a silence on the line.

"This is a very serious accusation," Fred commented.

"I know. I feel terrible saying this about someone who has been in your employment for longer than I have and whose services I know have been invaluable. But I feel that I wouldn't be doing my job honestly if I didn't tell you."

"What makes you think it is Boswell's?"

Bobby described what he had observed in the parking lot.

"Let us not do anything hasty," Fred said. "You have done your part. Now it is time for me to do mine. First, I'd like to call Yucun and congratulate her on her success. Tomorrow will be soon enough to confront Boswell. Bobby, I do appreciate your honesty. I realize how difficult it must have been for you to tell me."

"Thank you, Fred. It certainly goes against the grain to speak against a colleague."

VENICE, ITALY

MAY 14, 2018, 7:00 P.M.

Sarah kept reading the message from Bobby. She could not believe it. With only one more riddle to solve, she had thought that she had a real chance of winning. But Yucun had won. It was just so difficult to accept; she had started to believe she could build a new life in Switzerland as the director of the new institute. And maybe even dream about a life with Michael. She didn't believe in long-distance relationships. If she did go back to the States to continue her career, there was no way she could keep up her relationship with him. Dreaming about the possibility of having it all had been really nice, but now the time had come to face reality, and winning the competition had not been for her. She didn't know why this quote from Marcel Proust came to her, but she felt that it was significant for her future: *If a little dreaming is dangerous, the cure for it is not to dream less but to dream more, to dream all the time.*

Sarah decided there was no more time to waste on dreaming about a now impossible future with Michael and she grabbed her phone to book a flight back to Zurich. Fred had asked all contestants to meet for a debriefing. She was thinking how sad it had been to hear about Edoardo, Philip, and Jean-Pierre dropping out, especially the traumatic attack on the Edoardo. He had been very lucky to end up with "only" a broken jaw and some cuts and bruises. This vicious attack could have had much more dramatic consequences. Philip had also had his share of suffering when his companion had been involved in a serious car crash in California. But the contestants had received news from Philip that Julian was now out of the hospital and recovering at home in Pasadena. The situation with Jean-Pierre had been more difficult to understand, as the only explanation the other contestants had received was that he had been offered a unique opportunity to further his career at Columbia University in New York thanks to a large grant from a private foundation. Jean-Pierre had also written to all of them personally to explain that he had been so keen to be awarded this prestigious grant that he was ready to drop everything in order to take up his postdoc position at Columbia right after his thesis defense next month. Also, he had told his fellow contestants that he had realized that he was lagging behind quite a bit by having solved only two riddles after ten days and he was no longer really motivated to put a hundred percent of his time and energy into the competition. "*Place aux autres*, let the others proceed," he had said.

KLINGENSTRASSE, ZURICH, SWITZERLAND

As Corporal Regula Bischoff from the narcotics division of the Zurich police force followed Captain Martin Pfister and his five men up the stairs of Klingenstrasse 21, she thought how lucky they were to have Café Sofia nearby. The noise from the customers shouting and drinking provided the perfect cover. She was sure that it had allowed them to climb the stairs to the first floor undetected.

Upon reaching apartment number 7, Captain Pfister made a signal with his head that they all knew how to interpret. They stormed the apartment and in less than two minutes they had apprehended three suspects. A fourth suspect tried to escape through the window, but he was stopped in the backyard by two policemen. *"Keine Waffe, Keine Waffe,"* one of the men lying on the floor shouted, his hands manacled behind his back. No guns, no guns!

They started to search the apartment. They opened drawers, cupboards, undid beds, cut into mattresses. Every single box of food, whether it was pasta, rice, or soup was torn apart, even toothpaste tubes were emptied. It was a typical meticulous Swiss-style search. The informer had been certain that the police would find a large stash of cocaine, which had just arrived through Serbia and Austria. So far the search had been very disappointing. A few hundred grams of cocaine were found in a drawer.

"Peanuts," Corporal Bischoff thought, as she caught sight of what looked like a bit of panty hose protruding from a small crack between two panels in the wall. Inwardly, she laughed, remembering how she had hesitated earlier in the evening over whether or not to wear panty hose or socks beneath her trousers. She knew it sounded ridiculous, but panty hose kept her too warm when she did physical exercise and she had known there would be plenty of that this evening.

She tugged at the panty hose, trying to dislodge it from the crack. One of the panels started to move and fell to the floor. In no time, she removed a few more panels, revealing a cache. There they were, forty bags of cocaine, each bag containing what looked like a pound.

"Nice work, Corporal Bischoff," Captain Pfister congratulated her.

"Thanks, captain," she said as she put on a pair of plastic gloves. She reached inside the cache for a notebook with an ugly yellowing cover. As she turned the pages of the notebook, a newspaper clipping fell to the floor. It was from the *Neue Zürcher Zeitung* of May 2, 2018. She read the title of the half-page article: "The Lindenmayer Award: A New Boost for Alzheimer's Research." She had heard about the contest and had followed news of the it with much interest because her best friend's mother suffered from Alzheimer's. Talking with her friend about her mother had sensitized her to the symptoms of the disease to the point that her parents complained that she had become a complete bore. Every time either of them forgot something she immediately ascribed it to early signs of Alzheimer's.

On the back of the article, she found a blue Post-it with the name J. Boswell and a phone number. On the second page of the notebook, she read a list of five names: Edoardo Gardelli, Sarah Majewski, Yucun Fang, Philip Caldwell-Tyson, and Jean-Pierre Abdoulayé.

"Great," she said to Captain Pfister. "We may have gotten our hands on some bosses of the Serbian cocaine ring." "Vienna, Hotel Sacher, Zimmer 234" was scribbled on the third page of the notebook. The rest of the pages were blank.

POLICE HEADQUARTERS, ZURICH, SWITZERLAND

MAY 16, 2018, 2:00 A.M.

After returning to headquarters, Corporal Bischoff handed Captain Pfister the article on the competition.

"Why don't you read it," he suggested. She could tell that something amused him, and she feared that it was probably at her expense. She soon found the relevant passage. The five names in the notebook were none other than the names of the competitors for the Lindenmayer Award!

They had a good laugh. "So much for finding the bosses of a cocaine ring," Captain Pfister said. As for J. Boswell, they discovered that he was Fred Lindenmayer's secretary. All this seemed pretty mundane. What neither Corporal Bischoff nor Captain Pfister could

understand was the connection between the drug dealers, the contestants, and J. Boswell.

They moved to the adjoining office to begin the
interrogation of the only drug dealer who spoke
German.

"I not know," the man kept repeating. "I here for
drink," he insisted.

"Sure, sure," Captain Pfister replied with an ironic
tone.

While Captain Pfister interrogated the drug dealer,
Corporal Bischoff searched the Interpol database and
discovered that the man being interrogated was none
other than Cuno Milic, a well-known drug dealer, who
had been particularly active in Austria over the past
two years.

Once Captain Pfister had revealed to Milic the
picture and personal data he had gathered from the
Interpol database, the drug dealer's attitude changed
completely. He no longer tried to deny his involvement.
He even confided that Boswell had paid him.

"For what?" Captain Pfister said.

"Cocaine."

"But what is the connection with the Lindenmayer
Award and its contestants?"

"I don't know."

"It would be better for you if you did. Sooner or
later it will all come out. One of your accomplices will

tell us if you won't. As soon as we get a translator, I have no doubt that they will reveal everything."

"Okay, okay. Boswell hired me to create problems for the contestants."

"What kind of problems?"

"Delays," he said.

"Were you responsible for the attack on Edoardo Gardelli?"

"Not my fault. My men got a bit carried away. They were just supposed to scare him. You know, give him a fright."

"And this Boswell was paying for these impediments?"

"Impediments. I don't understand."

"Accidents."

"Yes, Boswell paid for everything. We had to stop all the contestants except one from finding the answers to the riddles."

"Interesting. Who was excluded?"

"Chinese woman."

"Yucun Fang?"

"Yes."

POLICE HEADQUARTERS, ZURICH, SWITZERLAND

MAY 16, 2018, 8:00 A.M.

When Jonathan Boswell was brought into the interrogation room, Corporal Bischoff suspected that it would not be so easy to elicit information from him. Boswell was dressed formally in a black suit and a freshly pressed white shirt. He even wore a tie with a gold pin.

She looked forward to observing Captain Pfister use his interrogation techniques. She had to hide a smile when Captain Pfister made his first mistake by addressing Boswell as Mr. Boswell.

After clearing his throat, Boswell said, "It's Dr. Boswell, if you don't mind."

"My mistake," Captain Pfister said. "Dr. Boswell it is. I'm curious. What kind of doctor are you? Doctor of philosophy?"

"No," Boswell said. "I have a medical degree. I used to do research."

"What made you change your mind?"

Boswell sat even straighter in his chair. "It happened so long ago."

"You no longer recall?"

"I didn't say that, but I very much doubt this information is necessary for your purposes."

"Perhaps not," Captain Pfister said. "Perhaps it was just a youthful mistake. Nothing more than that."

Corporal Bischoff knew what Captain Pfister was referring to. After all, she had done the research for him, but she admired the way he used the information.

"Do you know why you have been brought here?" Captain Pfister suddenly leaned forward.

"I have an inkling," Boswell said. Corporal Bischoff observed that Boswell's left eye kept twitching. Eventually, he raised one hand to his eyelid as if he could stop it from fluttering.

"Ah," Captain Pfister said. "And what do you surmise?"

Corporal Bischoff again had to contain her amusement. In Boswell, she suspected that Captain Pfister had probably met his match in terms of using elaborate, indeed arcane vocabulary.

"I would prefer for you to state your reasons."

"Well, I won't keep you in suspense. But a man who deals in certain substances has told us that he worked for you. Does the name Cuno Milic ring a bell?"

"Yes," Boswell said. "He provides me with cocaine. You know, for recreational purposes. I like to throw parties. That sort of thing."

"I see. You don't really strike me as the party type, but you certainly dress the part."

Here, Boswell moved uneasily in his seat. He cleared his throat.

"A glass of water?" Captain Pfister suggested.

"Please," Boswell said.

Captain Pfister waited for Corporal Bischoff to bring water.

"Okay now, let's get down to business," he said as soon as Boswell had taken a sip. "We know that you hired Cuno Milic to impede the contestants' progress, all but one of them, Yucun Fang."

Boswell lowered his head. He folded one long white hand over the other.

"What we would like to know is whether Ms. Fang was aware of your duplicity and was an accomplice, or if she is simply an innocent victim to your machinations."

"A victim, she is an innocent victim. In the same way I was a victim."

"How could you be a victim? It was entirely your fault. You chose to hire someone like Cuno Milic to threaten or hurt these young, talented scientists whose ambition was to win a medical award."

By then Boswell was even more bent and now he was trembling. His whole body visibly shook beneath the elegant suit.

With his fists and jaw clenched, he mumbled, "I can't stand those sons of bitches, they are a bunch of idiots. They don't deserve to win the award. I should be the head of the Lindenmayer Institute. That is why I have given her the solution to the last riddle, to make sure that she wins the contest and appoints me as codirector of the institute with her."

Boswell had just falsely accused Yucun of accepting his help. How could he have become such a cad as he continued to explain his devious plan to Captain Pfister? Back in control of his emotions, he confessed that since the intimidations had not worked and one of the candidates, Edoardo, had already solved four riddles, he had decided to move a step further and have him physically injured to stop his progress. Milic had many friends in Vienna and it was easy to arrange an assault. Milic was his angel and his devil. He was the one who provided him with moments of relief by selling the cocaine that helped him forget his gloomy life.

"Hmm," Captain Pfister said. "Any accomplice in all this?"

"No, no one," Boswell said hastily but forcefully. A long silence followed. Boswell stared up at the ceiling. He sighed with relief. His life had been one of cheating: cheating in science, cheating with Lindenmayer...it was a spiral of cheating...and it had finally come to an end.

ON THE PLANE TO VIENNA, AUSTRIA

MAY 16, 2018, 11:00 A.M.

Fred stared through the window of his private plane. He always enjoyed flying. In fact, he knew how to fly but had given it up. He loved seeing clouds up close. He loved flying over them. He wished he could emerge from the "clouds" of his own life, but more and more seemed to be gathering.

The flight attendant handed him the telephone. Heidi, his personal assistant, was on the line. He couldn't hear her very well over the static.

"Sir," she said, "Ms. Fang just called for Dr. Boswell. She did not wish to leave a message."

"Thank you, Heidi. Were you able to identify a number?"

"Yes, I checked it. The phone number is from Vienna. Hotel Sacher."

"We'll be landing in Vienna in twenty minutes. Do keep me posted if anyone else calls. Do you know on which return flight to Zurich Yucun is booked?"

"LX 1583 leaving at seven this evening."

"Good," he said. "We have some time before she leaves the hotel." He turned to Comina, who sat beside him. "I'm not looking forward to this meeting."

Fred dreaded the thought of confronting Yucun. She was such a talented scientist. She had made some very interesting findings at UCLA. In Max Fernshaw's view, she was a real star. Fred had secretly hoped, very early on in the contest, that she would win.

"She might be innocent," he said to Comina.

"It's possible, but very unlikely. After all, Boswell confessed that he had given her the solution to her last riddle."

"Such a waste of talent," Fred said.

"I know how you feel," Comina said. "In my many years of work with the police, I have seen so many cases where people who are basically good human beings cross the line that separates a law-abiding citizen from a cheater or a crook."

The plane made its landing.

"Nice job, Paul," Fred called out to the pilot. "I hardly felt it."

"Thank you, sir," Paul said, tipping his cap.

"Another call," the flight attendant said. This time she handed the phone to Comina.

"Yes, I see," Comina said, nodding. "We'll come directly. If you could just allow us a few minutes in private that would be terrific." He handed the phone to the flight attendant and then turned to Fred. He explained that Yucun had been taken into custody by the police in Vienna upon the request of their Zurich colleagues.

"We need to establish whether or not Boswell really helped her discover the answers to the riddles," Comina said.

"How are we going to do that?" Fred asked.

"Leave it to me," Comina said.

POLICE HEADQUARTERS, VIENNA, AUSTRIA

Sitting in the small office of the inspector in charge of the investigation, Fred felt very uncomfortable. He fidgeted with his wedding ring until Comina glanced at him. The door opened and Yucun appeared with the inspector and a female police officer. Yucun looked very surprised to see Fred and Comina.

"Fred, I don't know what I'm doing here. What's wrong? I don't understand." She was agitated and spoke very fast, looking from one person to the other.

"I'm so sorry," Fred said, starting to rise from his seat, but Comina put up one hand.

"Inspector, if we could just have a few minutes alone?"

"Of course," the inspector said after a moment's hesitation, as if surprised by the request, and left the room.

"Please take a seat," Comina said to Yucun. He rose from his chair and Yucun sat down while Comina positioned himself behind the large steel desk.

"Now let's begin," Comina said, looking at Yucun. "We just have a few questions."

"I don't understand. Why am I under suspicion?"

"Jonathan Boswell has been arrested."

Yucun grew pale.

It was only natural for her to be upset, Fred thought. There was still hope. He leaned forward to stare at her more closely.

"Why was he arrested?" Yucun asked after a moment.

"He was involved in illegal activities," Comina explained.

"But what has this got to do with me?"

"He was your lover, right?"

"So?" Her voice grew defensive. "That doesn't mean anything. I'm not responsible for him."

"Can you explain how you came up with the solution to the last riddle?" Comina asked.

Now Yucun grew more agitated. She glanced around the room, as if looking for an escape. Gradually, her face turned crimson. "I went to the Freud Museum."

"Yes, but what was the exact process of your reasoning? Give us the steps that led you to the answer."

She hid her face in her hands and broke down in tears.

She tried to regain her composure and started to tell what had happened with Boswell. How she had told him she wanted to quit the contest because she was scared of what could happen to her, and how he had offered to give her the solution to the last riddle.

She continued by explaining how she felt ashamed of quitting when her parents had given her the opportunity to follow her dream as a scientist. She confirmed that she had categorically refused Boswell's help, as she had been brought up by parents who valued honesty and courage. That is why, in the end, she had decided to complete the contest even if it meant that she would not be the winner.

"This is hard to believe." Comina had now become more confrontational in the interrogation. "How do I know you are telling me the truth?"

"I knew that Jonathan really wanted me to win because he wanted to work with me at Fred's new institute."

"Did Boswell make any hints to you during the contest that he would make sure that you would end up being the winner?" Comina was determined to get her to tell the truth or at least part of it.

"Yes, no, I'm not sure." Yucun seemed hesitant, but continued, "I somehow felt that he was too keen for me to win the competition. He made some comments that I didn't quite understand."

"What kind of comments?" Comina was trying to get to exactly what Boswell had told her.

"Well, at some point he did say that he could possibly tell me the solutions to the riddles, but of course I refused. I really wanted to win this on my own. And also…" But Yucun stopped as if she didn't want to tell them more.

"Yes, go on, we are not leaving this room until we get to the bottom of this story." Comina seemed adamant and Yucun went on.

"I thought he had understood that I wanted to win through my own efforts, but I now feel that he didn't understand my refusal to let him help me."

"And what did you know about Boswell's dealings with the attacks on your fellow contestants?" Comina asked.

"Absolutely nothing, I swear." Tears were now rolling down Yucun's cheeks. "If I had known anything, I would have asked him to stop immediately. What happened to Julian, Philip's lover, and to Edoardo was just awful."

"Okay." Comina seemed to be satisfied with her explanation. "But now we need to know how you solved the second part of the Vienna riddle."

"Of course, I understand," replied a still tearful Yucun. "It is quite simple, you see. A few years ago I had the opportunity to watch a movie called *Princess Marie*. It's the story of Marie Bonaparte's friendship and work with Freud. As I was walking by the Hofburg, it made me think of the famous Sissi, empress of Austria, and also of other princesses, like Marie Bonaparte. Then I remembered that I had read about the Freud Museum in a leaflet I had found in my hotel room. I put two and two together—Princess Marie and Freud—and I thought I could have found the solution."

"Thank you, Yucun." Comina touched her shoulder in an almost affectionate gesture. He got up and motioned to Fred to do the same.

"We'll be back in a while," he said and asked Yucun if she wanted a cup of coffee.

"Thank you." She could hardly speak and let her head fall into her hands.

After Comina had closed the door he turned to Fred: "I don't think she was an accomplice, but we'll let the police figure out the whole story. Her account is credible but she may have made it up. She is a smart cookie. It seems to me that she is more of a victim than an accomplice, but for the time being that doesn't change anything in the outcome of the competition, does it, Fred?"

"No, Marco, you are right. Given the uncertain situation we're in, as far as Yucun is concerned, we'll let the contest continue until we have confirmation that she indeed did not cheat. The Zurich police will have to continue interrogating Boswell to clear her name completely. I will immediately ask Bobby to let Sarah know that the competition is still on. Since she is the only contestant left, if she solves the last riddle, then she is the winner." Fred added with a big sigh, "It is sad that only two contestants will have made it to the end."

"Yes, Fred, I think so too," Comina said. "Now let's brief Captain Pfister about our discussion with Yucun and get back to the hotel."

Fred agreed it was now up to the police in Zurich to establish whether or not Yucun was guilty of any serious charges.

PIAZZA SAN MARCO, VENICE, ITALY

Sipping the cappuccino she had just ordered, Sarah thought she could not complain. It was true that she had been devastated after receiving the message that Yucun had solved the last riddle and was the winner. Even though Sarah knew that she had a promising future as a scientist, she had set her heart on winning this contest.

And she had put on a good front last night, as she was having dinner with Anna, her best friend from college in Minnesota, who was now living in Venice. Anna had sensed Sarah's disappointment and had done everything she could to lift her friend's spirits. She had prepared a delicious dinner: insalata caprese, spaghetti alla Bolognese, accompanied by a few glasses of Morellino di Scansano. She had also suggested they have their coffee on the roof terrace to admire the night sky.

Suddenly, as Sarah had the last sip of her cappuccino, the familiar beep of an incoming message interrupted her thoughts. Probably some stupid advertisement, she thought. Just in case it was important, she glanced at it. She could not believe what she was reading: *Dear Sarah, there have been new developments. Please ignore our last message. The contest is not over. Good luck! Fred*

Sarah was astounded and read the message again. It clearly said that the contest was still on. She checked her watch and saw that Anna was walking toward her. Sarah jumped up from her chair and darted to Anna, pulling her to the table and almost screaming: "There's no time to lose. I have to solve the second part of the last riddle. I can still do it, I know I can. Let's have another cappuccino and look at the riddle again."

But twenty minutes later, Sarah had to acknowledge that her elation had been replaced with disappointment. She still had no clue as to the second part of the riddle.

"Well," said Anna, noticing Sarah's discouragement, "you will probably not figure out the solution tonight. So let's call it a day and go for a drink at Harry's Bar. It's not far from here."

HARRY'S BAR, VENICE, ITALY

MAY 16, 2018, 6:00 P.M.

After Anna left to run an errand, Sarah ordered her third Bellini, the iconic drink made of white peach puree and sparkling Prosecco, named after the fifteenth-century painter Giovanni Bellini. She started reading a brochure that was lying on the table about the history of this world-famous bar, which was opened by Giuseppe Cipriani in 1931, on waterfront side of Piazza San Marco. Its specialty dish was Carpaccio, a plate of trimmed sirloin sliced wafer thin and dressed with mayonnaise mixed with lemon juice. Like the drink, it was also named after an Italian painter, Vittore Carpaccio, who was famous for his love of different variations of the color red.

What the regulars really enjoyed was the atmosphere, which hadn't changed since the bar opened. It was not too elegant or formal, but it had style, with comfortable banquettes and tables covered in yellow linen. "We simply like to be ourselves," Arrigo Cipriani, Giuseppe's son, liked to say. Arrigo had started working at Harry's when he was nineteen and was now its owner at eighty-six. This was not at all unusual. Most of the staff had worked at Harry's for a decade or two. The longtime local clients had the famed Senator's Table reserved for them. Ernest Hemingway had been a regular from 1949 on and the bar appears in his novel *Across the River and Into the Trees*. Orson Welles had sometimes ordered two bottles of Dom Pérignon at one sitting, and Truman Capote had favored prawn sandwiches. Today, during the Venice Film Festival many Hollywood celebrities pay Harry's a visit.

Lifting her eyes from the brochure, Sarah stared at the map of Venice that hung from the wall next to her table. In the upper left-hand corner, she read *Luigi Querci Editore, Aprile 1887*, and directly beneath it *Stazione della strada ferrata*.

"What a strange name for railway," she thought. *Strada ferrata* meant literally "iron road," an obsolete term that no one would use today. The map looked neither antique nor contemporary, as if suspended in space and time. Indeed, there was no context, no geographical markers that would allow one to compare it with the actual topography of the place. Unlike an antique map, it had no bumps, curves, or other oddities that one might expect. On the other hand, it did not look modern because the image was not sharp or precise and in no way like the pictures taken from a satellite. However, the map revealed the overall shape of Venice, and there was something very familiar about it, but she couldn't figure out what it was. She got up from her chair and stood a few inches from it.

At the center of the map an S shape, the channel of the Canal Grande, divided Venice in half. Each of these sections looked like a boxing glove. Together, they looked like two interconnected boxing gloves. No, that wasn't quite the right analogy. It was more like the joint of the hip—no, the elbow joint that connects the arm to the forearm. Yes, that described it perfectly! Well, enough of that. She was really losing it, and she was starting to draw attention to herself, standing there, gazing at the map. She sat down, leaned back in her chair, and tried to adopt a position she hoped suggested a casual attitude. But she couldn't help thinking that she was wasting her time. Here she was drinking her third Bellini alone in a bar. It was pathetic. Yet the map was like a magnet. She felt that she had missed something crucial. She kept puzzling over its strange shape, which seemed so familiar but which she couldn't quite identify.

Sarah got up from her chair again, attracting a young couple's attention. The woman whispered something to the young man and they giggled. They probably thought she was completely drunk. Little did they know, she was quite capable of holding her liquor, and her mind, right at this moment, had never been sharper.

Staring at the map once again, she noticed letters written across the S of the Canal Grande. The first two letters of Canal, a capital CA, puzzled her. In neuro-anatomical lingo, CA is the acronym for Cornu Ammonis, the brain area now called the hippocampus, but originally named Cornu Ammonis by early neuro-anatomists. Sarah remembered that the name Cornu Ammonis, or Ammon's Horn, came from the Egyptian God called Amun. Amun was represented as a ram with spiraling horns, which in the early neuroanatomists' imagination was associated with the convoluted shape of the hippocampus.

When she had worked in the tiny electrophysiology room at the University of Minnesota, she had, with her colleague George Higgins, recorded the activity of hundreds of neurons located in the hippocampus. "Fuck," George used to shout. "Would you listen to the little fuckers in CA3?" The three main subdivisions of the hippocampus are still defined as CA1, CA2, and CA3. One trick that neuroscientists used to help them "listen" to neuronal activity, when they have "caught" a neuron with their electrode, is to couple the electric signal to an amplifier and a loudspeaker. "Tack-a-tack-tack." The persistent sound of bursting neurons sounded like a machine gun firing at different frequencies. Sarah remembered her excitement when the article on the effects of the neurotransmitter acetylcholine on plasticity of CA3 neurons and its possible relevance to memory was accepted in the journal *Nature* and the ensuing libations with George.

Indeed the evidence suggesting that the hippocampus is involved in memory processes is quite compelling.

In Alzheimer's, one of the brain areas affected in the early stages is the hippocampus, where the disease manifests itself by the loss of neurons. A prominent feature of patients suffering from Alzheimer's is their inability to remember events that have just occurred, while their ability to recall old memories, such as those related to their childhood, is preserved. Therefore, the hippocampus appears central to the establishment of memory for recent events.

This was all very fascinating, Sarah thought, but it didn't get her any closer to solving the riddle. What could CA—hippocampus, memories—have to do with Venice? She read the riddle again: *Most serene, she lies in the arms of the sea: witness to glorious centuries, she hides in one of her many shapes the site of memory.*

Suddenly, she let out a cry, which immediately drew the attention of everyone in the bar. This did not perturb her in the least. She could not believe that the answer had been right in front of her. The map of Venice shared features with the shape of the hippocampus or Cornu Ammonis. That was why it looked so familiar yet odd to her. Seen from above, Venice looked exactly like a hippocampus.

Like a slideshow, hundreds of drawings of the hippocampus that she had seen in neuroanatomy books unfolded in her mind. Each one looked so much like the map of Venice. It was incredible. Could she really have solved the last riddle?

Section of the hippocampus

Aerial view of Venice

"Sarah," she heard someone call. Startled out of her reverie, she saw Anna standing next to her. "Are you all right?"

"Not just all right. Terrific." She hugged Anna tight. "I've solved the riddle of Venice. It's Ammon's Horn."

"What? I don't understand."

"Let's go back to your place and I'll explain on the way." She took her by the hand. She was about to step out when Arrigo reminded her that she had not paid. "I'm so sorry. How much do I owe you for the Bellinis?" She left an exorbitant tip.

As they hurried over canals and down narrow streets, dodging people, she explained her findings. She wanted to send the answer to Bobby as soon as possible. "Let's just hope that I have the right answer," she thought. "Why did it take me so long to figure it out? How many times have I looked at the shape of the city? Probably a dozen times, it is on every tourist map and every print in museums and art galleries." Although she was furious with herself for being so slow to solve the last riddle, she was also ecstatic.

"Sarah, calm down," Anna said.

Sarah didn't reply but suddenly stopped. "I'm so stupid. I forgot to take the picture. We'll have to go back to Harry's Bar."

"Do you know who you have to take it with?" asked Anna.

"No idea," Sarah replied, "but we'll find out."

They walked quickly back to the bar, where the barman recognized them. "Back already. Another Bellini, perhaps?" He gave them a big smile.

"No, thank you, we actually must…" Sarah seemed to have lost her ability to speak.

Finally, it was Anna who asked, "Have you heard of the Lindenmayer Award?"

"Of course, I have, and I suppose you forgot to take the picture with me?" He turned to Sarah. "I'm the head barman." He shook hands with her.

"Nice to meet you, I'm Sarah Majewski," she replied. "And this is my friend Anna."

"*Un piacere, signorina.*" The barman bent over her hand. "Now what about the riddle, *dottoressa?*" While Sarah gave the solution to the barman, Anna adjusted the iPhone and made sure that she also had the print of Venice in the frame.

"Now I must send the message to Bobby," Sarah said.

She typed the message, added the picture, and pushed Send. Then she read over her message again, as if she could not believe she had solved the final riddle: "'*Most serene, she lies in the arms of the sea: witness of glorious centuries*' indicates Venice, which is also referred to as the Serenissima (most serene). '*She hides in one of her many shapes the site of memory*' refers to the fact that the map of Venice shares features with the shape of the hippocampus or Cornu Ammonis (Ammon's Horn), which is one of the key brain areas for memory which degenerates early on in Alzheimer's disease."

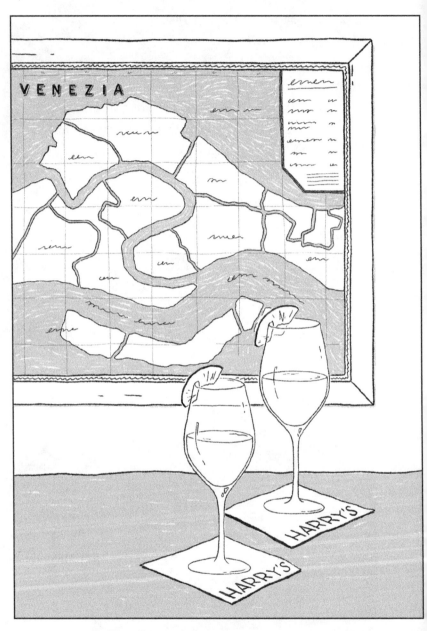

*Most serene, she lies in the arms of the sea: witness to glorious centuries,
she hides in one of her many shapes the site of memory.*

HOTEL SACHER, VIENNA, AUSTRIA

Standing at the window, Fred stared at the lit buildings. The last time he had stayed at this hotel, he was with Meg. Increasingly, he felt alone. Turning from the window, he glanced at the luxurious suite with its chandeliers and silk curtains. He was almost surprised to see Comina sitting in one of the capacious armchairs, sipping the gin and tonic Fred had offered him with a few minutes earlier.

"What a relief to have heard from Pfister that Boswell confessed his lies about Yucun," Comina said.

"Yes, I must admit I'm very relieved. You know I had a soft spot for her," Fred said, taking a seat opposite Comina. "What's going to happen to Boswell?"

"He will be kept in custody in Zurich until he is to appear in court."

Then Fred heard his cell ring. He pulled it from his pocket. "Hello?" he said, feeling very weary and fearing more bad news.

"It's me, Bobby."

"Yes, do you have any news?"

"One minute. I just got a message from Sarah in Venice. Let's see." Bobby now shouted, "She's got it! She's solved his fifth and last riddle."

Fred pulled his cell a few inches away from his ear.

"Did you hear? Sarah got Ammon's Horn right. She's solved the riddle."

Fred could hear Bobby yelling. But the words hardly seemed to register. It did not seem possible that after all these ordeals they finally had a winner. Then just as suddenly, Fred felt tears come to his eyes, and though he did his best to prevent them from spilling, he could not.

"I'm so happy," he said through his tears to Bobby. "I can't really believe it."

"I'll send you her message," Bobby said.

Comina passed a box of tissues to Fred, who wiped his eyes and then started to laugh. "Thank you for calling, Bobby. I'm going to call and congratulate Sarah now. But wait, I've just heard that Yucun is innocent. Boswell admitted his lies about her. What are we going to do now? We seem to have two winners, since we cannot disappoint Sarah now."

"Well, then we could just announce that we have two winners, and the two women contestants to boot." Bobby sounded really excited about his suggestion.

"This is excellent, thank you, Bobby. I rally to your suggestion." Fred was elated. "See you tomorrow in Zurich. Good night!"

After Fred got off the phone, Comina suggested he leave to let Fred get some rest, but Fred insisted that he stay for one more drink.

"Now we really have something to celebrate! Letting Sarah and Yucun know that they will be codirectors of the institute."

HOTEL SONNE, KÜSNACHT, SWITZERLAND

MAY 20, 2018

All five contestants were once again reunited at Hotel Sonne in Küsnacht. The last time they had met was under rather dramatic circumstances. But today was a bright day. The contest had ended a few days ago, with both Sarah and Yucun declared the winners. Tonight they would celebrate the end of three weeks of excitement and stress. Indeed, they had traveled a lot, worked relentlessly on solving the riddles, and met wonderful people, but they had also gone through difficult events riddled with anxiety and, sometimes, even fear.

As Fred had been driving to the Hotel Sonne that evening, he was reflecting on the past weeks. It had also been a very stressful time for him. A few times he had even considered putting an end to the contest, but every time he realized that he could not give in to the insidious hurdles that were put in his way. In the end, what was important was that he had identified an excellent director for his institute.

Fred raised his champagne glass to the five young scientists sitting around the table in the company of Bobby and Marco Comina. "So, dear friends, I do not want to get too emotional, which tends to become more frequent in my older years," he explained with a big smile, "but I want you to know, and I'm only going to say this once, what you have accomplished is just extraordinary! And I'm extremely proud to have had you as champions for my crazy project!" They all laughed.

Fred's voice took a more serious tone to brief them about the story of Yucun and Boswell. "Although I felt extremely angry with him for having broken the trust I had put in him, I decided that the only thing to do was to forgive. Boswell was taken up in a web of lies and resentment because of his unhappy, complicated life, and he tempted Yucun to become a consenting victim to further his own interests."

He continued, "As you become wiser with age, you acknowledge the power of forgiveness that will bring peace to your mind and maybe help the wrongdoers move forward in their lives too." Fred stopped speaking and smiled at the people around the table. "I do feel a little bit like a preacher," he admitted, "but please believe me when I say that this was certainly not my intention. So to finish on a lighter note, let me quote Oscar Wilde: '*Always forgive your enemies—nothing annoys them so much.*'"

"Thanks, Fred," said Sarah. "You have given us one of your short, to-the-point life lessons. And I think I speak for all my friends here when I say we are very grateful for the wonderful life experience you have given us in the form of this very special competition."

WORLD ECONOMIC FORUM, POSTHOTEL, DAVOS, SWITZERLAND

JANUARY 2019

Heavy snow was falling. Yucun and Sarah were wondering if Fred and Meg would make it in time for the Medical Research and Business Dinner given in their honor. Almost all the guests had arrived. There were many notable people from the medical, political, and business worlds. A former vice president of the United States and his wife, the prime minister of Finland, the chairmen of General Motors and Walmart, two Nobel Prize winners in medicine, and many more people, all personal friends of Fred and Meg's.

They were gathered in a splendid candlelit dining room of the Posthotel.

Sarah and Michael sat at a table with the other contestants and their significant others. Philip and Julian had just arrived from California. "My handicap came in handy," Julian said and explained that they had been given seats with extra leg room. He had just switched from crutches to a cane. Edoardo and Benedetta were deep in conversation with Jean-Pierre about their upcoming nuptials. Jean-Pierre suggested several good wines for their wedding dinner but insisted that a Sauvignon Blanc from the Loire Valley should be a must, for example one from the vineyards from his village.

Sarah was about to turn toward Bobby to share a joke with him when people started clapping. Fred and Meg were entering the dining room, still wearing their coats, covered with a light dusting of snow. Their cheeks were rosy from the cold and they laughed happily. After handing their coats to a hostess, Fred and Meg walked from table to table. They shook people's hands or hugged dear friends they had not seen for a long time. The atmosphere couldn't have been more festive. As Yucun looked at Fred walking toward the lectern to give his speech, she felt increasingly nervous at the thought of the speech she and Sarah had to give. She was hardly able to concentrate on Fred's words or to appreciate the gracious introduction that he gave both of them.

Fred had finished and now turned to Yucun and Sarah. The two winners stared at the crowd. People were looking up at them. Sarah tucked her notes into her pocket. She started their speech by telling them that she had rarely met a man of Fred Lindenmayer's gifts and generosity. Many people had generous impulses, but not many put their beliefs into action. In creating this award and, more important, the Lindenmayer Institute, Fred revealed his love not only for Meg but also for any person suffering from Alzheimer's and their family. Last week, Yucun continued, they and three other competitors—Philip Caldwell-Tyson, Jean-Pierre Abdoulayé, and Edoardo Gardelli—had laid the first brick for the Lindenmayer Institute in Rolle, a village famous for its vineyards, situated between Geneva and Lausanne. Indeed, some land overlooking Lake Leman had been donated to the institute by one of Fred's business associates whose father had died of Alzheimer's disease. Yucun announced that Edoardo and Philip had agreed to work with Sarah and her, to join forces and make a major contribution to the understanding of Alzheimer's disease. Jean-Pierre had decided to maintain his position at Columbia University. Each contestant had different skills that would complement the others'. Together they would form an extraordinary team. She finished by quoting, with a slight amendment, Ralph Waldo Emerson, the American philosopher and writer who, like Fred, had understood what it took for an individual to make a difference in the world: "It is easy in the world to live after the world's opinion; it is easy in solitude to live after our own, but the great man or woman is one who in the midst of the crowd keeps with perfect sweetness the independence of solitude."

POSTFACE

Where do we stand today regarding the treatment of Alzheimer's disease? The picture is pretty bleak: Not much hope can be offered to the millions of patients suffering from this disease, despite the billions of dollars that have been spent by the pharmaceutical industry and the thousands of research articles that have been published over the past three decades. Granted, the disease is complex, most likely involving many causes, including genetic, environmental, toxic, infectious, immunologic, to name a few. But isn't this the case for many other diseases that burden humanity? Take cancer: All the causes mentioned can be involved in the development of cancer in a given patient. Yet, massive progress in the cure of cancer has occurred over the same three decades. Only for a few cancers, such as cancer of the pancreas or glioblastoma, a form of brain tumor, are we still hitting a wall.

What is so special about Alzheimer's disease? Why is there such blatant and disarming lack of success? The cause may well lie not so much in the complexity of the disease but in an infatuation by the pharmaceutical industry and most scientists in the field with a single hypothesis for the cause of the disease: the amyloid cascade hypothesis of Alzheimer's disease. As years passed and dollars were invested, the hypothesis morphed into a dogma, despite a flagrant lack of convincing experimental validation and the failure of all of the dozens of clinical trials that tested the hypothesis.

Amyloid is a protein present in the membrane of most cell types, including neurons. The hypothesis calls for pathological mechanisms that would release a form of this protein that is toxic for neurons. The hypothesis states that the pathological protein accumulates in the brain and causes neurodegeneration. In 1906, Alois Alzheimer described the presence of amyloid plaques in the case of Auguste, as is mentioned in this novel by Professor Trümper. Yet this correlation does not mean that amyloid is the cause of the disease. By transforming such a correlation into a causality, a logical flaw has triggered the amyloid hypothesis race to cure Alzheimer's disease:

If amyloid accumulation is the cause of the disease, let's remove it from patient's brain and the disease will be cured. Unfortunately, three decades after the formulation of the hypothesis with more than $40 billion spent, the results are unequivocal: All clinical trials aimed at removing amyloid from human brains have failed. Some marginal improvements in cognition have been claimed, but the hard truth is that the target has been missed.

There is nothing wrong in formulating a hypothesis; science still works for the most part according to the hypothetico-deductive method. Propose a hypothesis, design the experiment that can prove it or falsify it, and move on. The problem is that despite an overwhelming accumulation of negative data and failure of clinical trials, to which the pharmaceutical industry and most scientists in the field turned a blind eye, the amyloid hypothesis has been alive and kicking. Even the US Food and Drug Administration approved, in 2021, despite the negative opinion of an expert panel, one of the drugs that failed in clinical trials. In July 2023 a second drug, only marginally effective, was approved.

Why, will you say, is there such a persistent obstinacy and stubbornness in face of irrefutable evidence? The reasons are probably multiple, but it is easy to imagine that it is difficult to "pull the plug" on a project in which a company has already invested hundreds of millions if not billions of dollars, while their competitor is following the same lead: It is likely due to the fear of missing out on and then being held responsible for a missed opportunity to develop a blockbuster medicine. For scientists working in the field, it is difficult to abandon a line of research that has brought them copious funding, highly visible articles, and in some cases even fame.

The amyloid hypothesis of Alzheimer's disease has been a very expensive and unfortunate mass delusion. Now the time has come to push in new directions.

So what are we left with now? The future is not as bleak as one may think. The first mental switch to be made is to acknowledge that, as is the case for many other diseases, the causes of Alzheimer's disease are likely to be multiple, meaning that a variety of mechanisms must be considered and targeted with drugs. There are candidates galore, they simply have not been taken seriously, overshadowed as they were by the amyloid cascade hypothesis.

Possibly first and foremost, there is overwhelming evidence that the brains of patients suffering from mild to moderate cognitive impairment, which in many cases precedes the development of Alzheimer's disease, are less able to use the glucose (sugar) present in the blood. The brain is the most energy-hungry organ of the body, using up to twenty-five percent of the glucose present in the circulation. The activity of neurons is tightly linked to their ability to have sufficient energy available. If such availability is impaired because less glucose enters the brain, cognitive functions and memory will be negatively impacted. In other words, Alzheimer's disease is a hypometabolic condition that could be counteracted by developing drugs that facilitate the use of glucose by the brain. In fact, such prototype drugs are showing encouraging results and should enter clinical validation soon. The cells that are central for the maintenance of energy delivery to neurons are a type of nonneuronal cells, the glia, and a particular subtype of them, the astrocytes. These cells are the gateway of glucose into the brain. Molecules targeting astrocytes to make them more efficient in importing glucose into the brain are a very promising focus for Alzheimer's disease.

There is also experimental evidence that inflammatory processes are at work in the brains of patients with Alzheimer's. Inflammation is a ubiquitous cellular process affecting many organs and leading to a variety of diseases ranging from inflammatory bowel disease, to cardiovascular and muscle diseases, diabetes, and even depression. The process involved in inflammation, initially geared at protecting cells from damaging occurrences, eventually become harmful for cells and tissues. In the brain, the main cells involved in inflammation are another type of glial cell, the microglia, for which there is considerable evidence showing that they are abnormally activated in Alzheimer's disease.

These two examples show that while neurons are eventually the victims of the degenerative processes leading to their demise, targeting glial cells, which represent at least half of the cells present in the human brain, to protect neurons from the negative consequences of inflammation or by providing them with adequate energy are viable and worthwhile new solutions. These solutions have been available in the public domain, published in high-impact journals, but not considered worthwhile pursuing for Alzheimer's disease because of the overbearing fascination and obnubilation by the amyloid hypothesis. It behooves the pharmaceutical industry and even more the venture capitalists to support this research in order to provide likely successful alternative directions for the development of new drugs for Alzheimer's disease. The results may come faster than might be expected because of the excellent science behind the approaches based on anti-inflammation and anti-hypometabolism.

And these are only some options. There are most likely many others that deserve attention. The key is to keep an open mind and think outside the box. In this regard the initiative launched by Fred Lindenmayer is a good example of hopefully more to come.

Pierre Magistretti
December 2022

ACKNOWLEDGMENTS

Many people, places, and cities have inspired us to write this novel. Harry's Bar in Venice is the place where we first had the idea for *Ammon's Horn*.

It took us three decades to write the novel, as we were busy bringing up our three children and dealing with our professional lives. It was also sometimes tricky to find some common quiet time to write.

We are grateful to many people who have encouraged and supported us throughout this project. A big thank you to all of them, in particular:

Our publishers, Odile Jacob in Paris, Judith Gurewich, and the whole team at Other Press in New York for their enthusiasm and professional support.

ACKNOWLEDGMENTS

Jane Nevins, Nicole Bokat, Sasha Troyan, Elizabeth Silver, and Daniel Levin Becker, five writers and editors who have helped us progress with the novel over the years.

Stéphanie Chuffart for her competent and gracious legal advice. Maria Encalada and Alyssa Frazier for their creative input on the illustrations.

Some of our friends who have read various versions of the novel. Their input and comments were much appreciated.

Last but not least, our three children, who were our most enthusiastic fan club over three decades. Thank you, darlings, for never getting tired of our discussions on *Ammon's Horn*. Your feedback and ideas were very valuable, and more importantly, you always believed that the novel would one day find its place in the world of published books!